ELFKING

SUSAN PRICE

Scholastic Children's Books
Commonwealth House, 1–19 New Oxford Street,
London, WC1A 1NU, UK
A division of Scholastic Ltd
London ~ New York ~ Toronto ~ Sydney ~ Auckland
Mexico City ~ New Delhi ~ Hong Kong

First published in the UK by Scholastic Ltd, 1996
This edition, 2000

ISBN 0 439 01401 8

Typeset by TW Typesetting, Midsomer Norton, Somerset
Printed by Cox & Wyman Ltd, Reading, Berks

10 9 8 7 6 5 4 3 2 1

CONTENTS

PART 1

PART 2

NOTE

PART 1

CHAPTER 1

Unwin Sassenach

The snow fell so thickly, it turned the darkness white. A traveller, his clothes plastered white, was slipping in the snow as he heaved at a miserable, exhausted donkey. Both of them were soaked, hungry, worn-out and so cold they could hardly move.

The walls and gate-house of the Royal Dun bulged from the whiteness of the blizzard, and the traveller wept and prayed to see it. He had not known it was so close. But when he dragged the donkey to the gates, the gates were shut.

A lantern hung outside the gates, its light hardly to be seen in the snow. A bell-rope dangled beside it. The priest reached for the rope, which he could hardly grip, and rang hard. In the snow, the clanging of the bell shrank to a tinkling.

There was a rattle as a panel, at eye-level, opened in the gate. The lantern-light shone on a nose that peered through the opening.

"Who rings?"

The traveller leaned against the door. "I am a priest. My name—"

"What do you want, priest?"

"Let me in. I—"

"The gates are closed and barred at sunset. They will be opened at first light tomorrow."

"I can't— Wait, wait!" The little door had begun to close. "It's cold, it's snowing –"

"Tomorrow, at first light," said the door-keeper.

"Is this hospitality?" the priest cried.

"Come before sunset," said the door-keeper, "and you'll be given royal hospitality. But this is a king's Dun, priest, not a tavern. At sunset the gates are closed. They open again at first light."

"I shall freeze out here."

An exasperated hiss came through the little door. "Go back across the bridge and turn to the right. You'll find a guest-house there, all stocked with fuel, blankets, food, everything you'll need. But these gates don't open until morning."

The door began to close again. "I must come in!" cried the priest. "I have news – Is it true, tell me, is it true that Unwin Sassenach is here?" He

4

knew by the door-keeper's silence that it was true. "I have news for Unwin. Take my name to him, tell him that Father Fillan is here. As God is your Maker, man, do that much!"

"Unwin Sassenach is not king here – or anywhere," the door-keeper said.

"But he is your king's guest!"

The door-keeper gave a heavy sigh. "Go to the shelter, father, and wait there while I ask. It may take a long time."

"I shall wait here," said Father Fillan, pulling his cloak about him. He was frozen, but thought God and King Lovern would grant his request more quickly if he suffered.

In King Lovern's hall, the household was at its evening meal. The hall would blaze for a feast, but that night it was only dimly lit, though warm. The lower tables were crowded with the commoners and slaves, and a great din rose from them, of chatter and shouts, the creaking of wooden benches and tables, the noise of knife-blades and wooden cups. The high table was almost empty, King Lovern having chosen to eat in his private lodgings. Close to the empty high-seat sat the big sassenach, Unwin Eadmundsson, together with the young Dane, Ingvi Jarlssen.

The food was plentiful, but plain: bread and butter, a thick broth of mutton and vegetables, fish, cheese, and milk to drink. They had both eaten all they wanted, and were merely lounging at the table, because the hall was warm. Ingvi was amusing himself by throwing up his dagger from his right hand and catching it in his left, then throwing it up with the left hand and catching it in his right. It amused Unwin less because the dagger was heavy and sharp and sooner or later Ingvi would miss it. There was a good chance, Unwin thought, that the dagger would hit *him*. But he didn't move, because that would have given Ingvi the chance to crow that the Saxons had less courage than the Danes.

Throwing up the dagger again – and catching it – Ingvi said, "I'm good at this. I haven't missed it yet, have I? And I've thrown it up, oh, twenty and twenty and twenty times."

Ingvi used "twenty" to mean simply "many". One of the things Unwin liked about him was that twenty was as high as he could count. As the dagger went into the air again, Unwin said, "It must be a useful accomplishment in battle." They could understand each other easily enough, their languages being dialects one of the other. But sarcasm passed by Ingvi's ears like the breeze.

"Well, it frightens the enemy," he said, "when they see how easy you are with your weapons. I can do this even when I'm riding." And up went the dagger again.

"I would be terrified," Unwin said.

Instead of throwing the dagger up again, Ingvi turned to Unwin and said, "People say *I'm* elf-born. I'm not really. Not like *your* elf-born."

"The thing is not *my* elf-born," Unwin said.

Ingvi wasn't listening. "It's just because I'm so dark." Certainly he was noticeable among his fair-haired, light-eyed, fair-skinned kinsfolk. They were famous for their height and hulking build while Ingvi, though tall, was slender. His skin was the brown of a ripe, polished hazelnut shell, while his eyes, shot through with green and yellow light, were the brown of a peat-stream, their lashes long, thick and black. Unwin's folk had always sneered that the Danes cut their hair to "bare the neck and blind the eye", and Ingvi's hair was cut just so, leaving the whole length of his brown neck exposed behind and curling over his brows in front. It was as coarse as dog's hair, as thick as thatch and as black as soot. There were plenty of dark-haired men among Lovern's Northern Welsh, but even they tended to have fair skins and light eyes, nor was their hair as deeply black as Ingvi's. Against all this darkness Ingvi's big strong teeth seemed as white as snow, and the whites of his eyes flashed. "I'm not elf-born at all," Ingvi chattered on. "My mother was an outlander. She—"

Through the heat of the hall came a faint, cool draught, and the light from the fires and candles flickered. The door of the hall had been opened. Dogs barked, and the chatter of the people at the hall's lower end changed its note. Unwin straightened in his seat and looked down the hall's length, and Ingvi broke off.

The door-keeper was walking the length of the hall, coming to pay his respects to his king's guests, even though his king was absent. He made a deep bow before the high table, saying something in his own language. Ingvi answered him, and the man began to turn away.

"Wait!" Unwin said. "What's the matter?"

While the door-keeper hesitated, Ingvi said, "He has a message for the king."

Unwin rose to his feet. "Is someone at the gate?"

Ingvi translated the question and the door-keeper's answer. "There's a man asking to come in – he has to tell the king."

"Why?" Unwin asked. "Ask him why he hasn't sent this man to the guest-house. Ask him what's so important about this man that the king has to be told."

Ingvi asked. The door-keeper turned once more to face the two of them, and made his answer, in what seemed to Unwin a truculent manner. Ingvi grinned as he passed on his words. "He says that it's King Lovern's Dun, and it's for King Lovern to know who's at his gate before any other."

Unwin walked around the end of the high table

and went over to the door-keeper. Ingvi followed. To the door-keeper, Unwin said, "Who am I?"

When the words were translated to him, the door-keeper seemed flustered for a moment, and then said, "You are a Saxon!" – words which Unwin understood very well without help.

"Who am I?" he repeated, and stepped closer to the man.

The door-keeper answered and Ingvi laughed. "He says if you don't know who you are, you must find some wiser man than he to help you!"

For an eye's blink, Unwin was quiet. Then he smiled and put his hand on the man's shoulder, patting it. "Am I your king's guest?"

Ingvi translated, and they could see the man struggling with the temptation to make a surly or impertinent answer. With Unwin smiling at him and holding him by the shoulder, he at last agreed that the Saxon was his king's guest.

"Am I of the Royal Kin? Am I a king's son? So now you will tell me who's at the gate, and perhaps we can spare King Lovern the trouble of leaving his fireside."

The door-keeper stepped back from Unwin and grumbled out something.

"There's a priest at the gate," Ingvi said. "Says his name is Fillan."

"Fillan!" Unwin said. The door-keeper made off down the hall towards the door.

Unwin stood still for a breath's space, and then he, too, started for the hall doors. Ingvi ran after him. "Where are you going?"

"To the gate."

"Why?"

"To open it," Unwin said.

They hauled open the door of the hall and passed from its heat into the night, where the air was so cold it made their flesh shrink. Snow crunched under their feet, and more snow swirled around them and clung to their clothes.

The guards in the gate-house were disturbed by their arrival, starting to their feet, trying to hide their food and drink and look alert. They hadn't the authority to stop Unwin going to the peep-hole in the gate and opening it, but they didn't like it.

Unwin peered out into the porch of the gate-house. Snow whirled white out of darkness, into the patch of lantern-light, and then into darkness again. He called out, "Fillan?"

Father Fillan had huddled himself into a corner of the porch, and had gone into such a daze of exhaustion and cold that at first he didn't hear the voice calling him. When he did, he started awake and almost fell from his corner, hardly able to move. "Here!" he said, groping towards the peep-hole.

Unwin saw him move into the light and

recognized him at once – Father Fillan, his mother's priest and his own instructor in the Christian faith. Stepping back from the door, he said to the guards, "Open the gate!"

Even after Ingvi had translated, the men refused to move. The gates to the king's Dun were closed and barred from sunset until first light, and it wasn't for foreign princelings, the one a refugee and the other a hostage, to order them opened.

"Dear God!" Unwin said, and set about opening the gate himself. Ingvi went to help him. They lifted up the heavy bar and set it aside, and Unwin took down the ring of keys that hung on the wall.

Orders were given in Welsh at that, and a man went running back into the Dun. "Gone to tell the king what we're up to," Ingvi said.

"Ah well," Unwin said as he tried the keys in the locks. "Sassenachs and Danes, both as mad as one another."

Ingvi laughed aloud, pleased to be counted on Unwin's side.

The right key was found, the lock turned, and Ingvi lent his help to pull the heavy gate back. Father Fillan fell through the opening. As Unwin caught him, and helped him further inside, Ingvi darted out into the snow to bring in the donkey. Not that the little animal needed much help. It trotted willingly through the gate, where it knew it would find shelter and food. As soon as Ingvi was back inside, the guards jumped to lock and bar the gate again.

"The donkey," Father Fillan said. "The bundle." Cold as he was, the man tottered over to the donkey and tried to untie its load with fingers as stiff as wood.

"Leave it and come to the fire," Unwin said. "One of the guards can bring it."

"Never, never! It's too – too –"

"I'll bring it," said Ingvi, and began to unfasten the bundle.

"Bring it to my lodgings," Unwin said, guiding Fillan away.

The Dun was a grouping of many buildings within its protective ditch and wall. Besides the Royal Hall, there were stables and kitchens, barracks and workshops – and many smaller halls, where the more important members of the court lodged with their households. Unwin, as a king's son and a royal guest, had been assigned one of these small halls, and provided with servants to staff it. The chief of these servants was even able to speak a little English. Unwin guided Father Fillan to this hall, and handed him over to his servants, with orders that he should be given warm water for washing, dry clothes, food and a place by the fire.

Unwin called aside the steward of his hall, and sent him to the king's lodging, with a message at once apologizing for his highhandedness in opening the gate and promising a full explanation the next day. "Tell him that the man outside the gate was bringing news to me, and that I have taken him into my hall, and he is cared for." The steward hurried away to assure the king that neither his hall nor his honour was in danger.

Ingvi came in, carefully carrying the bundle from the donkey. Unwin took it from him and led the way through the hall – where servants were already bedded down on the floor – to his private rooms. There he laid the bundle on the edge of the sleeping platform.

Ingvi brought a candle and they examined it together. The cloth was worn and stained from its travel, but thick and soft, and in the candlelight, gold threads glittered.

"An altar cloth," Unwin said. He suddenly knew what was in the bundle. Taking out his knife, he cut through the ties that held it and began to unwrap it. As the folds opened a faint but unpleasant smell began to rise from it, growing stronger.

"Faugh!" Ingvi said. "Something's dead."

Unwin threw back the last of the cloth, to reveal a long frail object, contained in a wrapping of silk which Ingvi only slowly recognized as a silken robe, stitched with gold thread and gems. And then he saw that the thing within the robe was

13

human – or had been. Those were blackened hands sticking out of sleeves, with rings still on the fingers, and stick-like legs outlined by the silk. The knob at the other end was a head, shrunken to the size of a skull and wrapped in a linen headdress. Its lips had drawn back from the teeth.

"Jesu!" Ingvi said. He had picked up Christian oaths during his time at King Lovern's court.

Unwin put his hand on Ingvi's shoulder and indicated the corpse with the other. "Ingvi – my mother, Saint and Queen, Ealdfrith," he said.

"Mother?"

Unwin sat down on the edge of the platform, by the corpse's head. "Your mother was an outlander. Mine was a Holy Saint of God. Here she is. Fillan is a saint too, for reuniting us – or has he brought her as a present for King Lovern, a precious relic for his chapel?"

Every word Unwin spoke was clear, and bitten off, and filled with such anger that Ingvi said nothing.

Unwin rose, and said, more calmly, "I have to hear Fillan's news."

Ingvi put the candle down on a chest and began to follow. Glancing back at the platform, he said, "Are you—?"

Unwin turned sharply and demanded, *"What?"*

Ingvi stopped short. "Only... Are you going to leave –?" He nodded towards the corpse.

"What should I do with her? Mother, would you like something to eat? Would you like to hear some music? See? She doesn't want anything. So let's leave her in peace. Unlike," he added, as he opened the door into the hall, "other people."

In the hall, most of the servants were still sleeping, reluctant to give up their few hours of rest and warmth. But one of the fires had been stirred up and there they found Father Fillan, still chilled, even though he was now in dry clothes and had eaten from the empty bowl beside him.

Unwin had seemed so angry that Ingvi expected him to speak angrily now, but Unwin sat down on the bench beside the priest and said quietly, "Well, Father? What is the news?"

The priest hung his head and drew a long sigh. "The news? Ah, the news!" he said, in English. "The news is all bad, my son. The Devil walks abroad in your land, seeking whom he may devour. Your mother's little chapel has been pulled down, stone by stone, and the earth has been dug and a yew tree planted in its place. I tell you, the light is put out in that land and the darkness come back."

Unwin blinked slowly, and said patiently, "My family?"

"Your father's brother, Athelric!" the priest said, turning towards him. "An unrepentant pagan ever! He is always at the Devil's side! He follows

15

at the thing's heels like a tame dog, and scurries like a dog at its word!"

Despite himself, Unwin smiled. "That doesn't sound like Athelric."

"I assure you!" cried the priest. "All his judgement is gone. He is bewitched. He fawns on the Devil so you would think he was in love!"

Ingvi, fascinated, sat on the floor in the straw to listen – the benches having been moved to walls to allow people to sleep. King Lovern, a Christian king caught between the pagan Saxons to the south and the pagan Danes to the east, spent much time listening to reports of events in both kingdoms. The Danes had caused him less concern over the past five years, since he had beaten them in battle and taken Ingvi as hostage to ensure the peace, but he still kept a close watch on both countries. News was always welcome.

Years before, Lovern had sent Father Fillan to the Mid-Saxons, to their Queen Ealdfrith, to teach her about the Christian faith. Now he sat on the bench beside Unwin, reeling off names of places and people that meant nothing to Ingvi. The firelight flickered over the priest, showing the wrinkles under his eyes and the grey in his black hair. He wasn't a big man, he didn't look bold. He wasn't the sort you'd expect to have the courage to go among the pagan Saxons – who were not friendly and civilized pagans like the Danes – and bring them the Christian good news they didn't wish to hear.

"My sons, Father?" Unwin continued.

The priest, tired, dragged a hand down his face. "They were with their mother, weren't they – at Unwin's Borough? I've heard nothing of them, my son, but –" He shook his head. "They are Christians, are they not, they and their mother? It is no good time to be a Christian."

Unwin straightened his back as he sat on the bench. "You think I should have some fear for them?"

"The Devil hates all things Christian: the Holy things infuriate it, and it destroys them. It grieves me, my son," Father Fillan reached out and took Unwin's hand, "but, yes, I fear for your Lady and your children."

Unwin looked straight before him, through the light of the fire. Ingvi admired the control with which he heard these words. Even more he admired the level voice with which Unwin asked, "And my brother?"

Father Fillan's hand tightened its grip on Unwin's. "The worst news of all, my son. I am sorry. Wulfweard is dead."

Unwin turned to face the priest. "You are sure of this?"

"In such a time, who can be sure of anything? I know for certain that Wulfweard was taken up from the battlefield, half-dead. And not so very long ago, as I was on the road, I heard it said that the atheling had died. Maybe it was Athelric they meant? But Athelric was in good health the last I saw of him. I fear – in my heart I felt it – the atheling who died was Wulfweard. I said prayers for him."

"You will say more," Unwin said. "So will I. And one thing I have to thank God for." Unwin smiled. "I no longer have to worry which brother will stab me in the back first, and when!"

Father Fillan patted his hand. "Ach, I know you loved your brothers."

Unwin pulled his hand away from the priest's and lifted up the gold cross, set with garnets, that he wore round his neck. "I swear," he said, "on this cross, before you and God, that I shall have blood for Hunting's blood and for Wulfweard's. I shall have the elf's drop's blood for theirs. I shall take his head."

"Unwin –" Father Fillan said.

"And Athelric, my own father's brother. I swear –" He spoke over the priest's protests, "I swear on this cross, before God, before you, that I shall cut off his right hand that struck against us, and I shall take his head."

"Unwin! If one strikes you upon the right cheek, turn and offer him your left. Forgive thy *enemy*! Yes, even thy enemy! Forgive and forgive and forgive! That is the Christian message!"

He found Unwin and Ingvi both looking at him blankly. Ingvi had heard the Christian message a hundred times while he had been at Lovern's court but, as a pagan, he had never let it trouble him. Still, he was surprised to find that there were some Christians who seriously expected you to forgive your enemies – not vague, possible enemies, but real enemies who had killed your brothers.

Unwin said, "I fall short of perfection, Father. I had two brothers. Now I am alone. The elf's drop killed them; my father's brother betrayed them to him. I shall kill them both."

Ingvi reared up on his knees. "Cut the blood-eagle on them!"

Fillan, aghast, had nothing to say.

"The blood-eagle…" Unwin nodded. If he was ever to succeed in taking back his own land, he would need the support of Ingvi's brother, Ingvald. A solemn vow to cut the blood-eagle on Elfgift would certainly impress the Danes. And then, when he led his Danish army into his own land, word would spread before it. Before each battle the Danes would cast the spear over the opposing army – the spear that consecrated every man beneath it to Odin. The Saxons would know, by that spear, that if they lost, every single man would be killed for Odin. And the leader, the king,

Elfgift, would take the blood-eagle. They would see how loyal the elf's drop's new subjects would be when that became known. "I swear –" He grinned at Ingvi's excited face. "I will cut the blood-eagle on the elf-born."

"Unwin –" Father Fillan said. "Unwin…" He couldn't think of any words that might be effective. When the Danes cut the blood-eagle they took a living man and hacked his ribs away from his spine. Then they spread out the ribs and the lungs to form the blood-eagle's wings. "How can you even speak of this?"

"Would you rather," Unwin asked, "that I crucify him?"

"Oh, now you blaspheme! You have heard Christ's words – have you ever listened? A man – God's creation! How can you talk of so mutilating and murdering a man and have Christ's words in your heart?"

"A Devil," Unwin said. "Not a man. You yourself have called it a Devil."

"Then I sinned! Because it is half a man! Your own half-brother, Unwin! Who might yet be won for Christ!"

Unwin turned sharply on him, leaning towards him so that the priest drew back. "It killed my brothers. I have nothing 'in my heart' except revenge. I have sworn what I shall do, and I shall not be disgraced before a half-grown Dane by going back on my word. Afterwards, Father, I shall come to you, and be confessed for my sins, and do my penance. But I shall do what I have sworn to do. Don't try to turn me from it again."

Unwin rose and would have walked away, but Fillan reached out and caught his hand. "My son, when God makes such great changes in our lives as He has made in yours, we should try to learn what it is He wishes to teach us."

Unwin looked down on him in silence for a moment. Then he spoke. "Father, it seems to me that when God tossed my kingdom into the hands of the elf's drop, He missed a catch in His juggling, and the best thing I can do is to put myself in the king's chair that should have been mine. Then maybe no one will notice that God was clumsy."

Father Fillan folded his hands into his sleeves. "It won't be to me that you'll come for confession then. I shan't even spend this night under your roof – I shall sleep in the Royal Hall. And tomorrow I shall ask the king's permission to return to my monastery, which I pray God I shall never leave again. You may call yourself a Christian, Unwin, but in your heart you are as heathen as that elf-born devil."

Unwin, who had been turning away, glanced back at the priest. "Then I shall get another confessor. They're plenty enough." Unwin walked away towards his private rooms.

Ingvi rose from where he was kneeling on the floor. "A good night, Father," he said, and hurried after Unwin, to ask if he could spend the night in Unwin's lodging instead of wandering through the dark yards to find his own sleeping place.

Unwin, he thought, was a grand man, as great as his own brother, Jarl Ingvald. He had not expected to hear a Christian speak so well of the duty of revenge. When Unwin rode out from Lovern's court to reclaim his kingdom, Ingvi intended to be riding with him.

CHAPTER 2

The Elf-Born

From the top of the gatehouse, where the wind blew strongly, the troop of armed men could be seen riding nearer. There was some comfort in the fact that they were approaching openly along the Royal Road. Surely men who meant to attack wouldn't do that?

The wind tugged at Kendrida's headdress, tugging at the pins set into her hair. She pulled her cloak more closely about her. "Do you..." She felt foolish for asking such a hopeful question. "Could it be my husband?"

The captain of the housecarls, standing beside her, was slow to answer. He plainly didn't believe that the horsemen were led by Unwin

Eadmundsson, but didn't wish to say so. "We have no news of him, Lady. If he was so close, we would have heard of it."

No news? That would have been easier to bear. They had been brought so much news, and all of it conflicting. Unwin and his brother Wulfweard were alive, in hiding. Both of them had run to the north and were at the court of King Lovern. Wulfweard had been killed, or had died – or both brothers had been killed in battle with the elfborn...

If Unwin was dead, how was she to keep her sons safe? Never had she been so eager to see her husband.

They stood watching the approaching horsemen. Soon they could hear the distant beat of the hoofs on the hard earth. The sun was not bright, but they saw light shine on helmets and spear points. Behind the troop of horsemen straggled a crowd, walking both on the road and off it. If they were soldiers, they were disorderly soldiers.

"Fifty men, and more on horseback," the captain said. "And then those behind. This is not Unwin, my lady." None of the stories had said that Unwin had won the battle at the Shrieking Stone, and this was no broken fragment of a troop. They were riding in good order, and all were equipped.

"Do you think it's *him*?" she asked.

Again, he took time to answer. He knew her

fears for her children. As the man charged with protecting them, he shared those fears. "Lady, I think it is."

She looked about her, at the steep-sided ditch below them, and the steep bank beyond it. From the height of the gatehouse, she looked down on the top of the timber walls. Enough to keep determined attackers out?

She did not wish to seem afraid before the housecarls, and reminded herself to stand straight. Inside her mind, her own voice cried, *Oh God! Oh God, help us! Oh Lady Mary!* And then: *Eostre, Lady, help me if the Christian God won't. Ing, if you'll help, please.* She was trembling, even her innards crawled with fear. This was not a hero-tale. The king was dead, and while the contest to decide who would be the next king was unsettled, all law was put aside. These men around her could all be so much butchered meat by sunset. *A feast spread for the ravens,* a poet would say. *When the warriors feasted the wolf.* She had listened to such poems in the past, and had felt her heart lifted with the glory of it. She did not feel her heart lift now.

When the housecarls were dead, then the butchery would turn to her sons, her little boys, with their soft skins and fragile bones. They would be butchered for their father's sake, run through with spears, chopped – she couldn't keep her mind from it. The trembling that was running through her almost shook a sob from her, but she swallowed it.

The troop of horsemen rode closer. Now they could hear the creaking of harness, the clanking of swords on mail – and they could see that it was a crowd of country people who followed, men and women, even children. Kendrida felt anger add to her trembling, that these people should have come to see – her murder?

Two men rode at the head of the troop. It was easy to tell that they were the leaders, but impossible to tell who they were. Both wore mail-coats, and cloaks over them. Both wore helmets, hiding the human faces behind faces of gleaming metal, with shadowed holes for eyes. Both wore swords at their sides. The hilt of one glinted whenever it caught the sunlight: highly polished, gold – an atheling's sword. The hilt of the sword worn by the other was dark and dull, but it was that weapon, not the gilded one, which held her eye.

Her eldest son, Godwin, had been telling her some tale he had heard about the elf-born. The Devil had been trained to fight by a Battle-woman who had given him a sword which looked dull and ugly, worthless and spiritless, like a farmer's tool, but which had been forged by the Devil-Woden. This sword had no weight in its bearer's hand and its blade was so sharp that it cut the wind. It would cut through anything. And as it was drawn, it screamed aloud and sang the spell of the Battle-Fetters, Devil-Woden's spell, that locked the joints of the sword's enemies with terror. Godwin's eyes had shone as he had gabbled out the story for her. The sword brought victory, Woden's gift, to its owner, and every time it was drawn it had to be fed with blood – a man's blood. There was no cheating it. If its owner ever sheathed it without blooding it, then it would turn on him and bring about his death.

She had said, "Godwin, your father would not want you listening to such stories or repeating them. You are a Christian."

"But everyone is telling it!" Godwin wanted nothing more than to be like his father. Still, the idea of such a sword had fascinated him. "Do you think it really screams when it's drawn?"

"We are Christians," she had said, but she had become a Christian only at her marriage. In the shadows of her childhood stood the God Woden, with His one blue eye that looked on life and growth, and the blind, gouged hole that looked into darkness and the world beyond Death. She feared anyone who claimed to have dealings with that God. She half-feared that everything Godwin had told her about the sword was true.

The troop came to a halt at the ditch that surrounded Unwin's Borough. One of the leaders spurred across the bridge until he was under the gatehouse. Kendrida leaned over the palisade and looked down on the metal mask. Was this the elf-born?

"In the king's name, open!" The horseman's yell boomed behind the helmet's mask.

Kendrida, who could not bellow, said to her captain, "Tell him that, since King Eadmund's death, we know of no king."

The captain filled his lungs and repeated her words in a shout that drowned out the noise of shifting horses and jangling harness.

The horseman raised both hands to his head and wrenched off his helmet, revealing a head of thick, fading fair hair. He lifted an ageing and haggard face which Kendrida recognized with a fresh trembling of relief and hope – Athelric, her husband's father's brother. A member of the Royal Kin, and her children's blood-kin. But even as she hoped he would protect them, she was afraid again. The history of the Royal Kin was regularly marked by the shedding of their own blood, and Athelric had taken the elf-born's side. As Unwin's half-brother, the elf-born had good reason to wish Unwin's children dead.

"Don't play games!" Athelric shouted. "Open the gates! In the king's name!"

But the garrison had to seek some sort of assurance. The captain shouted back, "In what king's name do you speak?"

Then the other horseman, the one who had remained on the far side of the ditch, suddenly rose in his saddle and yelled, "In my name!" His voice was at once muffled and magnified by the helmet. Kendrida's stare shifted to him in pure fear. That was the elf-born then! And that was the sword. As she stared a cracking cheer rose from the country people gathered around the edge of the mounted troop.

The captain spoke quietly to Kendrida. "Lady, we can't hold this place for long. Better to let them come in under orders than fighting." Raising his voice, he shouted, "Unwin Atheling's family are in my care. If I open the gates, do I have your word that they will be safe?"

Athelric started to speak, but the elf-born's voice silenced him. Guiding his horse a pace or two forward on to the bridge, the elf-born stood in his stirrups. He shouted, "If I have to fight my way through my own gates, I swear by Thunor that I will kill everyone inside! But if the gates are opened to me, then by Woden I promise they will be safe!"

The words brought a gasp from the crowd of country people, from the troops – perhaps the beginning of laughter. If so, it was laughter quickly silenced, and the silence spread throughout. Even the turning of heads and the lifting of hands quietened. Stillness came over them.

Kendrida, raised a pagan, understood the reason for the laughter and the sudden silence. Thunor was the God in whose name binding oaths were sworn; a vow made in His name was expected to be kept. But a promise sworn by the treacherous God, Woden, was double-edged. Woden, God of battles, promised victory to His followers, and kept His promise – until He broke it. Or He kept it, but coupled it with death or maiming. Hearing the elf-born's words, Kendrida could not help but think that there was no safer place for her children than the grave. Nothing could hurt them once they lay there.

She turned to her captain as he was turning to her. "Lady, we must open the gates," he said, just as she was about to order that they should never be opened. "Lady –" He put his hand on her arm – "We have more chance if we open the gates. We can't keep them out for long, and if they come in fighting mad…"

She couldn't speak. She nodded, and then ran for the ladder leading down from the gatehouse.

As she reached the yard, the gates were being hauled open. As the horsemen began to cross the bridge and thunder through the gates, she lifted up her skirts and ran across the yards to her lodging, without even waiting to welcome her kin-by-wedlock, Athelric. She wanted to find her children. If these men riding into her home had orders to find the atheling children and kill them, then she wanted to be standing in front of them, to fight for them as long as she could.

In normal times the preparing of guest-lodgings, the ordering of food, the allotting of sleeping places to the various troops of housecarls, would all have been part of her duties. But now she was not needed. The troops rode in and, with a great disorder of yelling and hoof-din, set about the stabling and the opening of the guest-halls themselves, under the instructions of their own officers. They would, she knew, be overlooking the stored food, relieving her captain of his command, and dividing his men among their own troops, to divide their loyalty. They would be counting the horses in the stables, the pigs in the pens, the hens in their houses. If they had consulted her, she could have managed the whole business much more efficiently, but now she would not leave her children – nor her four waiting-maids, whom she gathered about her in her lodging. They were all girls of good family, sent to her to be trained in the running of a household. She could not let them go wandering the streets of the Residence while strange troops were roaming everywhere.

So, shut into Kendrida's small room, the women talked about everyday matters, for the sake of the children. They told stories and sang while the girls spun, as they did every day. When shouts from outside drew the children to the windows, they pulled them away and tried to distract them with jokes, toys, nuts, anything. The eldest boy, Godwin, knew why his mother and her maids were so nervous, why their voices were so high-pitched as they rattled through their stories, why they laughed so often but looked at each other with frightened eyes. He knew that they were all in danger, and that his father might already be dead. The knowledge filled him with a terrified energy, and he stood at his mother's shoulder as she sat in her chair, determined to be everything she could need in an eldest son, determined to fight for her and for his younger brother and sister if need be. He breathed hard and grasped at the hilt of the little dagger in his belt, rehearsing the moves he must make in their defence. Or he roamed round and round the walls of the room, or went down into the hall to hear what the servants were saying, even venturing as far as the door to peer into the busy yard before running back to his mother's side to make sure she was safe.

The younger children, Godhelm and the little girl, Godhilda, were simply puzzled by the strain all around them, the shrillness of the voices, their big brother's bad temper, the boredom of being cooped up all day. It made Godhilda nervous and tearful, and Godhelm sulky.

Kendrida, like Godwin, wanted to rise and pace around the walls, wanted to strike the wood with her fist. But she bit down on all the anger and fear, and made herself sit still and play finger games with Godhilda, even while she was wondering if the child would still be alive for her to put to bed that night. But if she is dead, I shall be dead too, she thought, so I shall not have to grieve.

She tried to tell herself that she was being afraid of nothing, and that a Saxon woman should have more courage, but try as she might, the fear bubbled up under her breastbone, cold and fresh. She knew that if her own husband, Unwin, had been in the elf-born's place, then he would have ordered the killing of his rival's children as she would order the killing of lambs for a feast – as something necessary that hardly had to be thought about – indeed, the less thought about, the better. Oh God, oh God! she thought, and began to sway back and forth in her chair. Then she noticed Godwin watching her, and held herself still. Clenching her hands into fists, into hammers, she thought: *Thunor, let us survive this, and I swear I will leave the Christian God and return to You. Woden, You'll have my little ones soon enough; spare them this time, and I'll sacrifice to You, I'll give You blood. Eostre, Lady, You were with me when I wed, even though I left You for Christ; You were with me when I birthed. Three children, and all healthy, and I've never lost one or suffered overmuch. You have kept better faith with me, Lady, than I did with You. But keep my children through this, and if I live, I'll build Your God-house again, I'll sacrifice to You again, I promise, I don't care what my husband says.* And Ing, the Lady's young lover – some said He was also Her brother or Her son. Beautiful and gentle, He had always been Kendrida's favourite among the gods, since she had been a girl. *Ing, as You care for young and helpless growing things, please, please Ing, care for my children. Speak for me to Your Lady: help us, help us, oh Gods, help us, and I'll never kneel at a Christian altar again, I swear, I swear it by Thunor.*

As, with lowered head, closed eyes and clenched fists, she repeated these words to herself within her mind, there was a flurry of noise from the hall below – footsteps and voices. She looked towards the door as running feet sounded on the stair. Many people, coming to her room.

She started to her feet, feeling an energy of anger and fear fill her. Godwin came to her side, rigid, his hand on his dagger's hilt. Reaching out, Kendrida pulled Godhilda to her, and signalled frantically to Godhelm until he ran to his sister's side.

There was no knock at the door, which made her fear more. The latch was lifted, and the door pushed open. Framed in the doorway, in the shadow between the subdued light of the great hall and the brighter sunlight of her small room, stood the tall, slender figure of a man. Long hair hung about his shoulders, and light from behind turned the outer edges of the hair to a white blaze. He was a stranger.

She opened her mouth to demand how he dared enter her room without permission, but she had no voice.

"May I come in, Lady?" The stranger stepped through the door, and Kendrida's maids rose from their stools and scurried behind her. As the stranger came into the full light of the room's windows, his hair swung about his shoulders, losing its white glare and turning to a warmer fairness. Fear made her mind quick and fluent, so that many thoughts flashed, and turned and returned through it, like startled fish through a pool: he was beautiful – she knew him – he was poorly dressed for calling on her – she knew him and he was beautiful – he was wearing that dull black sword, yet he looked as if he had been working – she knew him.

"Wulfweard?" she said, her voice rising high in hope. They had heard that Wulfweard was dead, but nothing was certain and Wulfweard had always been a handsome boy, with just such long, fair hair. The face was like her husband's, but less harsh, gentler in every way, the eyes larger, the nose straighter, the mouth fuller and more smiling. But she had seen so little of Wulfweard in the past few years that she could not be sure. "Is it ...Wulfweard?"

He smiled and gave a slight shake of the head, which set the fine braids shaking beside his face, and the loose hair drifting and settling about his shoulders. He came further into the room, his shoulders sloping at the opposite angle to his hips, giving easily at the waist. He wore only riding-boots, leggings and a shirt, with the sleeves rolled up and the neck unlaced, even though the day was cool. To see a sword, any sword, belted round one wearing such poor clothes was strange, but this sword was so plain, its hilt the dull black-grey of an axe-head, that it was almost suitable. A smell of sweat drifted from him to Kendrida, and also a smell like hay, and a curious warmth.

"I am Elfgift Eadmundsson," he said, and seemed shy of saying it.

She was astonished, even as what he said made sense. That was why he was so like Wulfweard and Unwin, of course – they shared the same father. And the elves had gifted him with beauty. But he who claimed the kingship had come dressed – or undressed – like a field-hand, without ceremony. For escort, it seemed, he had nothing but a couple of armed men and a gathering of the idle and curious who were crowding the landing

36

outside her door and peering in – peering at him, gaping at him.

It flashed into her mind that he meant to cut the children's throats himself, with his own hands. That was why he had come without any company that mattered. Well, hadn't he, a bastard son, been raised like a farmer, used to wringing the necks of his own chickens and cutting the throats of his own piglets? With one arm she tried to push Godwin behind her, but he wouldn't move, pushing back against her hand.

"Yes, you killed Wulfweard Eadmundsson," she said. "We heard."

He looked puzzled, but then lifted his chin and nodded. "Oh, aye. I killed him, I mind. My sword screamed and leaped in my hand, drove him through, and he fell at my feet." As he spoke, his eyes moved to Godwin's face, though he did not smile. Godwin tried to glower back, but couldn't stop staring at the sword round Eadmunsson's waist. Did it scream?

Kendrida's eyes had flickered to the sword too. "Have you come to do the same to us?" She had to know. She couldn't bear to be subtle in the asking.

Elfgift pulled a stool towards him with one foot, pushed the sword behind him, and sat, his elbows on his wide-spread knees. He glanced around at the four frightened waiting-maids, the defiantly scowling boy, the frightened and defiant woman, and then looked long and thoughtfully at the two younger children who were peeping at him from around their mother's skirts.

"Lady, I came to tell you that I'm sorry for disturbing your peace, but this Borough is mine now. I shall appoint new officers. And I shall return the God-house to the Gods."

"And the Christ-priests?" she asked. They were her people, even if she had never had much true sympathy with their faith.

"They can go, unhurt," he said. He was still studying the children. "Or, if they'll set their altar beside the others, they can stay." Sitting on the stool, leaning his elbows on his knees, he watched Godhilda without smiling, but with nothing serious or grim about his expression either. He watched her as he might a bee in a flower, interested but detached.

Godhilda wriggled away from the clutching hands of a waiting-maid and moved forward a little to get a better look at him, though with one hand she grasped at her mother's skirt.

Kendrida looked down at her daughter and watched as Godhilda returned Elfgift's stare with a solemnity equal to his. First the little girl stood on one foot and swung her other leg and her skirts. Then, still holding a fistful of Kendrida's gown, she took a pace or two forward. Elfgift did nothing to attract her. He didn't smile. His hands remained motionless, hanging from his wrists as his arms rested on his knees. He simply looked at her. But Godhilda – who often refused to go to people who smiled and cooed at her and held out their arms – seemed to find something fascinating in this cool stillness. She let go of her mother's skirt and toddled forward.

Kendrida made to grab at her but, at the last moment, let the child go, though she felt Godwin start at her side, and then stiffen into stillness.

Godhilda went to stand between Elfgift's spread knees. She took one of his hands and lifted it in both of her small ones, examining it, finger by finger, nail by nail. Perhaps she was looking for the rings which most men of the Twelve Hundred wore: but Elfgift wore none. He let her move his hand as she wished, and tilted his head downwards to watch her, his hair falling forward and turning white in the sunlight again. She left his hand and moved on to his arm, pushing her fingers through the fuzz of hair that grew there. When she lowered her face to his arm and rubbed her nose in the hair, he gave a sudden, brief smile, but when she straightened and looked up into his face, he was as serious as ever. Not forbidding, or uninterested, but simply unsmiling.

She reached up and put her hand into his long hair, combing her fingers through it, and twisting it round them. He watched her, and let her.

Godhelm, more timid than his sister because he was older, began to come out from behind his mother, and stood chewing his thumbnail and watching his sister play with the stranger's hair.

Godhilda reached up and set the end of her forefinger in the exact centre of Elfgift's upper lip, where the deep groove ran down from his nose. Slowly, and with great seriousness, Elfgift opened his mouth so that her finger slipped inside it, and set his teeth gently around her finger-end. She giggled – still Elfgift did not even smile – and snatched her finger away, but almost immediately put it back to be bitten again.

Watching, Kendrida held her breath, thinking: *He cannot mean to harm them. Surely he cannot mean to harm them.* Godhelm took another step closer to Elfgift and his sister, and she let him go.

Godhilda now raised both arms to Elfgift, asking to be picked up and, when he seemed not to understand, she set about clambering into his lap herself, grasping the front of his shirt and pulling his hair in the process. He lifted her up and seated her on his thigh, where she laughed in anticipation of the game as she began to trace around his mouth with her finger. He moved his head slightly, making small openings and closings of his mouth as he tried to catch her finger with his teeth. All the time he was perfectly serious, but her giggling grew wilder each time he missed, and maniacal when he succeeded, and shook his head, as if worrying her, making his long hair flurry about them.

"Wolf!" she said. "Wolf!"

Godhelm had gone to stand right at Elfgift's knee and, breaking off the game with Godhilda, Elfgift turned and gave him the same long, thoughtful, serious look. Godhelm, shy, looked down at the floor, but moved even closer, and actually leaned against Elfgift before looking up at him.

Kendrida watched in bewilderment, unable to understand how her children had been drawn. She felt a sort of love, made up painfully of relief and hope. Would children, *could* they, so trust someone who meant to kill them? Fear told her, yes, the innocent often trusted their abusers. Still, she hoped.

Godwin watched the antics of his brother and sister with disgust. This was the man who had admitted killing their father's brother, Wulfweard, and who might have killed their father! Godhilda might be too young to understand, but Godhelm! Yet Godwin also felt the draw that came from the elf-born, like warmth from a fire. It was the stillness that drew them, the quiet eyes... Godwin, too, felt himself wanting to go nearer. He shook himself and said, "Did you kill our father as well as Wulfweard?"

Kendrida put her hand on her eldest son's shoulder, hoping to quieten him, but she said nothing. She also wanted to hear the answer to that question.

Elfgift shook Godhilda's finger away from his mouth and raised his head. With the little girl on his thigh, and Godhelm leaning against him, he turned to look at Godwin. "Atheling, your father is alive, in the north, with King Lovern. But he owes me a life. I shall kill him."

"If you can!" Godwin cried, and took a step towards Elfgift, though his mother tried to hold him back.

"I shall kill him," Elfgift repeated.

Godwin drew his dagger and, pulling from his mother's hold, rushed at the elf-born with the full intent, in his own mind, to kill.

The boy was so angry, and so clumsy, that there was little danger, except, perhaps, to the other children. While Kendrida shouted and the waiting-maids squealed, Elfgift rose and turned, swinging Godhilda round as if he were swinging her high in a game. His movement knocked Godhelm aside, and one of the waiting-maids grabbed the boy and pulled him well clear.

Godwin went blundering past Elfgift and into the chamber's wooden wall. He spun round, his mouth all awry, half-blind with fury and tears and unable to understand why Elfgift wasn't dead. He was holding his dagger as he had been taught, pointing upwards from his fist, ready to rip upwards. He glared about, wondering why he couldn't see his enemy; and then charged again, too angry to wait or think. Elfgift caught him from behind, and twisted his dagger-hand until he dropped the weapon. Another man, a complete stranger, bent and picked it up from the floor.

Elfgift pushed the boy away from him, and Kendrida, kneeling, grabbed him in her arms and hugged him tightly. "Don't hurt him! Please don't hurt him!" She had to shout to be heard above the babble of excited voices from the people crowded in the doorway.

Elfgift would have answered, but the boy wrenched himself from his mother's arms and ran at him again, punching and kicking. Elfgift raised his own arms high in the air, the hands open, and simply moved away, dodging most of the blows with slight movements. It was the other man who picked the boy up bodily and bundled him, as he continued to struggle, into the arms of a second man, a member of the elf-born's small escort, who had come in from the crowded landing.

Godhilda was crying, red in the face, and Godhelm, though he was beginning to consider himself too big for tears, looked as if he might begin to sob at any moment. The sound of crying frightened Kendrida: it was disturbing and she feared it might cause still more anger and bring disaster on them. She caught hold of one of her waiting-maids by the wrist, and pulled the girl towards Godhilda. "Take her," she said. "Take them away – keep them quiet. All of you – go!"

The girls fled, shooing the children with them. People made way for them on the stairs. Below were more private rooms, where the children and maids usually lived.

Kendrida pushed the door of her room shut on the curious faces outside, and turned to face Elfgift. He stood with his back to her window, his hair a white blaze, his face hidden in shadow. "Please don't be angry with him. He is only a child. He thinks he has to defend us. You are unhurt and—"

He held up his hands to silence her. "Lady, don't fear."

She moved towards him, clasping her hands. "Kill my husband," she said. "I don't care about him." They were alone, and she could say that: indeed, it gave her relief, and hope, to speak the truth so simply. She looked up and found him looking down at her with the same intent gravity with which he had watched the children. Her heart stirred as she felt the same pull little Godhilda must have felt. Now she was closer to him, she saw that his eyes were the greenish greyed-blue of lavender, each colour merging into the next, but specked with the ochre of lichen too. They were clear and beautiful. Elf-eyes, she thought: the Evil Eye. He could curse you, or even kill you, with those eyes. "It sounds wrong to say that, but – there has never been any love between my husband and me. I had to leave my home and people and my own Gods. I have given him three children – two of them sons – and I have never been unfaithful to him. He has never been faithful to me. But King – you see, I call you 'King' – I love my children. Please, spare my children. They are no threat to you." She took his hand, which surprised her with its warmth. "Please, will you swear to me by Thunor that you will never harm them?"

Elfgift saw her desperation plainly. Her terrible fear for her children moved into him with the pulse of her hand holding his. He knew that if her children died, it would be for her as if the world had turned dark and cold. And he looked clearly through that, and saw that whether her children lived or died, it mattered not at all. There would be hundreds of children in the world still.

But she, looking up at him, saw only under-standing in his face, and clasped his hand more tightly.

He said, "Lady, why should I care for your children?"

His face was so young: there was no more than

a handful of years between him and Godwin. She didn't want to understand what he had said. The light struck ochre and green-glass colours from his eyes. "But they're so little, they can't hurt—"

"I mean, Lady, why should I care for them more than for the thrall children in your villages? They die every day, and you don't even know their names."

Of course, he was uncanny. He would look young when he was as old as Athelric. She stepped back from him, feeling snubbed and furious. "My children are of the Royal Kin!"

"I am of the Royal Kin, a mannerless bastard raised on a hill-farm by goats and thralls." She looked up at him quickly, fearfully, shocked that he knew what was said of him. She saw him smiling, his face very young and gentle. "Lady, I shall no more hurt your children than I hurt the thrall children."

A groan of relief broke from her, and she was flooded by a warmth that made her so weak, she sank down on a stool. Tears ran down her face, and she felt the warmth as love for Elfgift.

He had moved to the window, a shadow against its light. Outside there was a growing noise, of horse's hooves, the crashing and creaking of carts, and yelling, shouting. "My baggage train has come in," he said. "Lady, will you put flowers on Wulfweard's grave?"

CHAPTER 3

Wulfweard's Grave

Kendrida strewed dried lavender flowers across the sheets in which Wulfweard would soon lie. Putting flowers on his grave.

Elfgift had led her from her lodgings and out into the yards, where her people and his people pushed, yelled, shoved, the crush increasing as the carts of the baggage train came through the gate, adding pack-ponies, oxen and still more people to the press. Elfgift offered her his arm, and she linked hers through his, and then wondered at his warmth, which came through his clothes and hers.

At first people shouldered against Elfgift, jostling him as they pressed by, noticing little of him but his poor dress. Sometimes it was her they recognized first, recoiling hastily from their Lady, and only then looking at her companion. But his height soon drew stares, and the long hair that blew about his shoulders in the fashion of the rich despite his rough clothes – and once they had looked at him, they stared.

People whispered to each other, punched others on the back, pointed. They began to follow, pushing and struggling in the crowd to get closer for a better look. In the noise around her, Kendrida heard the same words repeated over and over. Not "the king" but "elf-born – the elf-born – the elf –".

Jolted against him, she looked up at Elfgift to see what he thought of these attempts to get close to him, these whisperings. He was looking about, as if finding his way. He might have been alone, the people who collided with him might have been trees, for all the notice he took of them.

There were armed men in the crowd, wearing mail-coats, helmets and swords. Seeing Elfgift, they fought their way to him and, meeting each other's eyes, formed themselves into an escort, holding off the crowd with mailed elbows, straight-armed shoves, threats and shouts. It immediately became much easier just to stand, and Kendrida smiled at the men and thanked them. She saw their eyes move to Elfgift, and knew how little her thanks was valued against his – but he looked through the men with as little notice as he had given the crowd. The men responded by becoming ever more grim and self-important, shouting, "Way for the king!" and threatening anyone who came near with their spears. But it was as if Elfgift thought they were doing it for someone else.

He is making a mistake by snubbing them, Kendrida thought. They will remember. Her husband would have asked the name of each of them, and thanked them all, perhaps with some small reward. But then, however uncanny his birth, Elfgift hadn't been given the upbringing of a member of the Twelve Hundred.

Elfgift brought them all to one of the older quarters of the Borough, where Kendrida was in the habit of lodging the least important of her guests. A covered wagon, with oxen yoked to it, had stopped outside what was possibly the oldest, smallest and shabbiest of the guest halls. Kendrida was aghast to see a priestess standing beside the wagon.

The woman was of middle age, standing upright and calm amongst the yelling people coming and going about the cart. Her hair hung loose, like a girl's, instead of being gathered under a linen headdress; but what marked her unmistakably as a priestess was her cloak of striped cats' skins, trimmed with a fringe of feathers about the shoulders, and the tall wooden staff she held in her hand. A priestess was of high standing by virtue of her office alone, and might even be a daughter of the Twelve Hundred by birth. It distressed Kendrida that she should be standing there, in one of the poorest quarters of the residence. Even in Unwin's Christian Borough, it was proper to show respect to a priestess.

While she was wondering who had been housed in the better halls, and thinking how much better she would have managed things, Elfgift let go of her arm and left her side. She saw him jump up into the cart, and immediately men began to climb up after him, or to gather around the cart's tail-end.

A sling of blankets was lowered from the cart into the arms of those standing underneath, and the bundle of blankets and bedding, supported on many shoulders and arms, was carried into the guest-hall. The priestess followed, before Kendrida could speak to her. Then she saw Elfgift jump down from the front of the cart, and hurried after him as he went into the hall.

"Who was that, in the cart? There are better halls than this – this hasn't even a private room!"

He glanced at her, and turned away before she had finished speaking. She felt as if a door had been shut in her face. Who was this "king" that had been foisted on them? "Elf-born" perhaps, but not well-born!

Inside the hall fires were burning, warming the air and casting a fragile, golden light that moved like water over the wooden walls. But the walls were of bare wood! No hangings hid them. They weren't even plastered. It was to be hoped that the priestess hadn't brought many servants with her, because there was hardly a bench or a table in the place.

At the far end a curtain – of good cloth, thank goodness, but quite plain – had been hung across the hall's width, to screen off a private area. The curtain had been drawn back and, as Kendrida hurried up, the bundle of blankets was being lowered gently to the floor by the men – grooms and kitchen-hands mostly – who had carried it in.

Elfgift moved close to these men, looking into their faces, lightly touching the arm of one, the hand of another, thanking them.

They blushed, they grinned hugely and gathered close around him, even behind his back. True to their type, they went beyond what was proper, patting him on the shoulders, laughing in his face. He laughed with them. Well, he was one of them.

The men who had formed themselves into Elfgift's escort had drawn together in a knot. Kendrida saw their faces as they watched the thralls being thanked when they had not drawn a glance. She almost laughed – the men's expressions were so sharp with jealousy. She watched as the armed men gathered about Elfgift again – "to protect the King" they would no doubt say – and drove off their rivals. Then they looked at Elfgift, plainly hoping that now they would be praised for their attentiveness, but he looked briefly after the retreating thralls, and then walked away from his escort as if they were so many stools he had to pick his way among.

Kendrida shook her head. You may be elf-born and Goddess-chosen, she thought, but if you don't quickly learn how to keep the swords around you loyal, you will find one sheathed in your back.

The priestess was kneeling over the bundle of blankets. Elfgift crouched beside her and Kendrida, coming to his side, looked down on the patient wrapped in the bedding.

For an eye's blink, she thought she looked at a corpse. The face seemed as fragile as a bird's skull, its lips as white as the pallid skin around them, the eyelids blue, with blue shadows like bruises under the eyes. It seemed at once a worn, ancient face, and that of a sick child.

"Let me find a better hall than this," she said. The patient must be of high standing, to be travelling in a covered wagon, with a priestess in attendance. "One with a private room."

"Here is quiet," Elfgift said, seeming to speak to the priestess more than to her. Kendrida saw the priestess nod. "I chose it myself. It's far from the smithy and from the animal pens." Turning his head, he spoke directly to Kendrida. "Have straw laid in the streets."

The way he spoke to her only to issue an order angered her, though she knew he wished to deaden the sound of horses, carts and people passing. "We can't spare the straw," she said. "We need what we have for bedding and –"

He looked at her with a suddenness that seemed to have force behind it, and she took a step back before she could stop herself. Elf-eyes! They even seemed to have changed colour, becoming large and dark in the dim light of the hall. "Lay straw in the streets," he repeated. And he looked away, moved away, as if she had ceased to exist.

She was quite furious and felt a wave of heat pass through her. She remembered how his stillness had drawn her children to him, and how she had felt that same tug herself, whereas now... Now, she realized, she felt like the armed men, snubbed and jealous. Like them, she would forget her bad temper if, the next time his attention happened to light on her, he smiled. She considered these, her own feelings, with astonishment and dismay.

Servants came from the other side of the curtain, carrying a small, steaming tub, a jug and towels.

The priestess called them to her, and began to strip the patient for washing.

Kendrida looked beyond them to the bed. In this old hall, it was a plain one, built into a corner, with doors to turn it into a tiny room. The kind of bed a prosperous farmer might build for himself.

"Let me send for another bed," she said. "We have much better ones in store. I could have one brought here and put together in an eye-blink." She had in mind one in particular, with carved and gilded posts, and a high headboard with a projecting canopy, from which curtains could be hung to keep out draughts. She would fetch out her best linen and best down-filled coverlets. That would please Elfgift.

The priestess said, "He will be warm and quiet in this bed. That is all he needs. Let be."

Elfgift lifted the patient, propping him against his own shoulder. Kendrida looked at the two faces so close together, and was struck by the likeness, though one was so changed by sickness. "Oh!" she exclaimed, and both Elfgift and the priestess looked up at her. "It's Wulfweard!" Hadn't she mistaken Elfgift for him when she'd first seen him? "Oh – Lord! Wulfweard!"

She ran to the bed, to open the doors. Her young brother-by-wedlock, so sick he looked dead! Did Unwin know? It was small relief to find that the bed was already made up, and with linen sheets and a down-filled coverlet: she couldn't have chosen better herself.

On a shelf inside the bed-cabinet was a bowl of sweet dried herbs. Throwing back the coverlet, she sprinkled the dried lavender over the pillow and lower sheet. Strewing flowers on Wulfweard's grave... Did Unwin know that his youngest and favourite brother was – what should the message say? – still alive, or dying?

She looked over her shoulder and saw Elfgift lift Wulfweard and rise straight to his feet with the boy in his arms. The armed men all started forward, shouldering each other in their efforts to be the one to take the burden from him, but Elfgift ignored them, carried Wulfweard to the bed, and put him into it himself.

Before the covers were drawn over him Kendrida saw the dark, barely healed wounds across Wulfweard's chest, where every rib was outlined in shadow.

The priestess seated herself on the wall-bench that ran along the side of the bed. From the pouch at her waist, she took several slips of wood, laying them on the bench beside her. Taking a sharp little knife from a sheath at her belt, she took up the slips of wood, one by one, and carved into them the healing runes. She slipped them under the pillow and into the bed, near Wulfweard's heart and feet.

Elfgift leaned against the frame of the bed, looking down at his half-brother. To the priestess, he said, "He is no better."

The priestess broke off her work, dropping knife and wood in her lap. She sat back against the wall and sighed, then reached up and touched Elfgift's arm. Her hand slipped down until it reached his hand, which she held. "The spirit is gone," she said. "The heart beats because you keep it beating – and waste your strength." Kendrida saw the priestess's hand tighten on Elfgift's. "But Wulfweard is gone. The body will starve and the heart will stop, for all you can do."

Elfgift let his hand remain in the priestess's, and didn't speak or move.

Kendrida heard the word "starve" and said, "He must have something rich and soft – I shall make up a dish of groats, with cream and eggs, and sweeten it with honey. Even a little of that would do him good."

The priestess let go of Elfgift's hand and took up her knife again. She said, "We should take off the bed-covers, put out the fires and let him die quickly."

Kendrida took a quick step forward. "Not under my roof." It was unlucky to have any guest die under your roof, but one of the Royal Kin, one of Woden's sons! And suppose things fell out so she had to live with her husband, Unwin

Eadmundsson, again and he found out that she had let his youngest and favourite brother starve and chill to death. "I shall never allow that under my roof."

Elfgift knelt by the bed and drew back the down coverlet. She thought, for an instant, that he was taking off the covers, as the priestess had said, and she started forward to stop him. But before she could take a full step, she saw that he had pressed the palms of both hands to Wulfweard's chest. He lowered his own head so that his hair fell forward and hid his face and his hands from sight.

The priestess rose, took Elfgift by the shoulders and pushed him, so that he fell back to sit on his heels, looking up at her. She said, scolding, "When you haven't eaten all day!"

Elfgift rose to his feet and walked from the bed. He passed the armed men without noticing them, but they formed up and followed him. He turned to face them suddenly, and stopped. He looked at each of them, and then touched two on the shoulder and pointed to the bed where Wulf-weard lay – they were to remain, as guards.

Kendrida saw the faces of the men as they came back to mount guard. They were awed with the honour of it, and thrilled. They were happy men. *Me!* they were each thinking: *He noticed* me!

And the others, who had gone with Elfgift, would all be competing, all the more fiercely, for his notice.

Perhaps, Kendrida thought, the Twelve Hundred have nothing to teach the elf-born after all.

She went to the bed and drew the covers up to Wulfweard's chin. To the priestess, she said, "Not under my roof."

Kendrida's duties as Lady of the Borough had been usurped by Elfgift's officers, but she asked about her people. Her captain had been relieved of his command, but had been given another, and would be leaving with Elfgift when the troops moved on. It was good to know he had not been harmed or humiliated for his loyalty. And the strange troops seemed to have behaved well. She could find no incident of her people having been robbed or harmed. She was able to return to her lodgings and reassure her maids and children that they were safe.

She was in her room when the three Christian monks who served the Borough's church came to her, begging her to save them from being turned out on to the roads.

"What can I do?" she asked them. "The Borough is Elfgift's now – and he has told me himself that you can stay if you will set your altar up beside the others."

They only stared at her.

"What can I do?" she asked again. "Your church

was Ing's God-house before it was Christ's." The figure of Ing it had once housed had been a fine one, she had been told, and she often wished she could have seen it. Once again she realized how keenly she missed the festivals of her childhood from which her Christian marriage had exiled her. Ing's Feast fell just as the year was turning dark and cold, when Ing, in defiance of the dying all around, offered Himself as a target and spread wide His arms to receive the spears. His blood ran into the earth, and His spirit was taken into the Other World, to Hel's Hall. But it was always a cheerful feast, where people lit bonfires, got very drunk, and threw spears at a straw figure which was afterwards burned, as Ing had been burned on His pyre. They knew Ing would return.

Jul's feast fell in mid-winter, when the darkness had gone on for so long, and was still to go on for so much longer, that it seemed unbearable. It was held on the year's shortest day and longest night. After that, though it might grow still darker and colder, the nights grew shorter and the days longer as the sun returned. It was the Festival of the Dead, when grieving Woden made His way into the Other World, to plead with Hel to release His son Ing. Hel refused Him Ing, but allowed Him to bring the other dead back to earth for a single night. Kendrida remembered with what tenderness she had set places at table, served food, and sat down to eat with her dead, though they remained invisible.

And Eostre's feast, which began sadly with mourning for Ing. Everyone had prayed to help the Lady on Her way into the Other World to bargain with Her sister, Hel, for Ing's freedom. "All must weep for Him," Hel said, and so the women covered their heads, smeared ash on their faces, and keened. As a young girl she had luxuriated in the weeping, swaying and rocking with tears pouring down her face and into her mouth. Children wept easily, as they did at sad stories. Even men wept, and the madder sort among men and women cut their own arms with knives and drew blood.

The end of the day-long weeping was that Hel kept Her promise and released Ing, and the people celebrated with a feast even wilder and drunker than Jul. Eggs, the first of the year, were dyed red and everyone gave them to friends, with the words, "Ing is with us!" They were hard-boiled and rolled or cracked against each other in contests. People kissed and hugged, and pointed out catkins on the trees and primroses in the grass with cries of, "Ing is home!"

The Christian paintings on the walls of Unwin's church had been painted over friezes of Ing's Return to Earth, His Spring Ride. Kendrida said, "Unwin had the Gods burned and the Christian altar set up. Well, now the Gods have returned."

"Lady," said the abbot, "I think you are not displeased to see Christ thrown down, and us thrown on the roads."

"I am much concerned to think of you on the roads. If you insist on going, you shall have money and food. But you can stay safely here, under my protection."

The monks turned their backs on her and left her room. Nevertheless, she instructed her steward that if they left the Borough they were to be given food and money.

She was visited by Athelric, who asked to see the children, but endeared himself to them far less than Elfgift had. Godhilda, the maids said, had not stopped talking about "her wolf" all day.

Athelric spoke of Elfgift in a way that veered oddly from awe to fondness. He had an almost doting look on his face, as if he spoke now of a hero, now of a favourite nephew. She had nothing to fear, he said, "because we are all under the Goddess's protection now."

In that case, Kendrida thought, shouldn't we fear the Goddess?

That evening the Royal Hall was crammed, the benches and tables filled with the many, many people now in the Borough, who all had to be fed. Looking down from her place behind the high table, Kendrida decided that as soon as Elfgift's troops were gone she would have to check her stores. She led her maids from table to table, serving drink to all, but, as soon as that duty was over, and she had made sure that her children and maids were safe in their lodgings, she called for a servant with a lantern, and made her way through the dark streets to the shabby little hall where Wulfweard was lodged.

The hall was dark, the fires smoored, and the servants already bedded down on the floor. Making her way through them, she slipped around the edge of the curtain, hardly disturbing it.

The fire was still burning behind the curtain, though it was now low and its light red. The two guards were awake, seated opposite each other on the wide sleeping-benches. The priestess lay on the bench, asleep.

The guards made no attempt to stop Kendrida approaching the bed, but watched her. Because of them, she didn't go too near. One door of the bed stood a little open, the red firelight shone inside, and she could see that the covers were pulled up.

Someone was standing so close beside her they almost touched, and she gasped and stepped back, startled and angry because the guards had no right to come so close. But it was Elfgift.

He looked at the guards and, with a gesture, told them to leave.

When they had gone, he went to the bed and opened its doors wide. He sat on it and leaned into its shadows.

She remained standing near the fire, feeling snubbed once more, wondering if she should go, wishing *he* would go. Elfgift turned his head and looked at her. In the dim red light his eyes seemed black. "She's right. Only the heart beats: the spirit is gone. But I want a brother."

Tears filled her eyes. When she married, she had left her own country and her brothers and sisters behind. She doubted she would ever see them again. Her husband had fathered children on her, and yet there was no affection between them. All day, every day, she was surrounded by people to whom she was the Lady of the Borough, and she had her children to whom she must be mother — but there was no one who would both ask her advice and tease her, no one who would treat her sometimes as an equal, sometimes as an elder, sometimes as a child. No real friend; no sister or brother.

She had seen how people followed Elfgift and gawped at him, muttering about the "elf-born" — but he, too, must be as lonely as she. She went closer to him, and her hand moved by itself, reaching out to touch his shoulder, to let him know that she felt with him. Even before her fingers touched him, she felt that curious warmth that surrounded him, and he said,

"Lady, why won't you help me?"

She drew back her hand, startled, and then realized he had not been talking to her. He was looking out of the bed, towards her but not at her. It was as if she was not there, or was one of the house-trees that held up the hall roof.

Was he talking to the priestess? But the priestess still lay on the bench, asleep.

Elfgift was looking at the empty air in front of him. His voice, as he spoke quietly in his throat, seemed to thrum in the red-lit darkness. "Lady. Help me."

The darkness, smoke, firelight and flying sparks spun in Kendrida's eyes, spun into the shape of a woman. Before she could raise her hand in surprise, the woman had melted back into the flame-flickers – but then stood there again, beside the bed: a tall, straight woman with long hair hanging below her hips.

Kendrida's heart beat so wildly that she tried to hold it still with her hands. The woman had always been there, even before she had been able to see her. Elfgift had been looking at her. It was as if the dusk of the red half-light and smoke had been a fog, hiding her from sight.

Elf-sight, she thought: he has elf-sight.

She took a step backwards, wanting to run away, because she was seeing things that she should not see. But, afraid, she stayed where she was, like the bird that presses close to the ground and hopes the fox will pass by.

The woman of shadow and firelight drew close to Elfgift and he rose to meet her. She put her arms round him, standing as tall as he. Her long hair hung down, shining red and copper in the firelight. Her voice was a whisper in the darkness. "He died at the Battle of the Shrieking Stone. That was the weird woven for him."

Elfgift did not embrace her in return. "Lady, You choose the slain."

"You are asking me to choose another's life in place of his?"

"Aye. Take his brother's. Take Unwin's."

Kendrida, hearing that, began to shake in long shudders. She hugged herself but still she shook. She thought she had no love for her husband, but even so, to hear such words... It was dangerous even to think of killing one of the Royal Kin. Vengeance, and war, and many other deaths always followed. This is a dream, she thought. I am lying asleep in my bed, and I am peering into this red-lit cavern, and hearing these whispered, thrumming words. A foretelling dream foretelling nothing good.

The tall woman reached up and lifted Elfgift's long hair so that, except for the fine braids, it fell down his back. "But you are going to take

Unwin's life for me."

"Aye; and as I serve You, Lady, I ask You for this in return: Wulfweard's life."

"He is Woden's now. He waits outside Woden's Hall, until his body sets him free and he can enter in among the heroes. Are you not afraid of Woden?"

"You are greater than Woden, Lady."

"Oh..." In the darkness she chuckled, and stroked his hair again. "Don't put that to the test. I am Life and Death; He is Death and Life. I choose the slain; He chooses those to live. And Wulfweard is His now. When you need His promise to win your battles, are you not afraid to anger Him?"

There was a silence, and Kendrida stood staring in fascination at the firelit figures, the dying red light glimmering over their hair, now flaring and showing the curve of a shoulder and arm, the fold in a dress; now dying and letting them fall back into shadow. She thought: *I should not be seeing this!* and remembered stories of others who had glimpsed such things, overheard such words. They had been blasted, blinded, or turned to stone. She felt the hard coldness of stone closing around her. Her heart hardly beat, her feet didn't feel the floor beneath them, nor her one hand the grip of the other.

Elfgift spoke. "Lady, the day of my death, and the way of my dying, You chose long ago. Until that day, I need fear nothing. When that day comes, nothing will save me. But if I have served You well, please give me this: while I live, let me have a brother."

Another silence, as Kendrida watched the figures fade and glow, come and go, in the firelight. Then Elfgift lowered his head to the woman's shoulder and put his arms around her.

She lifted his head and held his face between her hands before kissing him. "Choose. Choose between your brother and your Lady."

Elfgift's head tilted down between her hands, as if he could not look her in the eye. Kendrida, waiting and dreading that she would be seen, held her breath and clenched her hands until they hurt. She saw Elfgift shake his head, still held between the woman's hands.

The woman released him. "I'll give you your wish. You must find for yourself the strength to live with it."

She moved to the bed, stooped and leaned into it. Her long hair fell forward over her shoulders and over the covers of the bed, hiding all within the bed from view. Then she drew back, her hair trailing over the bed, and straightened up. She looked at Elfgift and, turning her head, gave one look at Kendrida. Even as her head still turned, she was no more to be seen. Kendrida stood stock still, her hands gripping and twisting each other bruisingly hard, breathing in small, stuttering gasps. She peered, even squinted, at the empty air beside the bed, but the shadows, the darkness and the firelight would not be made into any shape now. No one stood there. No one she could see.

Elfgift seated himself on the bed and leaned into it, his head and shoulders swathed in its shadow. Kendrida moved towards him with tiny, unsteady steps.

The fire was dying, and it was dark in the room and growing cold. The interior of the bed was dark, and she could see nothing of Wulfweard. Yet, as her hand reached out to the bed-post and she leaned there, she saw a light within the bed, faint at first, but growing in strength, as if a candle had just been lit and flickered but then grew bright. By its light she saw Elfgift's hands, pressed on Wulfweard's chest. The light lit the fall of long hair that hid Elfgift's face, and touched the rounds and hollows of Wulfweard's chest and neck, even touched his face here and there. Slowly Kendrida realized that the light came from Elfgift's hands and was only seen because the room was so dark.

There was a warmth too, which didn't come from the fire, but from Elfgift – a steady strengthening of his warmth, which always seemed greater than that of other people. With the warmth came a scent, which might only have been the sweet, new-cut grass scent of the straw in the mattress beneath Wulfweard, and the scent of the wood in the walls of the hall.

She heard Wulfweard draw a long breath, and let it out easily and smoothly. He stirred in the bed, and sighed, and then began to breathe deeply, easily. The light that was brightest at Elfgift's hands faded, withdrawing from the corners of the bed, dimming and dimming until it was gone and the room was darker, blacker, colder than before.

The light seemed to have gone inside Kendrida, where it blazed in her heart and head. In the darkness, she smiled, from the deep and awed happiness she felt. *Gods*, she thought. *What I have seen!*

It is true, she thought, *it is* true.

What I have seen!

Despite all the stories, when she had heard him called "Goddess-chosen", she had thought it meant only that he had gone through the ceremony of king-making, and had set his foot on the Stone while the trumpets were blown. But what she had seen! The words "Goddess-chosen" were plain in their meaning and true and, because they were true and plain, they were immense and powerful. The Goddess had chosen him: he was Her lover, Her Ing, the day of his death and the way of his dying already chosen.

She could not stand. Her legs trembled and weakened under her until she knelt. And then, wanting somehow to make her gratitude and her fear known, she found his boots with her hands and lowered her head.

Startled, he put his hands under her elbows and pulled her up. She sobbed.

He stood, pulling her to her feet, pulling her with him across the room in the red dark. He kicked the fire with his booted foot, and it burned up. Small yellow flames sent a wavering, fragile light into the room and showed them, faintly, each other's faces. "What?" he said.

He folded his legs and sat by the fire-side, pulling her down with him. The flames were closer now and lit his face as he smiled at her, making his long hair yellow and his eyes grey. He was puzzled by her and shook his head slightly as he smiled, his expression wondering and even a little shy. He was so beautiful and so young that she reached towards him, put her arms around him and leaned her head against his shoulder. She wanted to embrace him and kiss him like a lover; she wanted to kiss his foot as she might have kissed the foot of the Ing-figure in the God-house; she wanted to cuddle him protectively as she would her sons. She felt more than a little crazy, and remembered how odd she had found Athelric's mixture of awe and fondness.

He supported her as she leaned on him, and his arms came round her, touching her head, her back, and then clasping her in a strong hold. She was lapped round with his warmth, and his scent of musk and hay, and his hair touched her face and was soft. Never had she felt so safe and happy.

"What is it?" he said.

"What I have seen!" She lifted her head from his shoulder so that she could look at his face again. "I *know* you! I am so scared – and so glad!"

He smiled at her again, shaking his head, young and puzzled.

"Now I know you," she said, smiling back, "now I *know* we are safe!"

The smile fell from his face. He took his arms from around her and rose to his feet, moving away from her. Without his support, she fell forward, her hands jarring on the floor.

He said, "Lady, there is no safety in knowing me."

CHAPTER 4

The Harper

Ingvald was a tall man, heavy in the shoulder and chest, with thick arms and big hands. He was bearded and, like all Danes, wore his light brown hair cut "to bare the neck and blind the eye", though he was bald on top. The feast that evening was being held in his honour and, having dressed in leggings of green and yellow stripes, and an expensive tunic of yellow silk, he was seated on his bed, bent over a small wooden chest, choosing the rings he would wear on every finger, and both thumbs.

Ingvi, already dressed in his best, sat on a stool by the wall. The brothers hadn't seen each other in two years and yet Ingvi had hardly spoken.

Ingvald kept glancing at him as he pushed rings over his thick knuckles.

Every other year Ingvald came to Lovern's court to renew his vows of loyalty, and Ingvi always looked forward eagerly to the visits. He was Danish again, in Ingvald's company – a Jarl's son and a Jarl's brother, not merely one of Lovern's hostages. Ingvald always brought him gifts and Ingvi, though he had almost nothing, tried to have some gift for his brother: a wolf-skin, or a stag's antlers, from beasts he had killed himself. Indeed, Ingvald was wearing a knife with a hilt of carved antler which Ingvi had given him years before. Whether he wore it because he always did, or whether he had found it out for this occasion as a compliment to his young brother, didn't matter. Ingvi loved him for it.

But on this visit, Ingvi was ashamed of Ingvald too. Ingvi had been present when his brother met Unwin Sassenach and had waited, smiling, to hear Ingvald speak of the men and arms he would give to Unwin.

Instead, before everyone, Ingvald had doubted that attacking the Saxons was wise. Better to wait. It wasn't certain that the elf-born could bring the Saxons under his rule. It could be that the Saxons would do their work for them. Then Unwin could return to his country as a king and hero, and it would be much cheaper.

Nodding to King Lovern, while turning his shoulder to Unwin, Ingvald had seemed to say: These young men, without kingdoms of their own, can make grand plans and never give a thought to how it will all be paid for. But you and I, Lovern... For himself, he couldn't think of such expense. The past three harvests had been bad. It was hard to equip his war-band, hard to keep them loyal. He was Lovern's man, and would obey any command of Lovern's, but...

Only stubborn loyalty to his brother had kept Ingvi from walking out of the hall. When they had all parted to go to their lodgings and prepare for the feast everyone had, of course, been on good terms. But though Ingvi had walked his brother to his lodgings, and though he was now waiting to walk with him to the feast, he had hardly been able to speak a word to him.

Ingvald, having put a gold ring on every finger, and bigger rings set with garnets on his thumbs, looked up at Ingvi and waited.

Ingvi tried to appear haughty, but when he saw Ingvald smile, he had to look away, and he fidgeted, as if it was *he* who was in the wrong.

Ingvald rummaged in his jewel-box. Whistling to attract Ingvi's attention, he threw him something which flashed in the firelight.

Ingvi caught it in both hands. It was a large, round brooch for fastening a cloak, shaped like intertwining dragons biting each other's tail. Each dragon had a garnet for an eye. "Wear it," Ingvald said. "Keep it."

"Thank you," Ingvi said, and that was all.

"Come here." The words had the ring of an order, and Ingvi went over to the bed. Ingvald sorted a handful of rings from the clutter in the chest and, taking his brother's hand, put them on his fingers.

"I thought you were poor," Ingvi said. "I thought the harvests were bad and you couldn't equip men."

Ingvald shook his head, grinning, as he closed the chest. Now he knew what was wrong. Alone here at Lovern's court, Ingvi had been listening to the Sassenach and dreaming of spreading a feast before the wolf. He was angry and sulky because Ingvald was not quite so ready to fight a Christian's battles for him.

But Ingvi, of course, lived among Christians. He had friends among them and looked to King Lovern for favour. It grieved Ingvald, but he wondered if he could afford to be entirely honest with his younger brother. A dreadful thing to think of your own brother, but Ingvald was not a big enough fool to refuse to think it.

"Has Lovern mentioned marriage to you yet?"

Ingvi looked up, surprised, from admiring the rings on his fingers. "No."

"He'll want to marry you to some Christian woman." Ingvi seemed unmoved by the idea. "I want to find you a wife in Denmark."

That did take Ingvi's interest. When he looked up, Ingvald saw all the doubts in his face. Ingvald himself was married to a Jarl's daughter from Denmark. If Ingvi made a similar marriage, making a stronger alliance with their homeland, then Lovern would feel slighted and threatened. And a Danish marriage would be pagan, blessed by Thor and Freyja, not Christ. Lovern would never allow his Danish hostage to be married to a woman from Denmark. So if Lovern would never allow it … What was Ingvald thinking of?

"Time we were getting to the feast." Ingvald picked up his cloak and swung it round his shoulders. They went out together, first into the hall of Ingvald's lodgings, where their escort met them, and then into the cold yards of the Dun.

All Ingvald had seen in Ingvi's face had been dismay at the prospect of being torn between Lovern, at whose court he had grown up, and Ingvald, to whom he owed family loyalty.

So he said nothing of his real reasons for being unwilling to join with Unwin. Why should a small pagan jarldom, already in thrall to one Christian king, fight another pagan kingdom in order to give it to another Christian king? Then there would be two strong Christian kingdoms, and the little pagan jarldom caught between them wouldn't last for long.

"One God above," said the Christians, "one king below." They wouldn't tolerate the worship of any God but their own, and every Christian king wanted to be the one king. Little countries, with their own Gods, their own customs, their own laws, couldn't hope to survive.

Ingvald wasn't strong enough to join the Goddess-chosen elf-born and help him to defeat the Christians. But maybe he could delay the war, or reduce the numbers that would go against the Elf. And maybe, if he was careful and watched for his chance, there would be a way of freeing his jarldom.

As they neared the Feast Hall, the firelight shining from its high windows and its open door, Ingvald wondered, if it came to war with Lovern, on whose side would Ingvi be?

On his side – his. It was unthinkable that Ingvi would fight against him. Ingvald dropped his arm across Ingvi's shoulders, and smiled as Ingvi turned, smiling, to him. Ingvi's darkness shone like jet in the torch-light. His outlandish mother meant they were as little like brothers as a grey cockerel and a raven. Ingvald could only hope their shared father was enough.

Bright, warm yellow light shone from the hall, and a din of voices came from inside. The guards, recognizing the Jarlssens, moved to open the door for them. Another man, tall and thickset, moved from the shadows against the hall's wall. He was wrapped in a cloak which, where the light touched it, was blue. The cloak's hood hung over his brow and hid his face. In his hands he carried a harp-bag.

"Take me in with you, Jarls?"

He spoke not in Welsh, but in their own Danish. They stopped and Ingvald, reaching out a hand, flipped the man's hood from his head so the light shone on his face. They saw a man of strong, healthy old age, his skin weathered into leathery wrinkles, his hair and beard iron-grey. The eye catching the light looked at them steadily, a bright blue. The other lay in shadow under the deep brow.

"Your name?" Ingvald asked.

"Ud Harper. I travel, Jarl, never long in one place. A stranger everywhere."

"Your father?" Ingvald said. "Your family?"

"Ud Udssen, son of Ud, son of Ud, son of Ud." Something about the man's voice suggested he was laughing at them. "I've been called Ud the Pleasant, and Grey-Beard and Long-Beard, and Ud Deep-Hood. But I am Ud Harper, and I wish to play for you tonight."

"I have a harper," Ingvald said, "and King Lovern has many." He doubted the skill of a harper who had no lord, and was reluctant to inflict a poor musician on the company.

"I have no harper," Ingvi said. He thought it stingy to turn the man away. "I'll take you in, and if you play well, I'll reward you." Thanks to Ingvald, he could give the man a ring from his hand.

"I am grateful," said Ud Harper and, bowing, drew the hood of his cloak over his head so that, as he followed them into the hall, his face was again hidden in shadow. Once through the doors, he left them, and found a place on the benches along the wall, waiting his turn to play. Ingvald and Ingvi made their way to the high table.

So many candles and torches had been lit from end to end of the hall that it blazed with light and heat. The long benches at the tables were filling up with men in their brightest colours, all wearing brooches, arm-bands, necklaces, belt buckles and rings that flashed in the changing fire-light. Their wives and daughters, as brightly dressed, sat at the tables with the men.

Ingvald, as guest of honour, was to sit beside the king, with Ingvi at his other side, while Unwin sat beside the queen. Both king and queen, when they entered, were dressed in long straight white robes, sewn with gold thread and many gems, while their heads were crowned with high-standing circlets from which golden crosses, studded with gems, hung to their shoulders on fine golden chains. They moved stiffly and slowly, hampered by their heavy, rigid robes, and seemed more like idols than people.

Wine was served by the queen and her ladies, and toasts were drunk while the food was served. Ingvi, his sulk long forgotten, pointed out to Ingvald various people of note, and passed on the gossip about them, ducking his head close to his brother's and speaking in quiet, rapid Danish. It was perhaps something of a slight to their hosts, but the whispering and shared language drew the brothers close again. King Lovern, seeing their heads rest together, gave a slight nod which set the jewelled crosses of his crown swinging and sparkling at the ends of their chains. He was reassured that Ingvi was not merely an expensive house-guest, but a valuable hostage. While he held Ingvi, he controlled Jarl Ingvald; though, in a few years more, he might do well to exchange Ingvi for one of Ingvald's sons.

Unwin, his attention taken by a burst of laughter from the Danish brothers, remembered once again that now he had no brothers. And while they sat feasting, the elf's drop might be murdering his sons.

The roasted carcase of a boar was brought in and carved up by the stewards and his officers. The choicest cuts of the meat were brought first to the king, so that he could make a show of giving them to Ingvald and to Unwin instead of keeping them himself. More wine was poured out, and the queen carried round baskets from which she distributed to her guests not only the best and whitest bread, but costly presents: brooches for cloaks and hats, rings, belt-buckles and such-like. For Ingvald and for Unwin there were swords with gemmed hilts and gilded scabbards. Impractical as weapons, but their great value honoured the guest.

By now the feast hall was so hot that the guests' faces glistened with sweat. The laughter and talk was so loud and constant that people had to shout to be heard by their neighbour. Smoke from the many candles and fires hung above the tables, and the golden light flashed across brooches and rings, blazed in the heart of gems, glittered on glass. The harp was sent round the tables, and the noise stilled to hear the music and the words – only to burst out in a thundering of fists on tables and crashing laughter at some clever rhyme or witty, jibing reference to another guest.

The harp came to the high table and an attentive quiet fell on the lower tables. Everyone in the hall knew that the Sassenach prince had asked for the aid of the Danish Jarl in winning his kingdom back. Everyone knew that the Danish Jarl had, politely, refused, and that their own king was not best pleased with his Danish vassal. Attention sharpened still more when Lovern himself took the harp. The king's voice, and the ringing notes of the harp were clear in the silence.

The king's song was short and simple, telling of a fish swimming in clear water and of a tree growing tall in the sunlight, spreading its branches wide and dropping its sweet fruit on the land beneath. Ingvi gave a small gasp, and leaned to his brother's ear to translate. The words seemed pretty and empty to Ingvald until Ingvi explained their meaning: the fish was the Christian symbol, and therefore the clarity of the water was to be understood as the clarity and excellence of the Christian message. It followed that the tree was the Christian church, growing tall and flourishing in the light of God, and giving its blessings to the land beneath – that was, to Lovern and Unwin's kingdoms.

Ingvald kept his face expressionless, but he understood. Lovern was making clear where his sympathies lay.

The king passed the harp to his guest, Unwin. Ingvald's eyelids flickered – as guest of honour, he might have expected the harp to come to him. But Unwin was a highly favoured guest too – there was no real cause for him to take offence. The Danish brothers didn't look at each other. They waited to hear what Unwin would sing.

It was a song with a lamenting tune, and the

harp's notes rang out and died in the listening quiet. Ingvald and Ingvi were among the very few in the hall who understood the words, and they understood as soon as the first lines were sung. There were Danish versions of the tale. It told the story of two brothers, devoted to each other, who lucklessly fell in love with the same woman. Each tried to behave honourably, but they ended by killing each other and breaking the hearts of their father and the woman they both loved.

At the end of the song, Lovern's people applauded with polite enthusiasm. Ingvald and Ingvi joined in the applause, and kept smiling. We, who share the same language, the song said to them, should behave as brothers and stand together. To quarrel brings tragedy.

Unwin stood and, smiling, passed the harp along the table to Ingvald, who took it, and strummed its strings with his fingers while he thought.

Ingvi ducked his head close to his brother's and whispered, "Call the harper!"

Ingvald raised his head. "I am ham-fisted with a harp," he said, and though it was a shameful thing to admit, he would rather that than enter into this battle of wits by song. "I'll spare your ears my clumsiness and let you hear a real harper. Ud! Come forward now!" A strange harper's choice of song would not be turned into a message from him, even if the music was poor.

Ud Harper rose from his place against the wall, amongst the servants, and came forward through the tables to the centre of the hall, before the high table and the fire. He had left his cloak and harp-bag behind him and stood, in the full light of fire and candles, dressed in good, plain cloth, but with no weapons about him except the eating-knife at his belt. His harp was a plain, undecorated instrument, unlike the carved and gilded one under Ingvald's hands. He turned his handsome lined face from side to side, smiling, and all saw that the harper was one-eyed. The eye that had seemed so deep-set in the shadows was a gouged, scarred pit. The queen raised her hand in distaste, to shield her own eyes from the sight.

A coldness seemed to shiver over Ingvi's skin, like the cold that touched him when dusk came through the trees and he remembered stories of hollow-backed elf-women. "I am called Grey-Beard, Deep-Hood..." And One-Eye too, and Wanderer – and – and... But as Ingvi's mind groped after images they retreated from him, leaving unease behind. As his mind tried to make his fear plain to him, the harpist's fingers brought a swift river of music from his strings.

The clearest, sharpest notes of the harp rang out like horn-blasts and brought everyone upright in their chairs and on the benches. Softer notes interwove, whispered in their ears and set the hairs on their necks and arms to twitching. Everyone turned towards the harpist. A silence fell, deeper than that for the king.

The harpist laughed – his voice was deep – and said, "Now, friends, we shall fly on the music's wings." And he brought from the harp another run of music that caught at the heart. Ingvi, sitting straight, his head up, felt his heart beating faster, filling his body with strength and his head with clarity – but he no longer gave a thought to who the harpist was, or to the strange familiarity of his names. Instead, his eyes wide, he listened so intently that he almost ceased to be Ingvi. It was the same with everyone else in the hall. People stopped eating, drinking, talking. They sat still and held their breath. They no longer felt the chair under them, or the heat of the fire. In all the brightness of the hall, they saw nothing but the one-eyed harper.

The music of the harp became soft and lapping, and the harper sang,

"Here come my darlings,
Beautiful,
Gold on their breasts,
Bringing drink for the heroes:
  Come Shield-girl,
  Come Raging,

Sweet Axe-time, fair Spear-girl,
Come Screaming,
Come Shrieking,
Come Host-Fetter, come Shaker, come
  Wrecker!"

They were the names of Battle-women, and as each name rang out, every man in the hall – and many women – felt the blood answer in their head. They drew long, shaking breaths as their hearts beat faster and their fists clenched.

"Come my darlings,
Make music for me.
Sound the call to battle!
Set war in the hearts of princes, hatred
  in the hearts of jarls.
Breaking of shields and death-screams,
  That is my music.
Axe-bite and raging,
  That is the song I love.
Fill my cup with battle's mead!
Feast the wolf, feed the raven!
  That is my delight."

Every man present felt his courage high, his muscles tensed. They heard the call to battle. The harp music softened and died away. Ingvi put his hand to his head, dizzied. He could not remember a single word he had heard, but the pumping of his blood, the drunken excitement remained.

Ud Harper tucked his small harp under his arm and drew a little nearer the high table, but in his dark clothes he faded into the smoke and the shadows between the flame-flickers.

Ingvald stood at the high table, in the full light of the torches, with Lovern's gilded harp in his hands. Ingvi remembered seeing his brother's fingers move on the strings, remembered his brother's voice raised in the song – *"Set hatred in the hearts of Jarls!"*

The hall dinned with applause. People clapped, cheered, banged their fists and cups on the tables, set the flames dancing with their shouting. All were looking towards Ingvald, praising him for the song that had roused them.

King Lovern called for more drink, and the queen's women hurried forward with the mead tubs to fill the cups again. Unwin, standing and holding out his glass towards Ingvald, called for a toast to the Jarl who was going to feast the wolf and feed the raven.

Ingvi jumped to his feet and shouted out, "King! Let me ask a favour, King!"

"Ask anything," Ud Harper said, "and you shall have it."

The people in the hall were astonished to hear their King Lovern speak these words. Once a king gives his word he should keep it, and Lovern was a close-mouthed man.

"Let me go to war with my brother and Eadmundsson," Ingvi said. "What I win, I'll give to you, King, if you let me go."

"I shall give you horses, weapons and armour," said Ud Harper. "Go to your war with my blessing." Ud raised his arm, and every man and woman in the hall broke into applause and cheering.

King Lovern graciously bowed his crowned head, wondering at the words he had heard himself speak – and which he could not take back. He had lost his most valuable hostage.

Ud Harper walked unnoticed through the tables to sit on a wall-bench among the servants. A long night, and many songs and much ale later, when the guests were leaving the hall to be torch-lit through the yards to their lodgings, Ud rose and stepped into Unwin's way.

Unwin peered at him drunkenly, wondering why the man had been allowed to come so near him.

"Atheling," Ud said, "make me your harper."

The word "harper" reached Unwin. Harpers received reward. He took a ring from his finger, gave it to the man, and went on.

Ud smiled, put the ring on his finger, and followed Unwin to his lodgings.

CHAPTER 5

News of Unwin

A clear, bright patch of sunlight fell through the open doorway of the little hall on to the straw-strewn earthen floor. Beyond that brightness, the light became dimmer until the further stretches of the hall were in shadow. A fire burned in the central hearth, and there was a smell of smoke and of the old straw in the thatch.

Godwin walked towards the end of the hall, where the curtain hung across its width. Lying on the floor, close to the curtain, was a plain, battered old shield, and a scabbarded sword, its sword belt still attached, as if it had been taken off and dropped there. A guard rose from the bench by the wall, lowering his spear so that its shaft and point swung down before Godwin's chest.

Godwin looked up at the man, at his helmet with its nose-guard, and his teeth grinning through his beard. "I've come to see my father's brother. I am Godwin Un – ." Perhaps it would be best not to mention his father's name, though it came hard. His father himself would advise caution. "Godwin Atheling."

The spear swung up and the guard leaned on it. "I think he's asleep." He nodded towards the shield and sword on the floor. "Tired himself out."

"I shall wait for him to wake," Godwin said, and moved the curtain aside.

A wind-hole high in the gable-wall made it lighter behind the curtain than in the main body of the hall. Light filtered down softly through the dust and smoke. Godwin looked round. His father's brother was not to be seen anywhere – but the doors of the corner bed stood open. Godwin went over to it.

The interior of the bed was in deep shadow, but when he was close he could see Wulfweard, propped half-upright on pillows, his head turned to the side and his eyes closed. His long hair, tied back, fell over his shoulder in a thick horse's tail.

Godwin waited, thinking Wulfweard might only be resting, but the deep, slow breathing soon told him that Wulfweard was asleep. Godwin put his hand to his mouth, to keep himself from laughing. It always seemed funny, to him, to be with someone who was asleep – you could play any trick on them.

There was a small stool beside the bed, and Godwin sat on it, being careful of the two eggs he had stolen from a hen-house and put into his belt-pouch. They were his excuse for being here. Having made sure they were safe, he studied his sleeping kinsman.

Wulfweard had gained flesh, thanks to Kendrida's coddling of eggs with herbs, her dishes of groats with cream, butter and honey, and her flavouring of warm milk with almond oil – but he was still thin. His jaw was as sharp as a knife.

The front of his linen shirt was unlaced, and through it Godwin could see the scar across his chest, well on in its healing now, but still a vivid red against the white skin. He wondered how much it had hurt, that blow, dashing hard against the ribs and opening the flesh with a sharp edge; and he felt his own flesh twitch on his bones. He owned a small shield, but only a wooden sword, and so far had only fought in play. One day, though, he would have to stand and take such blows. *How do men have the courage?* he wondered, but then he sat up straight and told himself that it came with growth. As his body grew, so would his courage. His father wasn't afraid to stand in the shield-wall and face the spears and axes, and nor had the men of his mother's family been. A boy took his looks from his father and his courage from his mother, and his mother came from a family of warriors too. He would be ready to fight when the time came. It was bred into him.

It was harder to understand how Wulfweard had the courage to fight and take the wound that had nearly killed him, and yet call the thing that gave him the wound "brother". The elf's drop had killed one of Wulfweard's brothers and exiled the other, and yet he called it "brother". How could he be so shameless?

He must have been bought with blood-money. The thought of a member of the Royal Kin taking blood-money for a brother from a bastard and an elf's drop was so shameful that Godwin blushed where he sat. *Even a kingdom*, he thought – *even two kingdoms wouldn't be enough to pay me to fight against my own blood!*

Looking at Wulfweard, Godwin thought: *I should stab him now. He shouldn't be allowed to live and shame us any longer. He's vile.*

Godwin took one of the bed's doors and slammed it hard, and slammed it again.

Light and noise – a thunderclap – broke Wulfweard's sleep. He opened his eyes and raised his hand to shield them from the dim light. A voice called his name, the sound arcing through darkness, his brother's voice calling... There was darkness all around and a dark sky above the moor. Was the light from the windows of the hall he had been trying to find?

"I'm sorry if I woke you," Godwin said.

Wulfweard lowered his hand from his eyes and stared at the boy bemusedly, trying to make sense of who he was and why he was on the moor, and slowly realizing that he was inside a hall – another hall. He looked at the wood of the bed around him, and put a hand to his head. He smiled.

Godwin looked away. The smile made Wulfweard look so like the elf-born, and he hated to see that. He opened his pouch and took out the eggs. "I brought these for you. To do you good."

Godwin held an egg in each hand, but Wulfweard was able to take them both in one hand. The wrists above his big hands, though, looked fragile. Wulfweard smiled again, but Godwin stiffened his face and kept it still.

"Did your mother tell you to bring them?" Wulfweard asked.

"I brought them myself. I thought of it."

Wulfweard's face became serious, and he gave a formal nod of the head. "Thank you, brother's son. That was kind."

Godwin tried not to let his mouth smile, but couldn't stop it. He felt foolish for being so pleased, but the thanks, so seriously spoken, warmed him. *No person so rich that he won't welcome thanks for a gift given* – but that was from a pagan poem, and he shouldn't be thinking of it.

Wulfweard held one of the eggs out to him. "You have one and I'll have one. Then we'll both be done good."

Godwin put his hands behind him. "No. They're both for you."

"Then thank you again." Wulfweard tipped back his head, cracked the egg against his teeth, and swallowed down the slippery grey and yellow. When he lowered his head, smiling, he had yolk and eggshell on his lips.

"I came to tell you some news," Godwin said.

Wulfweard wiped his mouth with the back of his hand, and raised his brows to ask what news that might be.

Godwin leaned forward, resting his hand on the high wooden side of the bed. "Not everyone knows this yet. A rider brought it to Mother this morning. She told me because it's about my father, and she made me promise not to tell anyone else – but she won't mind you knowing."

Wulfweard's eyes widened and his lips parted silently before he spoke. "Unwin?"

"He's crossed the border! He's here, in this country!" He watched Wulfweard's face closely, and saw in it only dismay. So Wulfweard was a coward! He was afraid of the battles that were coming. If he had ever had any courage, it had all run out of him when he took that wound.

Still watching Wulfweard closely and intending to inflict more fear, Godwin said, "Father has the North-Welsh and Danes with him. He's going to take his land back."

Wulfweard said, "Does Elfgift know?"

Godwin's mood turned cold and hard. That was Wulfweard's first thought: does the elf's drop know? "The Danes are throwing the spear over any who go against them," Godwin said. "When they catch the elf-born, they're going to cut the blood-eagle on him." He watched Wulfweard. Mention of the blood-eagle would surely make the coward go white in the face.

Wulfweard had been untangling his legs from the bed-covers, but he heard the angry, eager note in the boy's voice, and looked up. "Unwin is sacrificing to Woden? Has he left Christ, then?"

Godwin's head lifted sharply. "My father would not break his faith!"

"But I have?"

Now that he had to speak openly, Godwin was unhappy. Wulfweard was a grown man, if a young one, and Godwin couldn't look him in the face and accuse him of cowardice and faith-breaking. But he saw that he would be a coward himself if he didn't make some answer and so, fixing his eyes on a wisp of straw on the floor, he said, "The elf-born killed your brother!"

He waited for Wulfweard's answer. His

shoulders rose, hunching about his neck as he half-expected an angry shout, a blow.

Wulfweard said, "Hunting took men and went to kill Elfgift. He killed Elfgift's foster-elders and all his farm-people – burned down his house. When Elfgift killed him, it was in revenge for that."

"They were only hinds!" Godwin said. "He had no right to take revenge for *them*! Not against the Royal Kin – and him only a bastard!" Wulfweard sat on the edge of the bed, in his shirt and leggings, and said nothing. The open front of his shirt showed his scar. "Hunting was your *brother*!"

"Elfgift is my brother."

"No!" Godwin cried, and beat the air with his fist and stamped his foot.

Wulfweard, seeming angry for the first time, leaned over and caught his arm, jerking him towards the bed. "Elfgift is my father's son, and my father named him successor."

Godwin was so angry that he struck at Wulfweard's hand on his arm, and easily pulled free. "Hunting was your brother! My father is your brother! The elf-born is a bastard and a thing – a devil! It's made you break your faith! You should kill it!"

Wulfweard made no attempt to catch him again. Sitting on the edge of the bed, he said, "I tried. The first time, he could have killed me but gave me my life. The second time, he gave me this." He touched the scar on his chest. "And kept me alive."

"If he had killed *my* brother –!" Godwin said.

Wulfweard's head lifted. "What? If your brother had killed your brother, what would you do? If your brother, who twice gave you your life, had killed your brother, *what* would you do – you, who've never fought with anything but a wooden sword?"

Godwin knew what was right, and was infuriated that right and wrong should be confused with such cowardly questions. "You've lost your courage. You're so scared of taking another wound that you hide behind the elf-born. You'd let him – a bastard – kill any of us and not even squeak, because you're so scared. You're so scared you broke your vows to your Lord Christ." He struggled to think of worse things to say, all the time looking at the red scar on Wulfweard's chest, dimly aware of the fear behind his own anger. "You'd get down on your hands and knees and lick the dust off the elf-born's boots, you're so scared!"

If Wulfweard's face hadn't whitened at the mention of the blood-eagle, it was white now, and his eyes were wide with shock and anger. Godwin heard his own words repeated in his mind, and was aghast at what he had said. Insufferable, unforgivable insults! He remembered the sword that had been dropped on the floor, just on the other side of the curtain, and thought that Wulfweard would fetch it and kill him.

Wulfweard swung his legs into the bed again, and drew the doors shut on himself. Godwin found himself staring at smooth wooden panels.

He burst out laughing – at Wulfweard's cowardice in hiding from him, at his own relief, and because he had won. He turned, pulled the curtain aside and ran down the length of the hall, still laughing, though by the time he reached the door there were tears in his eyes, and he was forcing himself to laugh so that he shouldn't sob. He had realized that his safety lay in being only a little boy. Wulfweard wouldn't challenge him, or hit him, or even answer him, because he was just a little boy throwing a tantrum as little boys do.

Wulfweard could not be both the elf-born's brother and his father's brother. The elf-born and Wulfweard, he thought, are both my enemies.

In the darkness of the bed-cupboard, Wulfweard drew up his knees and bit hard on his own wrist to keep himself from crying.

In the darkness behind his closed eyes, the dark moors rose up to a black sky. He opened his eyes and, in the darkness of the bed-closet, the moors, the sky faded only slowly from his sight. If he fell into sleep, he knew, he would be walking those moors again, where all seemed half-hidden in mist, where all sound was muffled and fading even as he heard it.

To thorny moor you'll come at last, said the old funeral song, telling of the journey to the Other World. For so long he'd wandered there, climbing chill hillsides towards grey skies, following dark streams down into empty valleys, where no bird sang. He had heard, fading, muffled, the clangour of battle-din and had followed the sound endlessly, never coming any nearer. Once he had glimpsed a great hall, its walls melting into dusk or mist, its roof shingled with shields. Its long walls had held, it seemed, a thousand doors and in one there had stood a figure, black against fire-light, beckoning urgently. By its height, its frame, its movements, he had known it for his brother Hunting, his dead brother, and had started forward eagerly, thinking that at last he knew what he had been searching for, at last he had found an end to these chill, dark moors...

But then the hall was no longer in his sight. No matter where he turned, he could see no glimpse of it, hear no sound from it. Somehow, though the hall had been plainly before him, he had lost his way to it.

His body, a collection of bones covered with skin, a cage for a still-beating heart, had hampered him, holding his spirit back. And now, though it was said he was healed, the darkness and silence of the Other World lingered in his mind. He knew how close that other country was: as close as his own skin, just the other side of sleep. Weakness, weariness, brought him close to it. As he slipped into sleep, so he slipped across the border and walked those cold, empty hills again.

He tried to find strength. He ate all he could of what Kendrida brought him, and took up sword and shield again, to work his body back to the strength it had once had – but shield and sword were so heavy that even a few passes sent him crawling to a bed to rest.

Godwin, a child, had a body stronger and more solid than his. Godwin had easily broken from his hold, had brayed insults at him with more breath than he had.

Godwin, a child, could, with mere insults, shake him to tears. The dark country of thorny moor and silent streams waited for the weak.

Faith-breaker? He had broken no faith with Christ. True, he had once sworn loyalty to Christ – but it was as if he had sworn loyalty to a lord and then found that lord to be a scarecrow of old stick and rags. The oath was null.

Ah, but how could he deny that he had broken faith with Unwin, his own brother? Again he bit his wrist, leaving deep marks in the skin. The pain wasn't as sharp as the pain of shame and grief in his chest. Unwin had given him a beautiful harp, and had shown him how to play a few simple chords, which would always sound impressive when the harp was passed round in the feast-hall, even if he never learned more. Unwin had given him his first helmet, sword and shield and, in practice-bouts, had battered him to the ground many times. In battle-training, it was no kindness to go easy on a beginner. Unwin had also picked him up, kissed him on the forehead, pulled his hair and told him that, one day, he would be the winner.

He saw, with great clarity, that he should go to meet Unwin, who was his brother, whom he loved. And fight again for that scarecrow, Christ? Elfgift was his brother, too.

With the shadows of the Other World in the darkness around him, he could never break faith with Elfgift. But, even if he ever regained the strength to do it, he could never hurt Unwin in Elfgift's service.

He lay back against the high-piled pillows behind him and covered his eyes with his hands. He should lie back and sleep – let himself sink into that Other World and never leave it. He had begun to suspect that he no longer had the strength to live in the bright, brute world around him.

* * *

In the early evening a band of horsemen approached the Borough's gates, their horses sweating and dusty. The riders had shields slung at their backs, over their mail-coats, but all were bare-headed, so no time was lost in recognizing Elfgift as their leader. The gates were opened.

Inside the gates waited a welcoming party of maids with horns of ale and trays of bread. As Elfgift rode into the yard, Kendrida stepped forward from among them, to greet him. He reined in, but remained mounted. None of his men could dismount until he did. The grooms who were waiting to take horses stood at a loss.

Elfgift looked down at Kendrida, and she, looking up and meeting his eyes, felt a shock like a small push. There was an intentness in his stare – like a cat watching a bird – which disturbed her, and another quality, hard to name. It was too cold and distant to be called sadness.

Elfgift's eyes passed over her tall, solid figure and returned to the plain, pleasant face under the white linen headdress that hid her hair. The drape of her clothes over her breast and arms reminded him with hurtful intensity of warmth, scent, touch – all of which he missed. But She had said he must find the strength to live without Her – not that he was free of Her.

His eyes lifted to the shingled roof of the Royal Hall. Instead of defending it, he would have liked to burn it as his own home had been burned. The ashes would blow away in the wind. And the people? They could have the world's room to beg their bread. But he was not free to choose his actions. The hour of his death and the manner of his dying had been fated long ago. So had the manner of his life.

Kendrida, blushing, was holding a horn of ale up to him and telling him he was welcome. Leaning down, he took the horn, drank one gulp from it and handed it back. He dismounted then and, with groans of relief, his men swung down too, eager for their bread and ale. The grooms took the horses.

Kendrida offered him a tray of bread. As he took a slice, he looked beyond her and saw a scowling boy – her eldest son, the one who had attacked him. "Your name?"

The boy answered promptly, almost shouting. "Godwin *Unwinsson*. Atheling."

Godwin – *God's friend*. But not the Goddess's. "I'm going hunting for Unwin, Atheling. Do you want to be in at the kill?"

Shock wiped the boy's face clean of expression, then he scowled even more furiously. Kendrida stared, her mouth open. She could not believe she had heard Elfgift speak so cruelly.

"Pack your gear," Elfgift said to the boy. "You leave with me at first light."

Kendrida said, "No!" Elfgift's gaze swung to her and she fell silent, feeling that she had been lightly slapped in the face.

"First light. He comes with me." Biting into his slice of bread, he moved away from her into the Borough. His men were taken by surprise and three of them hastily handed back their horns and ran after him as his guard. They cursed, but Kendrida saw them grin at each other too.

"*Mother –!*" Godwin said.

"Don't worry – I'll speak to him. Perhaps he means to give you over to your father!"

"Wulf?"

The black skies and black moorland were broken with firelight and vanished into the vision of the firelit hall – and Elfgift leaning against the frame of the bed, looking in through its doors.

Wulfweard smiled and scrambled to the bed's edge. The shadow-land was never further away than in Elfgift's presence. "You're after the Danes." It could be the only reason for this sudden arrival.

Elfgift nodded. "We ride out before first light."

Wulfweard bowed his head. "I'm no use to you. I can't even use a sword and shield for more than an eye's blink." He hadn't even been wearing a mail-coat or a helmet.

Elfgift laughed. "I don't need you. I'm taking Godwin."

Wulfweard got to his feet. "Why?"

Elfgift shook his head, setting his hair shifting. He smiled, the gentle, half-shy smile which had moved so many hearts towards him. But it was too like Wulfweard's own smile to move his. "The boy is no threat to you! He isn't Goddess-chosen! He hasn't Athelric and all the Twelve Hundred with him!"

Elfgift's smile broadened, and he touched Wulfweard's shoulder reassuringly. "It's only that the boy hates me. With me, he may learn to know me."

Wulfweard studied him, frowning, and Elfgift looked back, straight and smiling. So many people, like Athelric and Kendrida, thought that because Elfgift was beautiful and warm and could heal, he was all kindness. When he seemed less than kind, they found excuses. Wulfweard knew the kindness could be trusted no more than fair weather. "If you are taking Godwin, I am coming too."

"You aren't strong enough."

"I will get stronger."

"Pack your gear then." Turning away, Elfgift looked back over his shoulder. "You can be in at the kill too."

Wulfweard sat on the bed and put his head in his hands. He knew what kill was meant.

CHAPTER 6

The Mad Girl

The gates of King's Borough, named for the rents it paid into the king's coffers, stood open. Inside the gates, in the yard before the Royal Hall, the people of the borough were gathered, waiting in silence. All were women or children. The men were either hiding or dead.

The mad girl sat in the dirt nearby, not of them but watching them. Her only clothing was a limp gown of grey wool, and it was stiff with dried mud where she had sat and even lain in dirt. Her uncombed hair was a thick, matted dark tangle stuck with bits of leaf and twig, and her odd slanting dark eyes peered through it like eyes of something wild peering through a thicket.

The borough's stewardess, the Lady Aeditha, stood before her people, waiting to speak for them. It was that responsibility which kept her, in all her linen and silk, from lying down in the mud and howling. The mad girl was something else to think about. She would be better – safer – standing among them than sitting there on her own. The lady held out her hand. "Ebba. Come here to me."

Ebba rose at once and came to her. She was not always so biddable. The lady caught at her hand as she came near, and drew her to stand beside her, doubting even as she did it whether she was acting wisely. The girl was filthy and smelled, and was also given to spitting and punching. But it was also true that Woden, the Raging One, favoured the mad. They needed Woden's favour.

Ebba put her face close to the lady and stared at her with those intense, mad, dark eyes. Then she said, "The Danes are coming."

The lady set her teeth and closed her eyes. Tears squeezed from between her lids. "I know," she said.

They had feared the Danes for weeks. Word had come of crops being ridden down, of fields and houses burned, of cattle stolen. And when the Danes had come nearer yet, the men had gone to meet them. The lady's husband and son had led them.

When sighted, the Danes had seemed few, and at the first attack had turned and run like hares before long dogs. So the Saxons, crowing, had given chase – scattering as they ran, breaking ranks. Then the Danes had turned, closing their shields into a formidable wall bristling with spears. Other Danes had sprung from the ground, chopping at the panicking Saxons from behind.

The Saxons had been mostly poor men, armed with home-made spears, sickles and long knives, lacking helmets or mail-coats. They had gone out in desperation to defend their families and fields. The Danes were landless men who had spent their lives fighting, armoured against farm tools in mail and helmets, with axes and swords. They had butchered the Saxons as animals were butchered for a feast – lopping heads as if for brawn, slicing flesh from bones, letting out guts and blood, jointing arms and legs.

The Saxons' old lord had been killed. His son had been captured alive, and the Danes had cut the blood-eagle on him. His screams, the survivors said, had followed them as they rolled down hillsides, struggled through thickets, splashed through streams and scrambled and ran to get away.

They had brought the news to King's Borough. It was for the widowed lady to say what they would do now. What was there to do? Their lord was dead, and they had not enough men left unhurt to defend the borough. No one would be coming to help. Their king, for all his supposed elvish powers, couldn't be in two places at once, and he and his army were far away, chasing another division of the Danes. So the lady had ordered the gates dragged open, and she had ale and bread waiting, as if for the arrival of guests.

The Danes came, sixty armed men on horseback. The crush of their horses filled the yard, pressing the women back against the walls of the Royal Hall. The noise rose, trapped between the walls: a din of horses trampling and whinnying, men shouting, metal on metal. A stink of horsesweat, and men's sweat, and blood. Sudden movement as horses clattered off down the streets in search of men in hiding.

The Danish leaders brought their horses to the centre of the yard and sat on them, waiting. Ebba, still holding the lady's hand, looked up at the nearer one. There was no doubting he was the leader. No one else could wear such mail – black, polished and studded with gold drops. His helmet was that of a king: a mask with scowling silver brows and golden lips hid his real face from view, and over the helmet's crown sprawled a golden dragon with garnet eyes. She had seen such helmets before, worn by Saxon athelings. Either this man had won it in battle, or... As he turned in the saddle, Ebba saw the long plaited tail of brown hair hanging down his back, and knew at once who he was. Unwin Eadmundsson. Danes didn't wear their hair long.

The man beside him must be a leader too, because he brought his horse so close to Eadmundsson, but his mail-coat was of plain grey links, and his helmet a simple iron pot with a nose-guard. He wrenched the helmet off, revealing a Dane's short hair – but hair as black as the bottom of a pot, and a young face as brown as a ripe nut. He was even darker than Ebba was herself, and she stared.

A Dane came to the stirrup of this dark man and handed him a large leather bag, which he emptied out in front of the gathered people. From the bag, into the dirt, thumped the severed hands, and the heads, of King's Borough's old lord and his son.

Ebba felt the lady's hand tighten hard on hers, hurting her. She looked and saw the lady's face, white as her linen headdress – but then women's voices were shrilly raised, and there was a sound of horse's hooves, and shouting. The armed men were returning from searching the streets, bringing with them Saxon men they had found, some so hurt they were slung across horses. In the yard, the prisoners were shoved to the ground, knocked down. The women in the crowd cried out more frantically, pushing forward. Horses shouldered them back.

The lady let go of Ebba's hand and, darting

forward, seized hold of Unwin's foot as he sat on his horse. "Atheling! Leave them!"

Ebba saw the golden mask turn down, towards the lady. But the killing had already started. The Saxon men were speared through, in front of their women and children, their throats cut. The disbelieving, despairing shrieks of the women rose to such a pitch that they set the dogs barking frantically, and the other animals squealing in their pens. Horses shoved the women back.

Ebba didn't waste her breath in screaming or pleading. She stood quietly and watched, through the tangles of her hair. She'd never seen anyone killed before, though she'd seen the bodies piled and burned afterwards. And she'd seen plenty of chickens and pigs killed. Killing men seemed easier, if anything. Most of them seemed to stand and allow themselves to be killed. Hard work, perhaps, like chopping wood, but there didn't seem any skill to it.

Ingvi Troll watched too, from horseback. His horse fidgeted a little at the smell of blood, but it was a trained war-horse, given him by King Lovern, and neither the smell nor the cries disturbed it much. Watching a man killed was no harder than watching a pig-sticking, he had found. It was hours afterwards, when darkness came, when you were sitting quiet by the fire or trying to sleep – it was then that the faces and cries started a trembling in the bones, and the shadows jumped like men in death-throes.

But that was the price of winning fame by feasting the wolf and raven.

Unwin had pulled off his helmet. He shouted, "I am Unwin Eadmundsson, of the Royal Kin and the Twelve Hundred, king of this land! These men died because they fought against their king! But if all here do as they're bid, these are the last who need die!"

He moved his horse forward slowly as he looked the crowd over, and then pointed to a skinny boy of about ten. "Him." Armed men reached into the crowd, to drag the boy out. Thinking he was going to be killed, like the men, the boy struggled and shrieked. His mother came to help him, shrieking herself, and was pushed aside.

Unwin yelled, "The boys will not be killed!" His voice could have carried across a valley. Even his men froze, staring at him. In the quiet, he said, "Lady, I want these boys as hostages. I want all the boys of his size and bigger. Tell your people, please."

The boys were pulled from the crowd and shoved together, terrified, under a guard of armed men. From the crowd on all sides came the sound of weeping. Ebba turned her attention from the Danes to these sobbing women. What were they crying for? Did they think it was going to make any difference?

"Lady Aeditha," Unwin said, "if one of my men dies while we are in King's Borough, I shall give two of these boys over to my blood-thirsty young friend here, Ingvi Troll. Do you know what 'Troll' means?"

"I think all Danes are trolls," the lady said.

Ingvi laughed out loud, his teeth very white against his darkness.

"Ingvi will send your boys to Odin." Ingvi, doing his bit towards terrifying the people of the borough, held an invisible noose above his own head, crooked his neck and poked out his tongue. "For every horse that's lamed, I'll give him one boy. I'll let you choose which boys, Lady. Now give me your keys."

Leaning down from his saddle, Unwin held out his hand. She unhooked the great bunch of keys from her waist and gave them to him: the keys of every storeroom and chest. He threw them to one of his officers, and only then dismounted. Ingvi swung down too.

Unwin was saying to the lady, "I will take the Royal Lodgings—" when Ebba snatched up one of the severed hands from the ground and, with a cry of laughter, smacked it in his face.

Unwin stepped sharply back, sending his horse dancing away. Ingvi came forward to deal with

Ebba, and so did several other Danes, weapons at the ready. It was Lady Aeditha who moved towards those weapons, grabbed Ebba by her long, tangled hair and dragged her back. "She's mad, Atheling! Don't you see she's mad?"

The Danes stopped short, Ingvi too. Ebba, still held by the hair, laughed and pointed at them, clapping her hands and jeering. Ingvi backed away. To Unwin, he said, "She's Odin's."

Unwin stepped in front of Ebba, folded his arms and studied her as she danced with pleasure at her own joke, ignoring the tugging on her hair.

He said, "I know her." He looked at Aeditha. "Later, when I have eaten, I want her sent to me."

He walked away towards the hall. Ingvi, after giving Ebba one stare, followed him.

Lady Aeditha pulled Ebba to her in relief. She looked about at the Danes standing in her streets, at her sobbing women, at her son's, her husband's heads lying on the ground, and she held her breath to keep from sobbing herself. "Ebba," she said. "Oh, Ebba."

Ebba was not mad. She knew that quite well. She was … a free woman. She was the freest woman on Middle-Earth, and if it took madness to set her free, then so be it.

She had been born a slave, and her life had been work. Carrying heavy buckets that wrenched her shoulders and back. Standing day-long in cold, wet fields to chase birds from seeds. Bending her back to gather stones. Working the grindstone, day after day, to grind grain into flour.

Her future had been easy to foretell: endless work, none of it for her own gain, none of it that she wanted to do. And she would be for the use of any man, free or slave. Free women could choose their lovers, could marry and divorce as they chose. A thrall-woman was as much for use, and had as little choice, as a spoon.

She had thought of running away: what slave hadn't? But to where? And as Hild had often said, "You sleep warm, with a full belly. What are you moaning about?"

And running away would have meant leaving Elfgift. She could no longer remember when she had begun to love him. He was in her first memories, a child like herself, working in the fields with her, playing with her, eating and sleeping with her. They had never been treated alike, though. Hild had let him play and sleep more, and had given him more food. More enviable still, she had hugged Elfgift, kissed him, stroked his hair and sat him on her knee. When Ebba, driven by furious jealousy, had demanded kisses for herself, Hild had pushed her away and, when she had screamed with disappointed rage, Hild had slapped her and driven her from the house, calling her "dirty slave".

Elfgift had come looking, finding her hiding behind the barn. Putting his arms round her, he had kissed her, and said that he would cuddle her if Hild wouldn't. He'd shared with her an apple which Hild had given him. They'd both been very small then. Elfgift had always been capable of such moments of sweetness. She had learned, slowly, that it was useless to expect them of him.

It was years before it became clear to her that Elfgift was not one of the farm people, but their owner – the only free-born among them. Even Hild was his slave, not his mother at all. She had simply been provided for him, to care for him while he was small.

Twice a year strangers came to the farm – rich strangers with thick cloaks and golden cloak-pins. Hild was afraid of them. They came to see Elfgift, and to make sure he was well cared for.

Those strangers came from the court of the king, because Elfgift was the king's son, though a bastard. That was why he owned them and the farm. She had believed this at first simply because she was told it. It had been astonishing, like turning round and seeing the house built of bread behind you, with the trail of crumbs leading to its door. All those stories of kings and lost princes were true, it seemed! Later she had doubted it, because life went on its ordinary, dull way – but it had turned out to be true nevertheless.

She had grown into loving Elfgift as she had grown into her full height, and she couldn't change any more than she could shrink. If he had loved her even one quarter as much as she loved him, then she would have had everything. The other men wouldn't have been able to touch her. She would have been free.

But Elfgift was as changeable as the light. Every time he noticed her she threw her whole soul into trying to please him, desperately hoping that, this time, it meant he loved her and she could begin being happy. She thought that hoping for it hard enough would make it happen.

It hadn't – and then the old king had died, and the law with him. Armed men had come to the farm and cut down the people as carelessly as corn-stalks at harvest. And as the farm that had been her only home, and the people who had been her only family, went up in flames, Elfgift had abandoned her. Truly, she thought, he felt more for the burning house.

And when she'd found him again, here at King's Borough, he'd been still further above her than he'd been as her free-born master. Even the bone-plaques she wore about her neck by then, which proclaimed her freedom, were of no use to her, nor was the gold she'd been given with them. To marry a king, a woman needed a country as a dower. And even if she'd found the magic quern-stone that ground grain into gold, a Woden's-son didn't marry a freed-woman.

So she'd stayed in King's Borough when Elfgift had ridden out with his housecarls. Her gold had soon been taken from her, but she hadn't cared. Even with the gold, she'd been no more free than before. The gold was meant to buy her a husband, but if she couldn't have Elfgift, what did she want with a husband who would only be another slave-master? Go there, do this, fetch that – and she would have to obey.

At King's Borough, a Royal town, there was always space in the guest halls for her to sleep warm and dry, and there was always food. But if she had stayed simply as a poor, free woman, she would have been found work, and someone would have remembered some free man who would pay his rents more promptly if he had a wife – a slave – to work for him.

Much better to be mad. Woden sent madness: it was a state both feared and respected. The mad, ridden by Woden, saw and heard things others could not. Mad, she could still sleep and eat in the halls, but was left alone. If someone dared to assume that she would work at their orders, she spat at them, shrieked, punched them, and pulled their hair, and they backed off as much in fear of Woden as of her.

It was wonderful. She did anything it came into her head to do. Sometimes she attacked people who merely looked at her. *That*, she thought, as her punch struck, *is for all the times I've been beaten.*

Being mad left her plenty of time to think of Elfgift. Magic, more powerful than his, seemed the only hope. Love-potions, love-charms, spells, bindings – one day she would find one that worked.

The king's private lodgings were above the Royal Hall. On a wall-bench, in the corner where the shadows were deepest, sat Ud, his harp on his knee.

In the candlelit centre of the room Unwin sat in a chair, while Ingvi sprawled full length on the sleeping-bench along the wall. "We do well," Unwin said. "We empty the storerooms and leave nothing but husks for the elf's drop. We've jointed the local musters and run away from Elfie – riding down the crops as we go!"

"If he splits his forces –" Ingvi said.

" – we'll come together and smash him. He won't split his forces; he hasn't enough men. So we'll run him ragged and leave him nothing but starvelings to work his fields and rats in his storerooms. We'll see how long they go on calling him 'Goddess-chosen' when they're hungry." Unwin drank again from his horn and lifted one foot on to a stool. "Harvest is coming. As soon as the corn begins to ripen, he won't have an army. But *we* will – thank God for landless men!"

Ingvi, laughing, toasted landless men.

"There'll be harpists coming to us soon," Unwin said, "bringing offers of a truce. I can ask them for news of my sons. And brother."

There was a silence. Ingvi, lying flat on the bench with his hands behind his head, began to be bored, and wondered if Unwin would play a game of fox-and-geese with him. They could play game after game until they were worn out and could sleep without dreams.

A knock at the door promised some distraction. Ingvi raised himself on his elbow. "Aye?"

A man looked round the door. "Jarls, the girl –"

Unwin twisted to look around the wide back of his chair at the man. "Send her in!"

The man withdrew, and Ingvi sat, swinging his legs to the floor.

The mad girl, dirty and unkempt as ever, was pushed into the room. Ingvi stood, eyeing her warily. The fear he felt of her was fear of the God who had blessed her with madness – Odin.

Ebba looked over her shoulder as the door closed behind her and saw a man sitting in the shadows behind the door. He held a harp on his knee. One eye caught the light and glinted. The other side of his face was hidden in darkness. He smiled at her.

Turning, she saw the two Woden's-sons looking at her – Unwin, of her own Saxon people (though she hardly feared him less for that) and the murderous young Dane who even called himself "Troll".

Once she would have cringed and tried to make herself small, but now she was mad – and when had cringing ever done her any good? So she held up her head and smiled at the Woden's-sons. With wide, dancing movements that set her filthy skirts swinging, she moved about the room, looking impudently at the weapons on the walls, stooping to finger the carving on a chest.

Ingvi left the wall-bench and went to lean on the back of Unwin's chair, though he kept his dark eyes on Ebba.

Ebba laughed, as if at a true thing that pleased her. Unwin held out his drinking-horn to her.

She came and took it from his hand, and drank from it, smiling at him. She had never tasted wine before. It made her shudder a little, but it was warm and sweet, as well as bitter. She liked it and drank more.

"Do you remember me?" Unwin asked. "The last time we met, you foretold that the elf's drop would be king."

Ebba, wary, said nothing but drank again, staring at them over the horn's rim.

"Only you said he would kill me, and that hasn't happened."

Ebba lowered the horn. "It might!"

Ingvi laughed. "It might," Unwin agreed. "You said that the elf's drop would marry you too. That hasn't happened either."

Ebba felt like throwing the horn at him. So she did. He ducked aside, and the horn hit the chairback, spattering wine over both men before hitting the floor with a ringing sound.

As Ingvi brushed wine from his sleeve, Ebba burst into frightened laughter.

Unwin rose, the better to brush the wine from his tunic. He wasn't much angered: his clothes were plain things, and had been stained with worse. But as soon as he stood, Ebba started to screech: long shrill cries like nails in the ears.

Wincing at the sound, Unwin raised both hands, palms outward, to show that he meant her no harm: but not until he sat again did she stop.

"Mad," Ingvi said.

"All those who have elf-sight are mad," Unwin said. "That's right, isn't it, Ebba? I wonder what you see now? What can you tell me? Pour her more wine, Ingvi."

While Unwin watched her with an almost tender curiosity, Ingvi picked up the horn, refilled it, and offered it to her at arm's length. As soon as she put her hand on it, he snatched back his arm.

"The Troll is more afraid of you than spears," Unwin said. They watched her drink. "What can you tell me, elf-sight? Of my sons."

Ebba saw that she could please the Woden's-son and win favour, but something in her, too quick for thought, refused. "Dead!" she said.

Unwin was quick to control his face. "And my brother?"

"Dead!"

Unwin nodded. "And the elf's get? What of him?"

"Dead!"

"I don't think so," Unwin said. "I spoke to him not long ago – there was a river between us, but it was him. He was in good health. It takes strength to be that angry."

"He will be dead!" Ebba said.

"Aye? When?"

If she told Unwin what he wanted to hear, he'd reward her. He might give her more gold rings, to replace those stolen from her. But she laughed and said, "After you're dead!" Holding the horn high, she whirled round in a circle-dance. "After he's cut the blood-eagle on you! Years after that he'll die! That's a true foretelling!" Giddy, she drank from the horn, staggered, and laughed at him.

Unwin sat quiet for an eye's blink, then rose, swiped the horn from Ebba's hand and hit her in the face so hard that he knocked her from her feet. Turning back to his chair, he said, "Have her kicked out at the gates."

Ingvi stayed where he was, behind Unwin's chair, looking at Ebba who lay, half-stunned, where she had fallen. Ingvi would not have dared to strike the girl, and didn't want to go near her.

"Get rid of her!" Unwin said.

Ud rose from his dark corner. "I'll take her away, Jarl."

Ingvi started, and Unwin turned sharply. Then both relaxed, as they remembered that Ud had been there all the time.

Setting his harp on the bench, Ud stooped over Ebba, lifting her up. Ingvi opened the door and Ud carried her out, down the steps into the hall where men still sat drinking at tables in the smoke from the fires.

Ud passed through them unnoticed. In the shadow against the wall, he set Ebba on a bench, and sat beside her. Taking her face in his big hands, he gently moved his warm fingers over her cheekbones and mouth. Her bruised flesh ached at the touch, and she looked up into one blue eye and one shadowed, gouged scar.

"Nothing broken," he said. "You'll go out at the gates – under my cloak."

"What happened to your eye?" she said.

"I sold it, sweetheart."

She laughed and leaned against him, put her arms round him and snuggled against his shoulder.

PART 2

CHAPTER 7

The Truce Meet

It was late summer. In the fields – in those left unburned or untrampled – John-Barley had grown a beard and was white-fair. The trees were in full, ruffling leaf, and winding their colour through the long grass, starring the turf, wreathing the corn, were the scarlet, pink, white, yellow and blue of flowers.

But one of the hillsides above the river was burned black, where fire from a burning village had spread before the wind had turned it back on itself.

"I shall not move," Unwin said, "until I hear the elf's drop is there, and waiting." He sat in the shade of his tent, on a stool. Behind him, seated on a chest, was Ud Harper and on the floor at Ud's feet the girl who, these days, carried his harp. No one paid them any attention. "Maybe I'll keep it waiting a day," Unwin said. "Or two. While its corn ripens in the fields and its men run away."

Unwin had dressed for the truce-meet with care, in clothes and jewels taken from the chests at King's Borough. He meant to impress all who saw him with the fact that he was an atheling of the Royal Kin. His leggings were of dark and pale blue stripes, his tunic of blue silk. Round his waist was a belt decorated with gold plaques, supporting a sword and dagger in ornamented sheaths. A cross of gold and garnets hung round his neck, and he wore gold bands on his arms and rings on every finger. His long hair was loose and shifted about his shoulders in a reddish-brown cape.

Ingvald and Ingvi hurried to Unwin's tent as soon as they heard that the elf-born had crossed to Council Isle from his side of the river and was waiting for them. Ingvald had dressed in yellow, belting on his most impractical bejewelled sword, and golden arm-bands, rings and a silver Thor's hammer. Ingvi wore another such hammer over his tunic of red silk, which was tightly belted because it belonged to Ingvald and was too big for him. A headband of red silk was tied round his black hair.

As they reached the tent, the warmth of the sun was just making itself felt. Looking across the brown river, Ingvi could see the tents and awning erected on the island. He was eager to get down to the water's edge and see the elf-born after so long hearing about him.

Unwin roused in his chair as they entered. "Welcome – have you broken fast? Shall we have a game of chess?"

Servants brought stools for the Jarlssens, and platters of bread and jugs of small beer. "The elf-born is already on the island," Ingvi said.

Unwin glanced at him, and began to set out the chess pieces. Ingvald sat down to play.

The sun rose further, making a bright, hot morning. The chess game was a slow one. Ingvi stood at the tent's entrance, staring across the river. The island was covered with short grass, with few trees or bushes, and Elfgift's men could easily be seen, the sunlight glaring on their helmets.

Looking back into the tent Ingvi saw Unwin capturing a pawn from his brother. Quietly, he left and made his way down to the water.

The muddy shores of the island were carpeted with reeds and pale lady-smocks, tall yellow king-cups and other damp-loving flowers. Elfgift walked there, followed at a distance by two armed guards.

Elfgift had come to the island in the chill grey of early morning. Now, in the heat, he had stripped off his padded coat of buff leather, and wore only a loose linen shirt over thin leggings of buff hide and worn, plain riding boots. He wore no gold. Only his long hair, white in the sunlight, braided into fine plaits next to his face and hanging loose down his back, told that he was no longer a farmer. Poor working men didn't wear their hair long and loose.

Across the water was the meadow where his force was camped. Sheep and goats, together with a few horses and cows, grazed among the widely spaced trees. Smoke rose from cooking fires and, following it into the air with his eyes, Elfgift saw the burned hillside above. He turned away. Burning houses, and worse. Burning fields, burning barns, the smoke rolling away to the horizon.

He turned to the end of the island and saw the other bank, where smoke rose from Unwin's camp. His fists were clenching. But he had to make a truce.

His housecarls – men whose business was nothing but fighting – were few. The rest of his army was made up of poor men poorly armed, called from their farms. They saw the grain ripening in the fields and were disappearing, not one by one, but by tens. Running home to their fields, to haymaking and harvest – and nothing, no threat, no reward, would stop them.

He would be a fool to stop them. The harvest promised to be heavy, but the Danish army ate hugely, wasted and destroyed. If, in addition, the corn stood in the fields until the weather spoiled it, then there would be famine next year. Hungry people ate horses and oxen, so next spring there would be too few horses for the mounted men, and too few oxen to pull carts. The men would be too few and weak to fight – and Unwin would win.

A truce had to be made, to buy time for the harvest, to stave off famine.

Unwin, with his force of landless men, fed on Elfgift's land, had no such troubles. He had so many men – from the north, from Denmark, from Norroway – that he could split his forces and raid wherever Elfgift was not. The killed and wounded were replaced by fresh recruits, and they opened storerooms, butchered cattle and feasted without caring when or how what they ate would be replaced.

Elfgift stopped among the reeds and mud at the island's edge, wrapping his arms about himself and lowering his head. Behind him, his guards stopped too, and leaned on their spears. They could see the tension in his hunched shoulders, but not that he was biting his fist as he held in the anger that filled him, that made him hot and filled the muscles of his arms and back until he was afraid of his own strength, which seemed likely to crack his joints. He had to hold in the anger. He had to make the truce.

He walked on, bursting from his stillness with a suddenness that set moorhens sculling through the water and ducks flapping up with cries and splashing of wings. The guards hefted their spears and hurried to follow.

He halted again where the coast of the island curved, and stood in the warm sun, watching the light run over the brown water. He said, "Lady, I am losing Your war."

She was always close, but gave no answer. Her silence spread about him, deep and deeper under the cries of the birds and the noise drifting from the encampments. She never answered him now – he had chosen Wulfweard above Her. Before making that choice he had ended every day in Her arms, comforted, healed, strengthened. Now every day ended in loneliness, and from that bleakness he had to gather himself up to go forward through the next long day; it was hard, and he was losing.

But he had Wulfweard.

He turned in a circle, for no reason except to use up some of the angry energy that filled him, and went on along the shore, almost running. He stayed among the reeds and mud because the going was harder.

Ahead of him a boat was crossing the water from Unwin's camp. In its prow sat someone in scarlet. Unwin coming at last?

Elfgift stopped again, watching the boat. He must put aside his anger and remember only the good manners due to a guest. The truce had to be made.

He climbed to drier ground and went on more quickly towards the landing-place. The guards, following him, saw how his boots were blackened with mud and water, and his shirt spattered with mud thrown up by his feet. They glanced at each other, and both grinned, one shaking his head. They wondered if their king would ever learn how to behave.

In the dim heat of the tent, a table was set with plates of bread and a mead-tub, full to the brim. Horns lay beside it, ready to be filled for the guests. Servants stood about, yawning, waiting.

In one corner, left well alone by everyone, Godwin was teaching his puppy to roll over and die for his lord on command, like any good housecarl. With grim patience he went over and over the trick, rewarding the puppy with scraps of meat.

Wulfweard had taught him the value of patience. "When your pup is stupid and won't learn, and you feel like kicking him – it's then you

133

must be most patient. And when he still gets everything wrong, you must be more gentle still, and more kind, and more patient."

"I can't!" Godwin had said. When you were angry, how could you be anything but angry?

"You can, if you try. If you can't, you'll always be a child, however big you grow, and your pup will be afraid of you."

Godwin had seen the sense of that, and quietly made up his mind to follow Wulfweard's advice if he could. Still, he had stuck out his chin and said, "My *father* loses his temper!" And his father was a bigger, better man than Wulfweard, and a better warrior.

Wulfweard then said something that had puzzled him ever since. "I've known your father longer than you, and I've never known him lose his temper. I've seen him pretend – that's a different thing."

Had all those rages of his father's, both frightening and exhilarating, been pretence, then? Why would anyone pretend to a rage they didn't feel? It was more manly, surely, to let your anger loose and cow everyone about you? Surely only children hid their anger, because they were punished for showing it.

Teaching the puppy had taught him that it was possible to hold down anger and show no sign of it, if you kept your purpose firmly in mind. He stroked the puppy's head and rolled it on its back, while it nipped his hand and wagged its tail.

Elfgift had given him the pup. One wet night Elfgift had come into the rank farmhouse where he and Wulfweard had been billeted, and dumped the puppy in Godwin's lap. Godwin remembered looking up into the beautiful face that he always found so intimidating. Elfgift had smiled, as if shy, and had left without a word. Godwin never found out where the puppy had come from, or why it had been given to him.

The elf's drop was trying to buy his loyalty, of course, which was laughable. He was only here, enduring boredom in this hot tent, to see his father. He was sitting alone in the stuffy heat to make it clear whose side he was on. He would only come out when his father arrived. Until then, he wouldn't sit with *them*, the traitors.

Even the little dog was a traitor, working for Elfgift. He had given it no other name but "dog". "Die for your lord, dog. Die!"

At the day's end, he would go with his father to his father's camp. He knew this was unlikely, but had chosen to believe it, to make it come true. God knew when he would see his mother, brother and sister again. But God would watch between them while they were apart.

The boat nudged the island's shore. Rush matting

had been laid down to keep the mud from the atheling's shoes, and Ingvi jumped on to it.

The guards were surprised to see Ingvi alone. He grinned. "I've come to keek at the elf-born. D'you ken where he is?"

One of the men, looking past him, gave a slight nod. Ingvi turned.

A tall man, dressed like a field-hand, was running through the reeds and mud of the shore towards them. His long hair lifted from his shoulders and flew about his head, white in the sunlight. Ingvi was about to turn away – a field-hand could have no business with him – when he glimpsed the man's face.

For an eye's blink he thought it was a woman – a giantess, a troll-wife, with such height and width of shoulder – but the face was so beautiful! He felt shocked.

Coming closer, slowing to a walk, the man held out his hand and smiled – an oddly shy smile that flattered Ingvi by suggesting that he could make this startling creature shy.

Ingvi knew then, before the guards stiffened to attention, that this was the elf-born. He felt his own mouth gaping as he stared at that sharp, clear, beautiful face. He made himself smile and stuck out his own hand while his thoughts hurried about in confusion – what can I say to make him like me, what can I do? – as if he was faced with a beautiful woman. Yet, as their hands met, his back twitched and his guts shifted inside him. Unwin said it was a devil – and the grip of its hand was strong and hot. Had it, Ingvi wondered, a hollow back like a rotten tree?

The elf-born was looking across the river. "Alone?"

Ingvi realized Elfgift had made no attempt to kiss him in greeting – and it was his place, as a king, to offer the kiss. He gave no answer. He felt something like a light slap to the face as the elf-born's eyes turned to him. "You are Ingvi Troll. You took King's Borough from me. Are you going to tell me our brothers won't be coming today?"

Ingvi had forgotten that this creature and Unwin were half-brothers. He studied the elf-born's face, seeing the likeness. Only when Elfgift's face turned aside, looking at him sidelong, amused, did he remember to answer. "They are playing chess."

Elfgift looked anxious. "Are they good?"

"Unwin is. And my brother not so bad."

"We are in for a long wait!" The elf-born began to lead the way along the path of rush-mats to higher ground. "Come and drink with us. We'll have our own meeting."

They climbed through green-smelling clumps of nettles and cow-parsley, where butterflies flittered. Ingvi felt slightly dizzy, because everything seemed so everyday, and yet he was in the company of this strange creature. The long back beneath the linen shirt looked human – nor, lower down, was there any sign of a cow's tail.

The path ahead was suddenly blocked with people, all chattering and squealing. Ingvi was reaching for his dagger and looking round for the guards before he realized that they were girls. Women. Girls with uncovered plaits and women in headdresses were pressing around Elfgift, all laughing, all with flushed, damp faces and bare arms – the women from the cooking-fires.

They were reaching out to touch Elfgift – his shoulder, his hair – but cautiously, as if they feared they might be burned. A pair of hands and bare arms raised a flowery wreath from the crowd and Elfgift lowered his head for it to be placed on his hair. A dozen hands stretched out to help. The laughter and chatter never stopped.

Elfgift straightened, lifting his head above them, and smiling down at them. His crown was of white and yellow day's-eyes, gemmed with blue cornflowers and flaring scarlet poppies. In the fashion of Miklagarth, it had chains of day's-eyes hanging down on either side, and the women fussed with these until they hung to their satisfaction. And then, like a flock of birds, they all suddenly took fright, squealed and ran away. Ingvi looked after them, rather hurt. Some had been pretty and he, though outlandishly dark, had never been thought ill-favoured.

But the path ahead was clear now and Elfgift, crowned with flowers, was walking on and looking back. Ingvi and the guards ran a few paces to catch him up.

The height of the island was covered with short grass, thickly spangled with small flowers of white, yellow, pink and blue. Two tents had been erected here, opposite each other. The awning between them shaded three big chairs: one set before the Saxon tent, two before the Danes'.

In one of the Danes' chairs sprawled an elderly man, his faded fair hair loose about his shoulders, his beard hanging over his tunic of yellow-and-green chequers. He might have been asleep. In the Saxon chair, one leg hooked over the arm, sat a young man who rose quickly and came towards them, looking at Elfgift's crown and laughing at it.

Ingvi wondered dizzily if Elfgift had used elf-craft to split in two and come at him from all sides, as ghosts were said to do, for this young man coming towards them was the elf-born dressed as an atheling in russet silk, with gold shining on his arms and fingers.

Then he saw that the atheling was not quite as tall as Elfgift, and, though he was handsome, his face was somehow blunter, lacking that quality of shining clarity that drew stares to the elf-born. Still, Ingvi was not sure that, if he met one of them alone, he would be able to tell which one it was. It was not hard to guess who the young man was, with his likeness to Elfgift and his atheling's clothes. "Wulfweard Eadmundsson? We had heard you were dead."

"And that I killed him?" Elfgift said, as Ingvi and Wulfweard exchanged greeting kisses. When Ingvi turned, it was to find Elfgift offering him a horn of mead, while the servant who had brought it stood by – a great honour, if he could be sure it was intended as such and not merely due to the elf-born's ignorance of how to behave. "This is Ingvi Troll," Elfgift said to Wulfweard. "His brother and ours are playing chess."

"We have a fox-and-geese board," Wulfweard said.

The board was brought and Ingvi settled to play with Wulfweard under the awning's shade and heat. Athelric roused himself enough to watch and offer them both advice, but Elfgift merely paced about the chairs. His friendliness had vanished: he neither looked at anyone nor spoke. Athelric often watched him rather than the board.

"This is more than a snub," Athelric said presently, his eyes following Elfgift. "This is an insult."

Wulfweard glanced quickly at Ingvi, as if fearing he would be offended. "Your move."

The sun grew hotter, parching the air to a thin,

dry stillness, drawing out the scent of the grass. Even in the awning's shade they grew hot and thirsty, and sent for milk. It was while drinking it they noticed that Elfgift had gone – and then heard the din of shields being battered. Athelric led the way towards the sound.

Behind the tents, watched by housecarls and women, Elfgift was practising. He had taken off his crown of flowers and tied his long hair back and, in the day's heat, was fighting three men. He was unarmed except for a wooden staff, and wore only his shirt and leggings. The men had left off their heavy mail, but wore helmets and carried shields, and were armed: one with an axe, another with a sword, the third with a spear.

Elfgift avoided all their blows, ducking, leaping, twisting, spinning. Again and again his staff slammed into their shields, or struck a dull, iron note from their helmets. Ingvi watched, growing oddly numb with astonishment. To leap above an axe-blow and, in landing, twist aside to dodge a spear while driving a staff at a shield, staggering its bearer – this speed, agility and unison of body, mind and eye could be achieved once in a while by a well-trained man in high spirits. But again and again and again – and yet again – in such heat!

Ingvi thought of his brother. We are fighting *this*? Ingvald, he remembered, had not wanted this war against the elf-born. He had been pushed to it by Lovern. Ingvald was no fool.

The three housecarls, panting and sweating, dropped out, and three more took their place, but the fight was cut short by running guards with news. Unwin was coming!

Servants and guards ran to their places. Athelric went to Elfgift and, pulling him angrily this way and that, wiped the sweat from his face, untied his hair and shook it out, tugged his tunic straight. "Change your clothes," he said.

"There is no time."

"Make them wait."

Elfgift moved away. A girl, tugging at his arm, got him to lower his head while she replaced the flower crown. The heat had made all the flowers droop, and the poppies were shrivelled. But the housecarls raised a small cheer, and one slapped Elfgift on the back, saying, "A king should have a crown, at least!"

Ingvi remembered that his own place was with the Danes and, shouting farewell, he ran to stand by the chair where Invgald would sit. He felt almost sad at parting from his friends of the morning.

He reached his place in time to see a small boy running from the Saxon tent, followed by a bouncing dog. Servants chased them and one of them scooped up the dog and carried it away, while another smoothed the boy's long hair and straightened the cross about his neck. The boy was dressed like an atheling, and the cross was gold. Ingvi wondered, as the boy took his place at Wulfweard's side, who he could be. Was he Wulfweard's son? Or Elfgift's?

He glanced at Elfgift, who was now standing before his chair looking – with his striking beauty, his atheling's hair, his sweaty field-hand's clothes, his crown of flowers – indescribably strange. The flower-crown... With a shock, Ingvi saw that the flowers were as bright and fresh as if newly picked, even the poppies. He felt something like fear.

Unwin sat in the prow of the boat, his long hair falling about his shoulders. The rowers grunted as the oars broke the water, splashing its welcome coolness over them.

Sunlight ran golden through the brown water and ahead was the bulk of the island where they would soon land. On that island – Ebba's heart filled her chest, she could hardly breathe – was Elfgift.

She sat in the stern with Ud, holding his harp on her lap. He had led her into the boat by the hand. Nobles had stepped back and taken other boats, as if they had not noticed Ud or had mistaken him for someone else. Now the boat thumped against the shore, and Unwin jumped out on to the rush matting as Ingvald's boat came to land close by. One of the rowers gave Ebba his hand to help her out. No one glanced at Ud behind her.

Horns were blown, the coarse, blaring sound announcing their arrival. With their escort of armed men, Unwin and Ingvald began the short climb to the meeting place. Ebba, with Ud at her heels, followed the nobles, often leaving the path to keep out of their way. Her heart beat so wildly, and her breath was so short, the blood pumped so strong in her temples, darkening her sight and making her head ache, that she could hardly see where she was going or remember why she was there. She simply followed the flashing of the gold worn ahead of her.

As Unwin came into the awning's shade the first thing he saw – his eyes flew to it – was his brother's face, framed with fine plaits and loose hair, crowned with day's-eyes, cornflowers and poppies. He was shocked: he had not remembered Wulfweard as so beautiful. But there were two Wulfweards.

Unwin's eyes flicked from one to the other. One – a more recognizable Wulfweard, a good-looking boy but not – and dressed like an atheling, not, like the one with the ridiculous flower crown, like a sweaty farm-hand. Unwin realized that, even if only for an eye's blink, he had mistaken the elf's drop for his own brother. He felt that a humiliating trick had been played on him.

Unwin strode across the grass to Elfgift, his arms outstretched, intending to offer the greeting kiss, as Elfgift's elder and superior. He had expected the elf's drop to try to offer the kiss first, but it seemed surprised by a kiss being offered at all and shied away. There was an awkward, shuffling moment before Unwin stepped back to stand before the chair set for him. Ingvald stood before his own chair, and their men gathered behind them. Ud was in the front rank, as if by right, and no one challenged him. He rested his hand on Ebba's shoulder as she stood in front of him. Her gaze was fixed on the bright cameo of Elfgift's face. A sort of calm had come to her, a calm of rage. She thought her heart would choke her.

She had thought Elfgift would be dressed like an atheling, withdrawn from her behind a barrier of rank. The fact that he was dressed like a farmhand seemed an insult to her, despite the long atheling's hair. And the flower crown! She had hung chains of day's-eyes on him in the past – who had made these?

Unwin's steward began the long recital of his titles and ancestry, going back, king by king, to Woden and then Noah. Unwin used the time to study Wulfweard, pleased to see that the boy looked no older and seemed strong and well.

Wulfweard looked back at him and soon smiled. Unwin had trouble keeping his own face straight.

Wulfweard, holding Unwin's eye, glanced down at a small boy who stood beside him and then looked, smiling, at Unwin again. Unwin looked at the child more closely – he had not done so before, since the boy was not big enough to be of any threat or use. The child stared back at him with ferocious concentration, his face bursting into huge, quickly quenched grins. But it was only when Wulfweard nodded to him that Unwin knew the boy. His own son! The elder, Godwin. It had been more than a year since he had visited his wife and seen him. So, he still had an heir.

He gave a brief smile to his son, who blushed, grinned, and seemed to shiver from head to toe. He seemed about to spring from his place and run to Unwin, but Wulfweard put a hand on his shoulder to remind him of what was proper. Unwin frowned and looked away.

Unwin's steward having fallen silent, Ingvald's was now reciting his master's lineage which, as Ingvald was a pagan, only went back to Odin. Unwin shifted his gaze to the elf's drop, allowing his mouth to twist with distaste. The thing's startling beauty was repellent, and he loathed its resemblance to his family. The poverty of its clothing was surely intended as an insult, and the flower crown worn in mockery of his gold.

Deliberately feeding his hatred, he looked into the thing's face and met its long, wide stare. He felt something like a shove, and the skin down his back crawled. He put up a hand and gripped his crucifix, steadying his gaze, refusing to look away.

Ingvald's steward reached the end of his recital and now Athelric – the traitor – began to recite the titles and ancestry claimed by the elf's drop. The presumption was insufferable.

Unwin said, "No king-list is needed here. Once you've said 'elf's get' there's nothing more to say."

Ingvald shifted his feet, offended by this gross discourtesy. Ingvi looked at the grass, embarrassed.

Only Godwin was impressed. Elf's get! That was the word for it – tell it to its face! He must, he *must* go with his father that night. Would he be allowed to take his puppy?

Elfgift turned and beckoned to his steward. Servants came forward to offer mead and bread to Unwin's party. Unwin's face showed contempt: these manners were tricks Athelric must have taught his pet. Certainly it had never learned such manners from the thralls that had raised it on its dung-heap of a farm. A pity that he hadn't been more thorough and taught it how to dress!

Unwin's own servants came forward, carrying horns and plates, and Elfgift's servants halted in confusion. They looked for orders, Unwin noted, to Athelric.

"This land is my inheritance," Unwin said. "You are my guests. It is for me to give you bread."

The silence was as heavy as the heat under the awning. Both Ingvi and Wulfweard looked away. Godwin couldn't stop grinning.

Elfgift nodded, beckoning to his servants who withdrew behind his chair. Unwin's servants pressed forward and Elfgift accepted a horn from one of them, but Athelric waved the proffered horn aside.

Taking a horn for himself, Unwin said, "I drink to your good health." Like one instructing the ignorant he added, "As guest and supplicant, you present your gifts first."

Elfgift said, "I am the guest? Is it custom to keep a guest waiting a day?"

"Aye," Unwin said, "when the host is a king and the guest a bastard-born farmer."

In the silence Godwin's giggle was shrill. He covered his mouth with his hand.

Unwin was glad to have made his son laugh, and amused by the expression on Athelric's face. He raised his horn towards Elfgift. "Another toast! To the beauty of the bride!" The wreath of flowers was like that of a bride. "You make a pretty girl."

"Do you run from pretty girls," Elfgift asked, "as fast as you run from me?"

Athelric laughed aloud, but it was Wulfweard's

smile which stung Unwin – and the way the grin dropped from his son's face.

Throughout the war, Unwin had withdrawn from meeting Elfgift in battle, choosing instead to harry and destroy local musters. It had been policy, not fear, and he had thought himself too old to care about gibes of fearfulness. Still, it nettled him that it was so easy to make him sound, in Godwin's hearing, a coward.

Only then did the other meaning of Elfgift's words catch him and knock the breath from him – that he ran from women. It even twisted his jeer about Elfgift making a pretty bride until it sounded as if he had spoken it in admiration. In front of his son! Blood reddened Unwin's face, his teeth set together hard, his fists clenched.

Godwin, alarmed, wondered, had his father truly lost his temper or was he pretending? He looked up at Wulfweard, but Wulfweard only appeared concerned.

Ingvald touched Unwin's arm. "It's time we spoke of why we're met. Of what you want from us, elf-born, and what we'll give you." He seated himself in his chair, leaned back and stretched out his legs. Ingvi moved closer and rested his hand on the chair-back, proud of the way his brother had guided the meeting when Unwin had been speechless.

Unwin and Elfgift remained standing, facing

each other. Then Unwin turned sharply away and dropped into his chair. His face still red, he said, "We know what it wants. A truce while it gets in its harvest."

Elfgift sat, and Athelric and Wulfweard moved to either side of his chair. "I want," Elfgift said, "to settle this war. I offer you, again, single combat. One of us to die, instead of many."

Unwin gave a huff of laughter. "And, again, I refuse."

"Is it this 'pretty girl' you fear?" Elfgift asked. "Or is your one god no match for the devils on my side?"

Unwin smiled, his anger now well hidden. "Lad, words won't goad me. Little boys call names in the street, and rats squeak in the barn. I pay no heed."

"If I matter so little, then fight me alone," Elfgift said. "You'll kill me easily. Then you'll have everything you want."

"It would do you too much honour. I don't fight farm-boys."

"Our brother Hunting said that to me once."

Unwin, his elbow on the chair's arm, set his clenched fist against his mouth and was silent a while. "No single combat, you thing. Now tell me of this truce you need."

Elfgift looked down at the flower-starred grass. When he raised his head, he said, "Atheling, I am sorry if I have offended you. You made me angry, and I couldn't hold my temper. If you will grant it, Atheling, I want to make a truce until next spring."

Ingvald nodded, appreciating the wisdom of these words and what they must have cost to say. Athelric reached round the high back of the chair to grip Elfgift's shoulder.

Unwin laughed aloud. "How about a truce until this time next year? Or the year after? Why should we make a truce with you at all? It's not our harvest. We aren't losing men."

Elfgift leaned forward. "You mean to winter here. You'll need food for horses and men. You will need to get in the harvests of the boroughs you hold."

"Why? You do the farming, farm-boy. We'll eat from your barns and herds – and kill your farmers and herdsmen."

Ingvald coughed. "I would be happier with full barns and men who know how to fill them. I've little interest in capturing barren fields."

Unwin looked sidelong at him, then decided to laugh. "To please the Jarl then, here's my offer. A truce until All Saints."

Elfgift looked up at Wulfweard, who stooped his head. "He means until Ing's Feast."

"Then to war again," said Unwin. "Plenty of grain for the horses and meat for the men. War until mid-winter. You'd rather fight than sit by the fire, eh, Athelric?"

That, Godwin thought, was what a man and a king should say.

The old traitor, Athelric, didn't answer. The elf's get leaned back in its chair, its face blank.

Unwin smiled at Wulfweard and Godwin. The boy laughed back at him, but Wulfweard's face remained puzzlingly serious.

Ingvald said, "A truce until spring could be bought, elf-born. What will you give for it?"

Elfgift raised one knee and hugged it, resting his heel on the chair's seat. "What do you want?"

"My land," Unwin said. "Give me that and I'll give you eternal peace."

Elfgift looked away from him, to Ingvald.

"Ten thousand pounds in gold and silver," Ingvald said. It would go towards paying King Lovern for his help, and news of the payment would draw more landless men to them. "Horses. Weapons – or iron ingots. Grain, ale, sheep. In return we'll give you your truce. Until spring."

"Until All Saints," Unwin said. "Until spring will cost more."

Elfgift hugged his knee. He rested his chin on it, the poppies and cornflowers and day's-eyes still glowing in his crown. "Ten thousand pounds of silver, for a truce until spring. Of the rest – nothing."

"The farmer wants his truce cheap," said Unwin. "But I'm not a farmer and I don't haggle. I named my price and won't change it."

Elfgift rose abruptly, turning as if he would walk away. But he turned back again, looking only at Ingvald. "Will you make a truce or not?"

Unwin clapped a hand on his leg. "The farmer's anxious to spit and smack palms!" Ingvald rose and went to stand beside Unwin's chair, stooping low to speak to him.

Elfgift walked behind his chair, leaned briefly on its back, and would have swung away and left the meeting if Athelric had not stretched his arm across Elfgift's back, holding him in place. His hand squeezing Elfgift's shoulder, he said, "They need the truce too. They can't go on fighting a war and feed their horses through the winter. They need to rest, give their wounded a chance to recover, toughen up new arrivals. Keep calm, lad. Unwin just wants you to beg."

Ingvald straightened. "A truce until Ing's Feast in exchange for ten thousand pounds of gold."

"Silver," Elfgift said.

Unwin said, "We haven't spoken of prisoners and hostages. Return me my brother and son, and maybe I'll agree to silver, not gold. Maybe I'll agree to a peace until spring."

Godwin jumped on the spot. As he had hoped! His father would drive the bargain home and the elf's get would crumble. He would row across the river with his father that night.

Above Godwin's head, Wulfweard spoke. "I am neither prisoner nor hostage. I stand here of my own free will."

Unwin looked at Wulfweard and saw the elf's get's face looking back. Even as his sight cleared, and he saw his brother's face emerge from the likeness, the chill remained in his belly. He had never been such a fool as to trust his brothers, not even the youngest and favourite, but Wulfweard could never have turned against him so completely. Perhaps there was more to the likeness between the two faces than their having been fathered by the same man...

"Whatever we agree," the elf's get said, "I shall never give up your son. He is hostage for your word. Break it, and I'll send him to Woden." Wulfweard's head turned sharply towards Elfgift. "A rope round his neck and a spear in his side."

Godwin drew a breath but held it, staring at his father. No need to be afraid yet. The last word hadn't been spoken.

Unwin kept his face expressionless. "It seems all the hostages are yours. Who will be hostage for your word? You have no family, do you, elf's get? So, stalemate again. Ten thousand pounds of gold for a truce until All Saints."

Elfgift considered, then rose from his chair. "No

truce. Not at that price." He turned away but spoke over his shoulder. "If I have to make war through the winter, then I shall make war like a farmer. I shall butcher."

"Wait!" Unwin leaned forward in his chair, holding out one hand towards Elfgift, in the manner of a man coaxing a dog to him. "Wait, lad. Jul's Borough is in your hold, is it not? Will you hold Jul there?"

Seeming not to understand, Elfgift turned to Athelric and Wulfweard.

Athelric said, "The king always holds Jul at Jul's Borough."

"Thank you, Athelric. Had you not held that lesson yet? Does your pupil know that Jul's Borough belonged to my mother, Queen Ealdfrith?"

"What is the deal you want to make?" Elfgift demanded.

Unwin leaned back. "My mother built a chapel there – at Jul's Borough. Is it still there, or have you pulled it down? It's where my mother died. I'd like to celebrate Christmas there – that's Jul, Elfgift – and pray to her. She's a saint, you know. Do you know what a saint is?"

Elfgift, still standing, stared at him. So did Athelric and Wulfweard. "Do you want...?" Elfgift began. "You want to – change a Borough you hold for –?"

"No. We will each hold what we have. But I would like to celebrate Christ's Mass in my mother's chapel, in her memory. Let me guest with you at Jul's Borough – you'll feast my company. That'll be the price of the truce until spring."

Athelric said, "Open our gates to a troop of your men?"

"Father's-brother, yes. There's no danger! Christ's Mass and my mother's memory are holy to me – more holy than your Jul is to you. It's a sin to break the peace on either side. And I shall be putting my life in your hands as surely as you risk yours by opening your gates to me. What have you to fear? But do me this favour, and I'll agree to a truce until spring."

Elfgift joined Athelric and Wulfweard behind the big chair. Athelric said, "It would be foolhardy. It would be the sheep inviting the wolves into the fold!"

"Are we sheep?" Elfgift said. "It would gain us the truce." He looked at Wulfweard.

"I hardly remember our mother alive," Wulfweard said, "but Unwin knew her, and loved her. He wouldn't use her memory in such a trick. And he's honest in his faith. You can trust him in this, Elfgift."

"It's Wulf who's too trusting," Athelric said. "Unwin has more love for the power his faith will bring him with foreign kings than he has for the faith itself. And he hates you, Gift." Athelric had watched Unwin's face during the meet, and had seen that Unwin hated the boy as a man hates spiders or snakes: with a murderous loathing. He put his hand on Elfgift's shoulder. "He means to get within your gates and behind your shield."

"But it would gain us the truce," Elfgift said, and turned back to the meet, pulling away from Athelric's hand. Standing before his chair, he said, "Ten thousand pounds of silver for a truce until Ing's Feast or – All Saints Day? And then to guest your host at Jul's Borough throughout Jul, in return for a truce until spring. Are those the terms?"

"Well done!" Unwin said. "You have it right. And to those terms, I agree."

"Then the truce is made?" The note of uncertainty in the elf's get's voice made Unwin laugh again.

"The truce is made," Ingvald said, rising. "Now we can eat!" It was late afternoon. Though still bright, the light was more yellow and the air, by the water, was growing cooler. "Tomorrow we can take the oaths."

Unwin rose and smiled towards Wulfweard and Godwin. "You'll eat with me, as my guests."

Elfgift said, "I shall eat in my own camp, with my friends." He turned his back on Unwin and moved away towards the shore. Athelric turned to

157

follow him.

Wulfweard snatched at Godwin's arm as the boy moved towards his father, holding him back despite the boy's outraged yells and thrashings.

"Wulf!" Unwin said. "You'll be my guest?"

Wulfweard, stooped over Godwin, looked up at his brother and then seemed to relent and allowed Godwin to drag him forward. Unwin put his big hand on the boy's head, and Godwin looked up at him so admiringly that he bent and kissed him. Straightening, he held out his arm to his brother, and would have embraced and kissed him too except that Wulfweard stepped back, out of reach.

"I am glad," Wulfweard said, "to see you alive and well."

"I am more glad than I can say to see you, Wulf. I was told you were dead. Eat with me tonight!" Wulfweard shook his head. Unwin reached out and caught him by the arm. "Is this truly your choice? You are not held by –?"

"Elf-craft? No. By my own free choice."

Godwin had put his arms round his father and was clinging to him.

"I can't believe," Unwin said, "that you are siding with that—"

Wulfweard began tugging at Godwin. "We must go now."

Godwin wouldn't let go. He sobbed, saying over and over that he wanted to go with his father.

Unwin, aware of the rules of war, was embarrassed. Elfgift's housecarls were coming to enforce his will. The situation was dangerous.

"Spend this one evening with me," Unwin said. "You and the boy both."

Wulfweard, still holding on to the boy, looked back with a blank, cold face that wordlessly refused. Even more than before, he looked like the thing, and Unwin was chilled. His brother had become nothing more than the Devil's reflection, doing its will.

Athelric came to them. "Elfgift orders that his company go with him. Release the boy to me: he is our prisoner." As Unwin opened his mouth, he added, "If you wish to spend the evening with your son, come to our camp – as Elfgift's guest."

Unwin crouched and held his son's shoulders, kissed the tearful face. "Tears are for children." The little boy struggled to still his sobbing. He tried to wipe his face on his own shoulders. "Go with them. You are their hostage but you won't always be. Do as I say now."

Unwin rose and watched as Wulfweard drew Godwin away. The boy walked backwards, looking at his father as long as he could. Wulfweard never looked back at all.

Ingvald, his arms folded, quoted the Words of Odin. " '*If there's a man you cannot trust, but you would have good of him, then use him with fair words, though your mind is false…'* If you'd remembered that, you might have been eating with your son tonight."

Unwin held his temper. He said, "My brother has changed. You wouldn't know, but he isn't himself. He's bewitched."

"They're the spit of each other, I'll say that. Not like me and Ingvi." He grinned at his own half-brother.

Unwin took offence that a mere Jarl should make any such comparisons. He turned and went into the tent.

Later, at table, while Ud played his harp, Ingvald went rumbling on, saying how good it was to have made the truce, and to what use they could put the time. Building up stores of food and weapons. Bringing in fresh men and training them up. And with the truce lasting until the spring, until Freyja's Feast, most likely…

"Until the Feast of the Rood," Unwin said.

…they'd have a chance to feed the horses up after the winter hunger. And time to see the fields planted at the Boroughs they held, to ensure another harvest, if the war lasted another year. Or even if it didn't. War or no war, you needed a harvest. Above everything else, a harvest.

Unwin grew tired of listening to Ingvi being instructed. "The war will end at Christ's Mass," he said.

"You know that?" Ingvald asked. "Is this some spirit-message from your God?"

"I shall celebrate Christ's Mass," Unwin said, "by cutting the blood-eagle on the elf's get. To free my brother from its spell."

No answer came from the Jarlssens. Through the silence, Ud's harp-music went rippling on. Unwin grinned at the Danes' faces.

"You'll break the truce?" Ingvi said. "You'll give your word, and swear by your God and your mother, and break peace at Jul?"

"I am a Christian," Unwin said. "No truce I make with a devil can bind me. I am working for Christ and His Victory."

The Jarlssens still stared. Ingvi leaned forward over the table, the better to look into Unwin's face. "But to break the Jul peace!"

"Jul is nothing to me. And when Jul's Borough is called Christ's Borough, Christ will forgive me."

"The elf-born is no fool," Ingvald said. "Neither is the old man who advises him. Whatever you plan, they will be ready for you."

"And they have your son!" Ingvi said. "You heard what he said – he will send your son to Odin!"

"How will it kill my son," Unwin asked, "when its ribs and lungs are spread in bloody wings?"

"If you fail?" Ingvi said.

"We won't fail."

161

"But if you do?" Ingvald asked.

Unwin leaned back in his chair. "If I fail … I have another son. And sons are easily made." The Danish brothers looked at him with something between awe and disgust, knowing nothing of the pain it cost Unwin to say this: the same pain he had always felt when he faced the possibility of treachery from his brothers. "Wulfweard is more use to me," he said, "once the spell is broken. He's old enough to fight."

Ud ended his music with a final chord.

Across the river in Elfgift's camp, Godwin lay in his bed-roll. His puppy lay against him, wrapped in his blankets and licking his face. He put his hand around its throat.

He would kill it, because he had been dragged back here. He would kill the dog and leave its corpse outside Elfgift's tent. No, he would carry the dog into Elfgift's tent under his cloak and leave it in the elf's get's bedding.

The pup wriggled out of his hold and licked his hand. He stroked its fur.

In the summer dusk, Ebba crouched on the height of the island, nibbling bread and breathing in the scent of grass, thyme and water. She looked across the water to the fires and lights of Elfgift's camp – and then started, her heart leaping and her arms jerking out as someone stepped close by her. Ud crouched at her side. She had not heard him come.

He smiled and, leaning close, kissed her cheek, his beard brushing her skin. Then he reached into the pouch that hung at his belt and took from it something like a tally-stick: a piece of wood, longer than it was wide, cut flat and smooth. He handed it to her.

The stick was carved with sharp, angular patterns. "These are runes, Master. I don't know about them." She tried to hand the stick back.

He drew her to him, his arm around her. He was so much bigger than she, he was able to put his arm around her, and still hold the rune-stick up in front of her. With his other hand he pointed to the patterns. "This is Ash ... this is Birch ... this is Oak ... this is Thorn... And here is Yew. Weapon, Torch, Gift, Grave, Need, Ice..."

CHAPTER 8

Holding Court

To step into the God-house was like stepping into a forest: its pillars were the straight, grained trunks of whole trees, and overhead were the interlocking cross-beams. The firelight of the candles flickered, catching the gilding of carvings and bringing them out of darkness for a moment, making the shadows shift like the movement of branches. And, for Jul, garlands of holly and ivy had been strung around and between the pillars, lending a green scent to the air and a green tint to the candle's golden light. Kendrida loved the place. In the God-house, she felt an awed contentment.

She led Godhelm and Godhilda by their hands

164

to the altars, and knelt, sitting on her heels, holding the children round their waists. There were stories they should have been told years since. "Look, that's Thonur in the middle, with the red beard. See His hammer?"

Thonur's face had been roughly chopped out with an axe. His beard was coloured red and grooved to indicate hair. Lower down, the beard turned into the hammer, and Thonur's hands grasped it. A golden ring glimmered about the thick wooden neck: the ring on which oaths to Him were sworn. It was not a beautiful figure, nor very human, but it retained all the power of the tree.

"And that's Woden, see? He has only one eye." Woden's face was disfigured by a deep, gouged hole. His tongue was carved protruding from His mouth – He was the hanged God. In His hand was His spear, its head gilded. "I'll tell you how He lost His other eye one day. And that one – look, that's Ing. See His yellow hair? And the corn in His hand?"

Ing's face was the most finely carved, as it had to suggest beauty and youth. The corn in His hand was metal, gilded. Some Ing figures held swords, but not this one.

The three God-figures loomed over them, darkshadowed and golden-lit, glimmering with gold. A three-fold God – just as the Lady was Maiden, Mother and Crone, so here was the Lord: Youth,

Warrior and Elder: Sword, Hammer and Spear. Kendrida almost felt Them welcome her back and she stooped her head and kissed her daughter's soft, fat little cheek, and then her son's. It was sheer joy to be here with them, before the altars of the True Gods. She only wished that Godwin was with them. Godwin would not enter the God-house.

"Are there stories about Thonur?" Godhelm asked. He had been taken by the red beard and hammer.

"There are stories about Them all – some are painted on the walls." Rising from her knees, she led them over to the walls, which were crowded with pictures. The shifting candlelight and the shadows of pillars and garlands made them hard to see. "Look, here's Woden again: you can always tell Him by His blue cloak and hood. He's leading the dead – look – bringing them back to us. That's part of Jul. We shall set the tables for the dead, so they can celebrate Jul, too."

Godhilda looked scared, and as if she might cry.

Kendrida crouched and hugged her. "No need to be scared! They will be the *good* dead: your grandfathers will be there. They come back to us for this one night in the year." When she had been as small as Godhilda, she had probably feared the homecoming of the dead too, as she would fear ghosts walking on any other night of the year now.

But she always remembered how lovingly, as a young girl, she had helped to make everything clean and welcoming for the returning dead. This year she looked forward to setting a place for her dead father. He should have a glass of the best wine. For so many years he'd been dead, and she unable to welcome him home because of her Christian marriage.

"Who are *they*?" Godhelm asked. He was looking at a painting of two naked youths, kneeling side by side with linked arms. In Their free hands They held swords. On Their heads, over Their long hair, They wore antlered helmets, as a sign that They were more than human.

"They are the Brothers." When Godhelm looked at her questioningly, Kendrida tried hard to remember anything she knew of Them, but shook her head. New Gods arose, and old Gods sank back into the shadows of the God-house walls and the darkness of forgetfulness.

"Lady?" A girl's voice calling.

"I'm here."

The girl stepped from the shadow of a pillar into golden light, one of the maids to the Borough's stewardess. "Forgive me, Lady, but we don't know which bowls and ewers to set out for the Atheling Unwin."

Kendrida sighed. She hated to be dragged away from the God-house and her children to give thought to her husband and his arrival to plague them all. But the feasting of Unwin and his company was the price they had to pay for the truce which had given them peace to gather in a lavish harvest. Despite the field-burnings and the riding down of crops, the barns were full, the apple-lofts crammed, the store-rooms stacked with baskets of nuts. Harvest-Home had been a true feast. The Lady was with them, and she was smiling. The thought cheered her, and she said, "The most costly, surely?"

"Lady Matilde thinks the most costly things should furnish the king's lodgings. But she's afraid to offend the Atheling and she's worried that the things left—"

"Oh, by all the Saints!" Kendrida said, and laughed at herself for still using Christian expressions. "I'll come." Perhaps she should have stayed at her own Borough, where she would not have had to think about Unwin or meet him, but she had wanted to see Godwin again. And to keep Jul where Elfgift was.

She stooped over the children and kissed them, wishing again that all three of them were there. "Stay here and be good, I won't be long. Godhelm, look after Godhilda."

She followed the maid from the God-house into the yard, where a thin covering of snow lay over the black mud and the wind blew cold. She had been trying not to think of it, but she had been dreading the time when she must meet Unwin and he would demand – as he certainly would – that she attend Christ's Mass with him. She would have to tell him that she could no longer do that.

You are your father's daughter, she told herself, and you trace your descent from Woden. You aren't afraid of Unwin Eadmundsson.

"One thing I've learned," she said to the maid, "Elfgift won't notice or care *how* you furnish his lodgings. We'll give the best to Unwin and keep him happy. Do you know where Godwin is?"

In the upper room above the Royal Hall, Godwin picked up a stool and carried it to the furthest corner, as far as possible from the others. Suddenly he wished for his father to be there so intensely that he shivered. When Unwin arrived, he would go to Christ's Mass with him, and people would see him by his father's side and know that he was his father's right-hand man. He would tell his father how his mother was making Godhelm and Godhilda into heathens.

In the centre of the room stood a brazier filled with hot coals and, beside it, a big, high-backed armed chair meant for the king – but Athelric was sitting in it. Elfgift was sitting on the floor, leaning against the chair's side, his head resting on his raised knees and hidden in his arms. Wulfweard was kneeling on the straw- and herb-strewn floor, using his dagger to try and broach a small cask, one of the many presents given to Elfgift in court that morning.

From his corner Godwin watched the dagger work at the cask's bung and thought that the cask should have been in his father's hands. His father should have been holding court. His father, if he had been there, would be sitting in the chair, like a King, and Athelric would be on a stool. But his father *was* a king, and behaved like one – not like a farmer, a bastard, a *thing*!

The Royal Court held that morning had been like a fair. Courts were always crowded, but that morning the hall had been so packed that nobles in gold and fringed tunics had been pressed against farmers in wool and leather, and ladies had been jostled by sheep-stinking shepherds in coats of woven grass – or even by slaves and beggars, people with their feet wrapped in rags. Most of them had no business at the court, no case to be heard or petition to present. They had come simply to stare at the elf's get.

The shepherds and farmers and thralls had brought their women with them, and none of them had any idea of how to behave in a Royal Hall. Staring and pointing wasn't enough. They had whistled and bawled, waving their hands in the air, yelling out, "Elfgift!" and even "Giftie!"

Their ceaseless noise had gone beyond anything forgivable. Three times Athelric, as steward of the court, had ordered the guards to beat their shields until the crowd had fallen silent, but each time the silence had given way to whisperings, growing louder and louder, and then shouts and calls and whistles, until the din was as bad as before.

The crowd had thrown things towards the throne-chair – bags of nuts, bundles of cloth, rolled up tunics, packages of braid for trimming sleeves and hems, skeins of dyed wool. Several guards and clerks had been hit and Wulfweard, leaning on the back of the throne-chair, had been forced to duck as a package had flown past his head.

Some people from the crowd had dodged the guards and interrupted proceedings by running up to the throne-chair itself, to present Elfgift with flasks of ale and mead, cheeses, sucking pigs, fish, bags of apples. When Athelric had announced that the next such interruption would be punished, they had given their presents to the guards and tried to persuade them, or bribe them, to deliver their presents for them. They had no shame, these people. Nothing could make them behave. And it was all because of Elfgift. The slaves and farmers were only there in such numbers, braying and bawling, because of Elfgift.

The lower sort knew he was one of them – well,

in so far as he was human at all, he was, having been raised by thralls. And he pandered to them. In hearing after hearing, he found for the farmers and against the nobles. The farmers and the thralls had cheered, and their women had shrilled, and their noise had set the birds flying and screeching about the rafters. Even Godwin, young as he was, knew the stupidity of flattering commoners like that. When next war came, let Elfgift try raising an army from among the farmers and thralls! He would see how quickly and willingly the fighting men of the Twelve Hundred gathered to a king who set thralls above them.

Wulfweard at last succeeded in producing a spout of liquid from the little cask, and his cry of delight roused Elfgift, who scrambled on his knees to fetch the cups set out on a nearby chest. A king, scrambling on his hands and knees in straw and holding out cups to be filled like a serving man!

Elfgift, on his knees, twisted round to hand a filled cup to Athelric. Seeing Godwin in the corner, he called out to him, "Where's the pup?"

Godwin looked up to see the thing smiling at him – that shy smile that flattered you, and almost made you feel sorry for it. Godwin looked away. *Don't try to charm me*, he thought. *I'm a Christ-man: it won't work on me.*

When the silence went on too long, Athelric said reprovingly, "Godwin." They were all under the elf's drop's spell.

"I left the dog at my lodgings," Godwin said.

"Why?" Elfgift asked.

"I didn't think he had any business at a Royal Court." Although the place had been such a fairground, he could have brought terriers and hunted rats, and no one would have noticed.

"Come and eat," Elfgift said. There was a plate on the chest, piled high with bread, and a jug of ale. Godwin glanced up to see Elfgift set a cup of mead on the furthest corner of the chest, the corner nearest Godwin.

Godwin was only allowed small beer. Whether Elfgift offered the mead as another trick of charm, or because he was ignorant of what Godwin was allowed, Godwin didn't know – but he suspected trickery. Still, the mead bothered him. He wanted to stay aloof on his stool, but the chance to drink mead with the men might not come again soon. And he was hungry. A fighting man should eat when he could, and keep his strength up. It never made sense to go hungry out of pique. He left the stool and went over to the group about the chest.

Elfgift pushed the plate of bread towards him, but Godwin picked up the cup, trying to seem unconcerned. The first sip was warming and sweet, but made him shiver.

"You've done well with the pup," Elfgift said.

Godwin gritted his teeth. He knew that he had

173

done well with the pup, and praise was always welcome, but it was almost painful to be praised by the elf's get. He wanted to sneer and pretend he didn't care, but found himself smirking before he lowered his face into the cup, to hide it. The mead was sweater and warmer with each sip.

An idea came to him. If the elf's get was so set on winning him round, he might as well get some good of it. He banged his cup down on the chest and went to his knees, his movements all a little more clumsy than they should have been. He knelt before Elfgift like a man asking a favour of a king, though Elfgift should have been seated in a chair instead of leaning against one. "A favour, King!"

Elfgift seemed puzzled. Athelric said, "Godwin, behave!" Court games weren't for little boys.

Elfgift, straightforward as a farmer, said, "Let's hear what you ask before I say owt."

"Only a little favour, King – a very small favour." He had heard those words in a story. Quickly, before Athelric could stop him, he went on, "After Jul, when my father leaves, can I go with him? I'm his eldest son – I ought to be with him!"

Wulfweard looked away. Athelric shouted, "Godwin! I told you to behave!"

Elfgift continued to look at him with that serious, intent expression which always seemed to show more interest and sympathy than any smile.

Godwin, staring back, saw the thing's eyes shift colour in the sunlight, from grey to the greenish-gold of glass. His hopes rose. The thing hadn't agreed with Athelric yet.

With a movement so slight that it didn't disturb the fine plaits that hung beside his face, Elfgift shook his head.

Godwin felt he had been taunted. He floundered to his feet and started furiously for the door.

Behind him Athelric shouted, "Where are you going?"

"To my lodgings! With your permission, sir."

Athelric was standing in front of the big chair. "It's not my permission you should ask, but the king's."

As Godwin shook with anger to hear the thing called "king", he heard Elfgift say, "Let him go." Rather than look into those eyes again, Godwin pulled the door open and ran down the stairs.

Godwin sat alone in the private room he shared with Wulfweard. His pup ran about the room, sniffing in corners and then scurrying to the door before coming back to put its paws on Godwin's knee, telling him that it was time they went out.

He cuffed it away from him, and it ran to the other side of the room, cringing.

Godwin was crying, though the pain at his heart was rage as much as sorrow. To think of his father leaving after Jul, while he remained with these traitors and heathens was intolerable.

He had enemies all round him. Godhelm and Godhilda were just babies, and his mother! She was sinking back into the worshipping of devils his father had saved her from, and pulling his brother and sister down with her. She even asked him to break his vows to his Lord Christ. She was bewitched.

If he could, he would kill them all. He ought to kill them. Even his mother. Tears filled his eyes and his heart ached as if it was gripped in claws.

He jumped up and went to one of the storage chests, rummaging through it until he found a belt, while tears fell on his hands. Stooping, holding out a hand, he called the dog. It ran to him, tail wagging, glad to be forgiven.

Godwin looped the belt through the dog's collar and buckled it. He heaved the dog off the floor by the belt.

The dog kicked and whined, jerking the belt in his hand. One of its claws raked down his arm, but couldn't hurt him through his thick winter's wool. But the way it struggled weakened him, and he dumped it on a wall-bench.

Frightened, the dog tried to run away, but Godwin was still holding the belt, which pulled it up short. As he reached for it, the dog snapped at him, then cowered, ashamed.

Godwin was ashamed of his own cowardice. How could he kill men, when he was full-grown, if he couldn't even kill a dog? What he had set his mind to do, he should do.

Climbing on to the bench, he heaved the dog off its feet again. Setting his teeth, setting his heart, he ignored its struggles. A bracket projected from the wall, where a lamp could be hung. He hooked the belt over the bracket, and jumped down from the bench. In the middle of the floor, he turned to watch.

The collar sank deep into the dog's throat. It couldn't whine. It kicked, more and more frantically, scratching the wall. Godwin wiped tears from his eyes and fixed his face in as calm and manly an expression as he could, struggling against the sobs that rose in him, and the pain of them. He refused to think of how the dog had slept against him or run after him. It was no different from killing a hen or a pig, which thralls did every day. It was less than killing a man, and when he was a man, he would have to watch the death-throes of men if he wished to earn fame.

But the dog was still struggling when he ran from the room and out into the yards.

Wulfweard brought the dog's body to Elfgift.

Elfgift lifted it by the belt that had throttled it and held it out at arm's length while he studied the swollen and distorted mask, the tongue hanging out as if to pant.

Elfgift's face was utterly still and gentle, as if he gazed into the distance, at nothing.

After all, what did the life of a small pup matter? Scores were drowned, unwanted. Against all the life and all the pain in the world, this pup's carcase was unimportant.

But how much it had mattered to this small body. The pain, the desperation, the fear that had swelled inside the pup began to seep into Elfgift, bringing with it a thousand, thousand echoes: life hungry, life in fear, life wounded, in pain, drowning, dying – everywhere, all about. And none of it mattered, because other life crowded up behind, to take its place, like grass growing over the plot of a burned house.

He turned on Wulfweard a smile so beautiful it was disconcerting. "I think Godwin's foretold his own future."

Wulfweard couldn't smile.

CHAPTER 9

Sword Dance

Ebba had spent most of her life among people who dressed always in the grey, black and brown of undyed wool, and it thrilled her to see the many colours worn by the people in the hall: chequers and stripes, fringes and embroidered braid, all in bright reds, blues, yellows, green that seemed to flicker and throb in the candlelight. They wore gold too, which constantly caught the light and threw it back in flashes and sparks.

The hall itself was decked for Jul with bunches of green leaves and glowing red berries set among the gilded carving. She sat beside Ud on a bench against the wall, his blue cloak bundled beside her and his harp on her lap. No one glanced at them, but she was able to look about and stare as much as she wanted.

The high table was the best sight. Crowns of holly, ivy and burning candles hung from the rafters above it on long ribbons. Shifting candle-light ran up and down the table, glittering from arm-bands and brooches, from the rings on gesturing hands to golden collars. It glittered and darted from the goblets of green glass as they were raised and set down. Ebba had never seen glass before and it fascinated her almost more than the gold. She longed to touch it, to see if it felt cold, like ice.

Elfgift had ridden out the morning before, to meet his Jul guests on the road and escort them into the Borough. Unwin had not been pleased, on riding through the gate, to find his wife waiting to greet them with bread and ale, acting as hostess for his usurper. But he had smiled, and greeted his wife and children with kisses.

Kendrida, accompanied by Athelric, had walked with the guests to the halls where they would be lodged. They would eat in their lodgings that night with their companies – the food provided would not be stingy. The following night they were invited to the Royal Hall, to a feast to celebrate Jul's Eve.

"Wear no weapons," Athelric had said.

Unwin had kept smiling, though invited to a

feast in a hall he considered his. "But Athelric, the peace won't have begun. It will only be the Eve of Jul."

"The peace begins at midnight. Wear no weapons."

"I made a truce and I shall keep my word," Unwin said. "Lady, you will pour ale for us tonight?"

Kendrida had been standing with lowered head and hands clasped before her. Now she raised her head. "I don't wish to anger you, Unwin, but … I have spoken before witnesses and unwedded us. I shall send my maids to wait on you, but I am no longer your wife and no, I shan't pour ale for you."

Even through that, Unwin smiled. He only said, "So be it. Until tomorrow night, then, at the feast."

Unwin had made an impressive entrance into the feast, walking at the head of his party, dressed in blue silk with gold at his neck and on his arms and hands. The belt round his waist had a large golden buckle and was decorated with gold plaques, but no weapons hung from it – only a small dagger for cutting meat. Behind him came the Jarlssens and their company: tall Danes and Christian Welsh in their dark plaids.

Athelric came forward to lead Ingvald to the seat beside him, and Wulfweard brought Ingvi to the seat next to him. The seat beside Elfgift, at the centre of the table, was for Unwin.

As he approached his seat, Unwin looked to see if the elf's get was wearing the tall golden circlet which was the Saxon crown – but Athelric, anxious to keep the truce, was not flaunting his pet's claim to kingship. Elfgift's crown was a Jul crown: a tightly woven wreath of straw protected the wearer's head from the spikes of darkly-shining holly, jewelled with scarlet and crimson berries. Otherwise Athelric had dressed his puppet like one of the Twelve Hundred: a tunic of scarlet silk and a twisted gold collar about its neck, the finials set with garnets. Its long hair, combed back from its brow and falling to below its shoulders on either side, was white in the brightest light and amber in the shadows.

Unwin, caught by the eyes, stared. Surrounded by the sheen of silk, the glitter of gold and sparkle of glass, the creature seemed to radiate light. Its face was startling: such sharp, perfect lines. The solemn eyes were dark, and then caught the light like the greenish Roman glass. The dark green and scarlet of the holly crown glowed as gold could never have done. That must be what an angel looks like, Unwin thought – and was furious that such a thought had entered his head. It was elf-craft, the same craft it had used on Wulfweard. But he was stronger than Wulfweard.

Unwin had caught the thing's hands in his own

182

and, smiling, had spoken for the whole hall to hear. "I am honoured to share your feast tonight. I hope it will give no offence if I and my followers leave before the Guisers come. I am a Christian, and my vows to my Lord forbid me to worship any other God."

The elf's get's gaze shifted, to look over his shoulder. Athelric was somewhere behind him. Looking to its trainer.

"A guest may leave when he will," Elfgift said, his eyes returning to Unwin. "We shall take no offence."

Unwin nodded, and leaned forward as if to give Elfgift the greeting kiss due from an elder to a younger.

Elfgift drew away from him, pulling his hands free. As they all seated themselves, Unwin was smiling. Everyone had seen him offer a brotherly kiss to Elfgift, and everyone had seen the thing refuse it.

In the chattering din and heat of the feast, Ebba was standing, the better to see Elfgift. He was so beautiful, it made her want to cry. She couldn't tell if what she felt was hate or love. She saw many other people looking his way, and jealousy would flare in her, and then she would want to shout out for everyone to look at him. It grieved her to think that the night would pass, and the memory would fade, its colour and clarity dying. And once the blood-eagle was cut...

To Ud she called out, "You should make a song about Elfgift."

As always, the hole in Ud's face stared much harder than his one eye. "Aye. I shall make a song for him."

The Lady Kendrida and her maids were going about the hall, serving drink to the guests. Unwin, watching her, was careful to smile. She had always irritated him – too tall, too plain, forever doing the right thing – but having married her, he had honoured the contract, always acknowledging her as his wife and giving her three children. She repaid him with the insult of breaking their marriage. He saw her smile as she poured mead for Elfgift. It wasn't hard to see under whose influence she had fallen.

The women began to distribute Jul-cakes – small cakes baked from the last grain gathered in the harvest. Those shaped like boars were eaten in honour of Ing, those like stags in honour of Woden, and those like birds for the Lady. Unwin rose. "I can stay no longer. But it's good we've eaten bread and salt together." The words were meant to be reassuring. It was treacherous beyond expression to attack those with whom you had shared bread and salt.

Elfgift rose too. "We're sorry to see you go. But we wouldn't have you break your faith."

All through the hall, Unwin's Christian followers got to their feet, some more than a little drunk. Unwin gripped Elfgift by the shoulders and kissed him on both cheeks. He felt the thing tense under his hands, pulling away, and he was both amused and annoyed. If he could bring himself to touch the thing, for the sake of good manners, then Athelric might have trained it to stand still and accept a kiss politely.

As Unwin led his North Welsh from the hall, Elfgift looked down the table and met Athelric's eyes. The old man gave a slight nod, assurance that things were in hand.

Ud rose from his seat against the wall to follow his master. He wrapped his blue cloak round him, looking at Ebba.

"Can't we stay?" The feast would last for hours yet, and she could look at Elfgift.

Ud's one eye stared, and she hastily picked up his harp and followed after him. She kept turning her head, snatching every last look she could at Elfgift standing at the high table, blazing in red silk and red gold, his holly-crown glowing, the candles burning round him, the glass shining. Then she was through the door, and the cold made her flesh shrink on her bones. The dark robbed the light from her eyes. She was homesick for the light and warmth of the feast-hall.

At the end of the high table, Ingvi drank from

his mead-cup and stayed because Ingvald stayed. When Wulfweard said something to him – unheard in the din – and smiled, he felt wretched. It sickened him to stay in the hall when he knew what was planned. But which was worse? To betray a man in whose hall you had feasted, or the lord with whom you had taken service? Both were unforgivable.

In came the Guisers, bringing with them gusts of sharp, cold air which shook the candle flames and sent shadows jumping. They banged on the floor with their tall staffs and carried smoking torches which showered red sparks. Their bodies were clothed in tangles of leather twine strung with bones and flashing rings of bronze, while their faces were hidden behind animal masks: tusked boars, antlered stags, horned goats. Two of them wore swords – the only weapons in the hall.

Everyone rose, laughing and clapping to the Guisers' song, and people formed into lines between the tables to follow the Guisers in their dance round the hall, and follow them out into the night again. Ingvi couldn't help but grin, despite his bad mood. It was so like keeping Jul at home in Ingvald's court.

Outside the hall, wrapped against the cold, were crowds who hadn't been allowed into the feast: the poorer sort, and women. They began laughing when the Guisers appeared again, and tagged on to the noisy, drunken, laughing procession as it made off through the Borough's dark streets.

Near the procession's head, close behind the Guisers, Elfgift and Athelric drew together in the red, flaring light of the torches. "I have set guards," Athelric said.

Elfgift nodded. To post armed guards was to break the Jul peace, but with the enemy inside their gates, not to post them would have been foolhardy.

But Elfgift's skin tingled, his mind was full of shadows, and cold water seemed to move through his limbs. It was not the mead he had drunk. He knew the feeling; it had warned him many times before. If he allowed it to form itself into words, it would whisper: *Something bad coming*.

He prayed: *Lady, be with us* – but knew that She was not with him.

So he repeated over to himself: *The day of my death and the manner of my dying were fated long ago*.

The light of the torches and lanterns made a crack in the darkness as the singing, chanting, cheering, noisy troop made its way through the Borough gates and down through the orchards to the fields, calling out, "We are coming, coming!"

They marched and danced around the frozen fields, the light of the torches sweeping suddenly across black earth and scattered snow, then leaving it to darkness again. They rang bells, clapped, shouted and called out that it was Jul, Jul, and they had come to wake the fields from winter sleep. The night's silence was broken by the crunching of feet in snow, the whistles, the calling of thanks to the trees.

And then the Guisers led the way to the grave-field.

To the guards, Ud Harper said, "I can't bring the feast out to you, lads, but I can sing you a song!

Oh, he was as good harper
As ever plucked upon a string,
And he could drive young women mad
With the tunes his wires could sing.
He could harp a fish from the salt water
Or blood from out a marble stone
Or milk from out of a maiden's breast
Though baby she had none!"

He could harp cold into a man's bones, and sleep into his eyes, and he left every one of Athelric's guards sleeping and freezing. When Unwin led his men cautiously into the Borough's empty streets, there was no one to call them to a halt or to sound a warning.

As Unwin's men passed, feet treading quietly on the hard ground, weapons scraping, Ud came out of the shadows of a doorway and joined with them. Ebba was with him, wrapped inside his blue cloak and carrying his harp.

The grave-field, the field where the dead were sown. A low stone wall surrounded it, and the crowd leaned on the wall, sat on it, even stood on it. Torches were wedged in the stones, the wind carrying the scorching smell of burning wood. Lanterns hung in the guardian thorn trees, and leaping light played over the grave mounds.

The Guisers jumped the wall and to the music of pipe and drum – music frail in the big darkness – danced over the graves, their fantastic costumes of strings thrashing and whirling about them, their big masked heads eerie. Then the Guisers fell back to the wall, leaving only the two who wore swords facing each other in the middle of the graves.

A silence fell: children and other chatterers were hushed. The Guisers drew their swords and flourished them in the air. They were about to strip off their masks and tattered robes, to strip naked as newborns and dance for the dead, before leading the risen ghosts back to the feast-hall.

But instead they turned to where Elfgift and Wulfweard stood, side by side at the front of the crowd. The Guisers held out their swords to them. Elfgift and Wulfweard looked at each other, already half shaking their heads, but the crowd broke into murmuring and then shouts. When Elfgift threw aside his holly-crown and unclasped his belt, the shouting broke into cheers. Wulfweard, grinning, began to strip off his own clothes.

They had been warmed by drink and running after the Guisers, but as they pulled off their clothes the air of the winter night was sharp. The snow and hard ground stung their bare feet, and they did not linger before snatching the swords from the Guisers and running to the centre of the grave-field. Only the dance could keep them warm, as they danced above and for the cold dead.

The swords were poor, cheap things, sharp of edge, but clumsy in the hand. "With these, we could kill each other," Wulfweard said.

Elfgift grinned. "If you can!"

The music started, the pipe thin in the open air, and the drum sounding distant, and they struck their swords together with a jarring, ringing clash. Then spun away from each other, swinging round so that Wulfweard leaped over a blow from Elfgift's sword, and then Elfgift leaped over Wulfweard's. The swords rang again, and the dancers turned, twisted, ducked, leaped, imitating the actions of a sword fight and risking a wound at every movement. Boys in training were taught the sword-dance.

The silence of the crowd deepened as they watched. It seemed they watched Elfgift fight, or dance, with himself. The hair of the dancers flew; their faces, turning into the light, were intent, laughing, twin. The torches showered red sparks, and red light ran like water over the muscles of the dancer's arms, backs, legs. Into some minds there crept a memory of the God-house wall, of a fading picture that no longer had any story: two long-haired, naked youths, armed with swords: the Brothers.

The swords rang again, and the wind soughed through the thorn trees, flinging showers of sparks from the torches. Shadows moved in the grave-field's dark corners, and people turned sharply towards them. The dead were rising from their graves to watch the sword-dance with their living friends. They could be felt in the cold touches on cheek and neck, the shudders down the back. They were standing among the living now, shivering in the wind and hoping the dancers might shed some blood to feed and warm them before they joined the feast in the hall.

Unwin's men fell without warning on the rear of the crowd. The battle-shout was raised and people turned to find shields in their faces, to glimpse swords and axes coming down. They screamed, cried out to children and friends, scrambled over the stone wall and stumbled through the graves. The armed men followed.

The crowd's rush carried many from their feet: they were pushed down, trodden down. Swords drove into the fallen and running. Cries of pain and shock brought answering shrieks of fear. The grave-field was filled with another kind of frantic dance.

Elfgift and Wulfweard were pushed apart by the people struggling to escape through the graves. They struggled to stay on their feet and reached to each other through the crowd, fingers straining to link and so stay together. They raised their swords high, to keep their edges from the terrified people shoving past.

Ingvi, hearing the battle-shout, struggled in the crowd as if fighting to swim in a strong current, turning his head, looking for Ingvald. But the darkness was only fitfully lit by the wavering torches and faces were blurred in the dusk. Ingvi couldn't see his brother, nor could he catch sight of Elfgift or Wulfweard. Had they been cut down already?

If I had a sword, he thought, I would fight for Elfgift – but he had worn no sword in honour of Jul's Eve. Raising his hands high, he yelled, "Dane! Lovern!" and hoped that would preserve him as he fought to reach the grave-field's wall.

Some escaped over the wall and through the

lines of armed men into the fields and woods. Others were captured, or fell and were trodden on, or were chopped down. So the crowd thinned and the struggle lessened until the culling left Elfgift and Wulfweard alone at the grave-field's centre.

Unwin stood on the grave-field wall, the torch-light catching the golden studs on his black mail, glimmering over the mask of his helmet and down the length of his sword's blade. He nodded towards Wulfweard and Elfgift. "Take them alive."

The North Welsh, with shields on their arms and swords or spears in their hands, began advancing into the grave-field.

Wulfweard and Elfgift stood back to back and waited. Even to the Christians, they were an un-canny sight. Standing among graves, lit by the golden-red flaring and fading light of the torches, their long hair blowing about them, armed only with swords, as alike as twins and naked as ghosts, they brought old fears into Christian heads.

But Unwin had given his orders. The boldest of them began to test the brothers' unshielded sides.

With a shriek that tore her throat, Kendrida yelled her children's names, desperate to be heard above the shouts, the clash of metal and shields, the sound of running and yelling. People slammed against her full-tilt and she heaved them away, using her fists and nails to force her way through the buffeting crowd. She glimpsed a child's face – there! – here! – again! – soon snatched away in tumult, and her frightened mind made every one hers and sent her lunging in a new direction.

Desperation had carried her unharmed through the battle, she neither knew nor cared how. She had to stay on her feet so she could find her children, that was all.

There was some memory in her head of a helmet looming at her, a sword raised – even of pushing the sword aside because her children were beyond it.

Her knees and shins met the hard stones of the wall, her hands scraped on rough stone. Hauling up her skirts, she clambered on to the wall's top. The wind snatched at her, snapping her skirt, whipping at her torn headdress, chilling her. But she saw Godhilda and Godhelm. Catching her breath, she peered through the darkness. They didn't turn into strangers as she stared: she knew Godhilda by her little head, the way her hair fell. She had leaped from the wall and was running towards them, her heart racing thankfully, her mind a babble of thankful prayers to any and all gods, before she saw anything else.

Then she saw that they were standing beneath a thorn tree, dappled by the light of a swinging lantern hung in its branches. Athelric was with them, standing before them, standing off the men who came at them with shields and spears. In Athelric's hand a small knife caught the light – his table-dagger, the only weapon he wore as Jul's Eve turned into the Jul Peace.

Kendrida hauled her skirts up about her knees and screamed like a Valkyrie as she ran to join Athelric in battle. Still running, she saw the spear driven into him, shaking him to his knees. He grasped at the spear, and a sword, blazing in the lantern-light, came down on him from the other side. Dark figures, jumping over him, covered Godhilda's small figure from sight. Godhelm staggered as he was hauled away by the arm.

Kendrida threw herself bodily into the shield hiding Godhilda, and it was like throwing herself into a wall. She battered at the shield with her fists, reaching over it to the helmet behind, her fingers clawing into the eye-holes.

The man holding the shield heaved and threw her backwards, but she kept her feet and went forward again, grasping the edge of the shield and trying to pull it away, to get behind it. She was screaming Godhilda's name, thought she heard an answer and, with manic strength, tore at the shield again.

Arms held her from behind and lifted her from the ground. Men laughed and shouted words she couldn't understand. She kicked and pulled at the arms clasped about her, fought until she felt her joints cracking, but more men came to help those who held her, and she was lifted, dumped to the ground again, dragged. Never had she been so man-handled.

She was loosed, and fell hard to the ground. On her hands and knees in the snow, she looked up and saw the grave-field wall. A torch wedged among its stones lit two small figures standing by it – she saw only them. Godhelm and Godhilda, both wailing but both – Oh, thank the Lady! – alive. Godhilda tried to run to her, but a man held her back.

Another man stood on the wall. The light gleamed on the gold studs on his mail but didn't light his face, and Kendrida hardly noticed him. She had seen Godwin beside him. All three safe! Kneeling on the ground, she shook and sobbed.

The man in the gold-studded mail jumped down with a ringing of metal and, before she could think or move, was hauling her to her feet by her headdress. It was pinned to her hair, and his hand tore hair from her head. She came clumsily to her feet, crying out as she tried to loosen his hand with her own. Why? she thought. What have I done? Even when she had her feet under her he didn't let go, but pulled her this way and that by her hair. She could only take stumbling steps, almost falling, while her scalp felt as if it was being torn from her skull.

When her hair was torn from its pins and plaits and hung about her face and shoulders in dishevelment, the man let her go and said, "Now you look like the whore you are!" She recognized Unwin's voice.

She thought: at least the children are safe – he's their father. As she lifted her head he hit her in the face, so hard that she was lying on the ground, looking up at his shape against the black sky and stars before she knew what had happened. She didn't know if the pain was from his blow or the shock of hitting the ground. Her mouth was full of the taste of blood.

He hit me! she thought, astonished. *Me, a king's daughter!*

Turning away, Unwin said, "Put her with the other women."

Kendrida was clambering dizzily to her feet when men stooped over her and lifted her up. The children shrilled behind her as she was pulled away, their voices full of panic.

"Unwin! Let the children come with me – please!" The men holding her stopped, as if in sympathy.

Unwin came and pushed his face close to hers. "What children? You have no children." She gawped at him, his words making no sense.

The men pulled her forward again. For a

moment she went with them, stunned, but then her fury rose and she fought them to get back to her children. But they picked her up bodily and carried her away and, in all her fury, she could do nothing about it.

Unwin climbed over the grave-field wall and walked across the graves towards the centre.

Behind him, two of his children sobbed and were held back from running after their mother. But Godwin stood on the wall and lifted his head up with pride as he watched his father go. When Unwin came back to the wall, he would be bringing the elf's drop's head.

The sword-dance went on. The first man to come forward had taken Elfgift's sword-blow on his shield, but his knees had bent under the force, the blow shuddering through his every joint. Splinters of ash-wood flew from the shield.

Others, pressing the attack, had found Elfgift's sword swinging at them. One man fell, wounded in the leg – he hadn't seen the sword sweeping under his shield. Another man's shield was shattered on his arm and he stumbled back, fearing his arm was broken.

The North Welsh gave way. They hadn't known the speed with which Elfgift could move. Born from a devil, they reminded each other. Less human than he looked. Stronger, too. He looked a cub, but struck with the strength of the full-grown bear.

By the light of the torches and lanterns, Elfgift waited for the next attack. His eyes were stretched wide and watchful, and where he looked it was as if he dealt a light blow. His enemies flinched from his face – a face of frightening beauty that might have been a hero or a Valkyrie.

Better leave the Devil alone! The human boy would be easier to capture.

But though Wulfweard had no shield, he had Elfgift at his back. Any approach to Wulfweard's unshielded side brought helmet-breaking blows from Elfgift, chopping through spear-shafts, splintering shields. Then he would jump back to his place at Wulfweard's back and throw his sword to his other hand, to fend off any who risked coming at his other side.

The Welsh withdrew again, to think better what to do. While they drew off, Elfgift stooped over a fallen man, finished him, and wrested the shield from the corpse. He gave it to Wulfweard.

Glumly, the Welsh watched Wulfweard fit the shield to his arm. Now he would guard the Devil's back, and they dared not approach the Devil's face.

Unwin shouldered through the Welsh. He took off his dragon-helmet and tossed it to one of the men, who dropped his sword to catch it.

Unwin drew his own sword but held it pointing to the earth. Even his shield he held on a lowered arm. Unhelmed and half-disarmed, he walked up to Wulfweard, who watched him come over the edge of his shield.

Unwin said, "We have no quarrel, brother. Come to me. No one will hurt you."

Elfgift, his back touching Wulfweard's, felt him move as he drew in a quick, deep breath. The edge of Wulfweard's shield touched his shoulder, and Wulfweard's sword-arm jolted him as Wulfweard drew back for the blow. "Stand!" Elfgift said. Wulfweard was guarding his back.

Unwin said to Wulfweard, "It's we who should stand together."

Wulfweard looked at Unwin sidelong, disbelieving. He remembered how he had argued with Athelric, saying that Unwin could never be so treacherous. He felt cheated, as if some precious thing he had been keeping safe had been stolen and replaced with trash. And now Unwin assumed that he would leave Elfgift to die while he took shelter behind Unwin's shield.

"Come," Unwin said, and held his shield-arm wide, uncovering his body to Wulfweard's sword, safe in the knowledge that Wulfweard was too weak, or too afraid, or too loving of his brother to attack. With all his strength, Wulfweard drove his sword at Unwin.

Unwin leaped back, as one of his Welshmen threw himself forward to cover him with his own shield. Another man, coming at Wulfweard from the side as he made his forward lunge, buffeted him with his shield and sent him sprawling. He caught himself on his hands, but they were kicked from under him, and someone stamped on his sword-arm before wresting the sword from him. A man dropped on his back, pinning him to the cold ground.

Now Elfgift had no one at his back, and no shield, no helmet, no mail – nothing but a sword, and that a clumsy, heavy Guiser's toy. As Wulfweard was dragged to his feet, his hair whipping about his face, he yelled out in fury and frustration.

If Elfgift had followed Wulfweard, he would have thrown himself on the spears and swords of the Welsh. Feeling Wulfweard leave him, he jumped forward instead and, turning in the air, landed to see Wulfweard, disarmed, fighting with the men who held him.

Unwin put his helmet back on, covering his face with a golden mask surmounted by a ruby-eyed, snarling dragon. Men came to him from all corners of the grave-field. Elfgift, turning, saw the torch-light flicker over their helmets and shield-mounts.

Unwin said, "Lay down your sword – it's no

better than a kitchen-cleaver." Elfgift's attention shifted from him, back and forth among the men who circled him. "Your people are killed or captive. Your Gods are wood. You've been Athelric's pawn."

Elfgift made a short dash at a man who hastily fell back. Spinning as in the sword-dance, Elfgift faced off another coming at him from behind.

"Lay down your sword," Unwin said, "and I'll let you go back to your farm."

Elfgift was watching for the slightest movement in the uncertain, shifting light, listening for the lightest tread on the hard ground. He turned, fast, and swung a blow at the head of a man behind him, who couldn't raise his shield fast enough and, taking the blow on his helmet, fell to his knees. If the sword had been Woden's Promise he would have been skull-split.

Turning, Elfgift met the attack of those who had rushed at his back, leaping over a blow aimed at his legs, chopping at a man's neck, battering back a third with blows to his shield. The Welsh fell back again, looking to Unwin.

"One man!" Unwin shouted. "Naked! All but unarmed!" But his men noted that he showed no eagerness to test himself against the Devil's speed and strength. The Welsh fell back, leaving Elfgift alone at the grave-field's centre.

All round the grave-field were gathered the

survivors of Jul's Borough, guarded by Welsh or Danes. The Saxons, seeing their king still sword in hand and undefeated, straightened their backs and looked at their captors. The Danes, who were not Christians, saw, standing among the graves, a naked, long-haired youth who might have been one of Odin's chosen, a Valkyrie's companion. They began to look at the Welsh.

Ingvi, pacing round the wall, came upon Ingvald and jumped down to stand beside him. Ingvald stood with folded arms, glowering across the graves to where Elfgift stood. Ingvi guessed that Ingvald felt as shamed as he did to be skulking at the edges of a fight. Guessed, too, that Ingvald was as reluctant as he to fight for Unwin.

Ud took his harp from Ebba and walked across the graves to Unwin. "I have a song for the elf-born," he said.

Unwin looked at him in astonishment, but Ud was already striking the first notes from the harp. The music of the pipe and drum had been almost lost under the wide, dark sky, but each note plucked from the harp rang as clear, sharp and true as if it had been played within walls.

The notes pierced Elfgift as if with ice, and the trill of the strings ran through him in shudders. The fierceness of the battle had kept him from feeling the cold, but it was as if the music drenched him in ice-water. The cold of the winter's night bit hard on his flesh; the sword weighed heavy in his hand.

> *"The frost-cup brimming with winter rain;*
> *The mountain stream, running from the ice;*
> *Beneath your feet, the corpse cold-wrapped in*
>   *clay..."*

Elfgift shook his head hard and changed his grip on the sword's hilt, bunching the muscles in his arm. He wrenched himself round, ready to face any who might be coming at him from behind. His movement seemed to shatter a thin layer of ice that had wrapped him round. He was free again, like a thawed spring.

The harp sounded its cold chords.

> *"I bind you with Ice-rune!*
> *Cold gem, painful to hold.*
> *I bind you with Hail-rune!*
> *Coldest of grains, corn-destroyer –"*

The cold stole into Elfgift again. The marrow of his bones was freezing, making his limbs heavy as stones, bowing his head. Gathering together all his strength, he struck with his sword at the wizard with the harp. The wizard, though grey-bearded, jumped back, and laughed.

"I bind you, I, who have the power!
With Grave-rune I bind you!
Hear me well!
Chill rain shall fall —"

When great cold drives the blood from the fingers, they become stiff and blue-white, as if turning to unmoving marble. Struggling, Elfgift strove for each step as he tried to reach the wizard. No other threatened him now.

"Snow shall fall and cover your grave;
Dew shall seep through you, in your long lying!"

Elfgift's sword-point fell. His arm would not bend to lift it. He could not lift his head to see where the wizard stood.

"I bind you with Grave-rune!
The rigour of the cold corpse."

Elfgift could not unclench his teeth to speak. He tried to move, but fell like a felled tree.

Ud looked round, his missing eye a glaring darkness. "You need fear him no longer. Where swords and spears could not win, the sweet harp has triumphed."

The men came forward then, clustering round Elfgift. His eyes moved to look at them, but had lost their power to shock. They could see the muscles move beneath his skin as he tried to raise the sword against them, but he could not lift his arm. They unclenched his fingers from the sword's hilt, one by one. Yet they did not kick or punch him. They still feared him that much.

Onlookers were leaving the grave-field wall. Ebba ran to Ud's side, and Godwin went running to stand by Unwin. Both looked down at Elfgift, lying helpless in the mud churned up from snow and grave-mould. Godwin laughed up at his father, who smiled and put a hand on his head. Ebba hid her face against Ud's cloak, and he stroked her head while his eyes remained on Elfgift.

Unwin said, "Lift him up."

The men took Elfgift by the arms and lifted him to his feet. The light of a lantern fell on his face. Unwin studied it, calmly noting its insulting likeness to his brother, and glad that he would soon be rid of it. "I am going to send you to Woden. Thank me." Elfgift making no answer, Unwin backhanded him across the face with his fist, and nodded to the men, who dragged Elfgift away from the grave-field, back towards the Borough.

Ud took Ebba by the arm and drew her after him as he followed behind the soldiers. No one noticed them go.

CHAPTER 10

Woden's Promise

A Saxon woman lay dead on the cold ground, wrapped in a cloak. Unwin tugged it away from her, rolling the body with his foot. He carried the cloak to where Wulfweard stood by the grave-field wall, still naked, with Welsh guards about him. Unwin held out the cloak.

Wulfweard studied Unwin's face: the lines on his brow, the harshness of the cheekbones, the way the beard outlined the lips. He saw the likeness to his father's face and all the time he thought: How can this be my brother? He loved his brother. He did not love this man.

"Put it on," Unwin said.

Wulfweard turned his face away.

Unwin threw the cloak to the nearest guard. "Put it on him."

The guard shook out the cloak and held it out. Wulfweard ducked away, but another guard held him. He stood still and allowed the cloak to be draped around him. It would be, eventually, whatever he did. Straightaway he felt warmer, and looked at the ground, angry that he could take such comfort – and that it had come from Unwin.

"Are you hurt?" Unwin asked.

Wulfweard's fist lashed at him. Unwin dodged, and the guards grabbed Wulfweard by both arms, hauling him back. The cloak slipped to the ground.

"Bewitched," Unwin said.

Godwin peered around his father at Wulfweard. There was no bewitchment, he thought. Wulfweard was a traitor and a coward, betraying his own kin and breaking his vows to Lord Christ because he'd thought the elf's drop could offer him better protection. He deserved to die like the elf-born. Godwin wondered if he would win praise for saying so. He didn't quite dare to try.

A party of men approached from the darkness beyond the torch-light: men of Unwin's old warband. They carried a body among them, which they flung down at Unwin's feet.

It was Athelric. Godwin went to stand by the head and look down curiously at the bloodied tunic and staring eyes. Kendrida reached out as if to call him to her, but her guards pushed her back.

Godwin glared at her. She would have to learn that he wasn't a baby, to live with women, any longer. He looked down at the corpse again. It wasn't so bad. He could look at it. Strange to see Athelric's face, always so ready to shout – dead. But Athelric was a traitor.

Looking up, Godwin saw Wulfweard, his lips drawn back in a way that had nothing to do with smiling. Godwin felt triumphant. Wulfweard couldn't stand the sight of the body half so well as he could. Coward!

Unwin took an axe from a nearby Dane, then crouched over the body as if to close its eyes. He took the right arm, which had not yet stiffened, and pulled it straight. Raising the axe, he chopped it down on the wrist.

Godwin flinched and took a step back. Kendrida covered her face with a cry. Wulfweard watched disbelievingly as the axe came down for a second time before he shouted, "Stop that!" and lunged forward. His guards grappled with him.

Unwin, looking up, said, "Take him back to the hall. Take them all back."

Wulfweard wanted to get the axe away from Unwin and hit him with it. That foreigners, Welshmen, should hold him back from his quarrel with his brother enraged him, but though he fought off one and almost freed himself from two, he couldn't fight them all. He was taken away.

Kendrida went with her guards eagerly. She had hidden her eyes, but had still heard the butchery of the axe hacking into bone. She felt ashamed as she hurried back along the path to the Borough, keeping her head down and flinching at the shouts of the guards – but her children were in the Borough, and where was the good of being heroically dead? She glanced at her fellow prisoners and was as fearful for them as for herself. Could any words of hers save them from harm, or would they simply bring Unwin's anger down on her? Or, worse, on her children?

It came into her head how much they had all been looking forward to the time of Jul Peace, and how much faith they had had in Elfgift. And how completely Unwin had destroyed both.

A feeling of helplessness, like falling. Though Elfgift's muscles twitched and jumped, they would not obey him, and he was carried along like a straw man. He knew the grip of magic in the music that had brought him down: he knew the Lady's note. The day of his death and the manner of his dying She had fated long ago. She had given him to Unwin, and he knew the death Unwin had vowed for him.

He exerted all his will and strength to break

free, but the greater his effort, the more tightly the magic web wrapped about him, and the colder and heavier his body became. His will was like a corpse in a grave: buried in cold clay.

The harper, Ud, pushed open the doors of the Royal Hall. Inside the long tables were still spread with food and plates, the fires still burned, crackling; the candles were still alight, but the people had gone.

The firelight was redder, the shadows darker as they leaned in from corners and dropped down from the rafters, where sleepy birds twittered. The great wooden pillars, the roof-trees, emerged from the shadows as the light washed round their boles, and withdrew into shadow again as the light died.

The high table's dais was framed by two roof-trees. With a nod, Ud signed to the men to bring Elfgift to the roof-tree on the left hand, and it was Ud who tied Elfgift's hands to the tree, above his head. The rope held him upright – his legs would not. He could not even hold up his head which, for all his efforts to lift it, sagged forward, too heavy.

Someone was near him, brushing him with cloth, smelling of earth and rain. A hard grip fastened on his jaw, and his head was lifted without his willing it. A man's voice asked, "Do you know me?" The breath that stirred in his face smelled of earth.

Elfgift opened his eyes with effort, as if against

an extreme of weariness. He saw a blur of candle-light and darkness and, closer, the light and move-ment of a living eye and the deep, unlit darkness of a place where an eye had been. He tried to say One-Eye's name, but his mouth would not shape the word.

"Ready for the road?" One-Eye asked. "It's hard travel, but you chose it when you took Wulfweard from me. And at the road's end I shall be waiting."

Elfgift tried to draw a deeper breath, but the power of the Grave-rune wrapped him round. Ebba, standing by, saw his eyes widen, as if with fear, catching the light like green glass.

My prayers are answered! Ebba thought, and was afraid. She wasn't even sure who she had prayed to – Christ, or Woden or Ing. Still less, who had answered.

"Grave is hateful to all men," One-Eye said. "Lifelong you struggle against that crone, Age, and even the strongest She overcomes. But Grave's blessing is this: have courage, and your fame will burn like a torch to light the way of those who come after."

Elfgift wished to shake his head, to say no, but could not move or speak. "I give you this rune," One-Eye said and, with the forefinger of his free hand, drew on Elfgift's forehead.

Ebba followed the movement and she knew the rune: a diamond shape, with tails above and below. The rune Ing. She spoke the rune's meaning, as Ud had taught her.

"*Every winter Ing leaves us and crosses the whale's road. But bone-fires and laughter and holly in the fire rouse Him from His cold sleep, and He comes back to us with sheaves of corn in His arms. He it is, Ing, who loosens frost's letters and drives away winter: He it is who brings grass to the fields and crowns the trees with green.*"

One-Eye lowered Elfgift's head again, and Elfgift could not lift it, could not break the ropes that held him or move against Grave's grip.

My prayers are answered! Ebba thought again, and gripped her hands together and stared into a blank and terrified amazement.

From the streets outside came sharp, shrill cries and yells. Ud drew Ebba with him into a shadowed corner.

The hall doors were thrown open and guards herded people through, shoving them against tables and stools. Kendrida was pulled aside, stumbling, and made to stand close to the dais. She saw Elfgift tied to the roof-tree and quickly turning her eyes aside, saw, on the wall behind the high table, the black sword Woden's Promise. Her throat drew painfully tight. Woden's promises were always broken.

Wulfweard was brought on to the dais and dumped on the boards by four Welshmen. He scrambled to his feet, but stood quietly enough. Kendrida could see him gasping for breath as he looked about the hall, at the people crowded below him, up at the rafters, at the walls, as if he had never seen the place before. For Kendrida too, the familiar hall – a place of order and decorum – was turned strange and frightening, the air so full of fear that it crackled about their ears and stung their skins. Unwin's North Welsh stood at the doors and about the walls, laughing.

The people massed in the hall jostled and staggered, struggling for a place to set their feet, fighting to keep themselves from being pushed into the fires, but when they saw Elfgift a long cry rose from them. There was a press forwards, towards the dais. The guards leaned on the crowd with their shields, pushing them back.

The noise and movement stilled when Unwin came on to the dais. He held up, in a bloodied hand, a bloodied object which Kendrida recognized even in the eye's blink before she turned her face away: Athelric's head.

Unwin held up the head until the silence was absolute. The flames could be heard eating at the wood. The letting go of a held breath, or the stirring of a foot in the straw, were loud.

Then Unwin said, "A king should keep his promises and his vows. I made a vow to kill the traitor who kept my crown from me and killed my brother—"

"Liar!" Wulfweard was held back from Unwin by his guards.

"Killed my brother Hunting—"

"Liar! Hunting was not—"

Unwin turned on the guards. "Keep him quiet."

A guard stopped Wulfweard's mouth with a handful of cloak, while others held his arms. The crowd watched and understood that not even the Royal Kin were safe.

"I vowed I would take the traitor's right hand and head," Unwin said. "I keep my promises." He dropped the head on the dais. Everyone heard the thump as it hit the wooden boards.

"I made one other promise." Unwin walked to the edge of the dais and stood beside the roof-tree where Elfgift was tied. Wrapping his hand in Elfgift's hair, he pulled his head up and back. "This is the king Athelric gave you. 'Goddess-chosen'!" He looked round as if he expected laughter, but those who understood him, the Saxons and Danes, were silent. "You see whose God has given him victory, whose God is the One True God. But my friends, the Danes, have not yet come to the One True God, and I promised them a sacrifice for their God. Ingvald, here's your sacrifice – a king, Goddess-chosen! Odin should be pleased."

The silence was broken by gasps, and a swaying of the crowd as all strove to see Ingvald.

Ingvald was close by the dais, his dark brother beside him. Both stood with folded arms and sealed lips.

"Ingvi!" Unwin said. "I know you've cut the blood-eagle. Here – win more favour with Odin!"

Ingvi's arms unfolded, his mouth opened – but Ingvald caught him by the arm before he could speak and shook his head. Angrily denouncing Unwin would do no good for the elf-born, and would only make things hard for them, as Unwin's allies. But Ingvi could not be entirely silenced. He called out, "Be your own butcher!"

"I am a Christian." Unwin spoke over the heads of the crowd, to the guards about the walls. "Isn't there a man here who wants to win Woden's favour?" He saw their faces turn from him.

Behind Unwin, the guard had uncovered Wulfweard's mouth. Half-stifled, he had stopped fighting. He watched the crowd and listened, his chest heaving for breath.

"Isn't there a man here who wants *my* favour?" Unwin asked. "I'll give land and gold to the man who saves my oath."

Now men looked at each other and whispered. Two Danes came forward, raising the axes they carried. They saw Ingvald scowl, but what did they care? They were landless men, come to get land, and if they could get a king's favour with it, then almost anything was worth it.

"Can you cut the blood-eagle?" Unwin asked.

"All it takes is a strong arm," said one, and hefted his axe. "And a strong belly."

Unwin stepped back. "Then go to it."

"Unwin, no!" Wulfweard's guards held him only by one arm. He strained towards his brother, reaching with his free hand. "Please, Unwin! No!"

The Danes hesitated, but Unwin nodded to them, and they hefted their axes again. The guards dragged Wulfweard back, but his shouts went on, ringing through the shocked silence of the hall.

All the din of the hall and Unwin's words had been little more to Elfgift than a buzzing in the ears, but Wulfweard's frantic shouting of his name broke through Grave's grip. He woke to the pain of his weight on the rope about his arms and, with all the strength and will he had left, he heaved up his head and faced the Danes as they came, though he saw little but blurred shadows against blurred light. This was the day of his death, and this the manner. There was no avoiding it.

Seeing him lift his head, the crowd sighed and shifted. A low, grumbling murmur rose from them, broken with shouts. The guards jabbed them with spear-butts, shoving them back.

The first axe-blows, Elfgift felt: shocks against his ribs that burned and burned, the heat growing fiercer, spreading throughout his body. He let go one cry that flew up to the high roof and echoed among the rafters, setting the roosting birds flapping and crying. Looking up into the rafters, Elfgift saw the fire that burned him, a lake of flame. He felt the heat, and fell, upwards, into it.

At his shout, the crowd had hushed again. The sound of the Danes' work, their breathless gasping, was loud. Some among the Welsh tried to raise cheers, but they were thin and scared against the deep silence underlying them, and soon were silenced too. Through the hall crept the smell of the butcher's block.

Kendrida lowered her head so she could see nothing, and she forced her fingers hard into her ears, and shuddered and wept and shook her head again and again.

Wulfweard tried to watch. It seemed to him a keeping of faith with Elfgift, to watch. But soon his head hung. His arms were still held: he couldn't block the smacks of the axes and the breaking of bone from his ears.

Ebba hid her face against Ud, covering her ears. She had prayed for this death but, in her mind, it had never been like this. She had not imagined such noises, nor thought it would take so long.

Unwin watched every blow, nodding as they fell. At his side Godwin, shivering, tried to watch. His hand went to his father's sleeve, but withdrew, because he would not be seen to cling. He kept his face turned towards the butchery, even when he could stand no more and was looking aside. He knew the killing was right: there could only be one king. His tears were of shame at his own cowardice. When he was a man, he would have to watch such things, as his father did. He should harden himself – but he could not turn his eyes to the sight again.

Ingvi watched to the end, while Ingvald stood with folded arms and his gaze on the floor. The hair moved on Ingvi's head. His breath would not come. This hacking of living bone from bone, this bleeding, was a thing that started the heart straining and shudders running through the flesh. He remembered scarlet poppies, broken-stemmed but living through a hot, hot day. Corn is killed to make bread, animals slaughtered for the feast. Without death, there is no living. In the trees round the god-houses of Ingvi's people swung the carcases of horses, oxen, boar and men, and Ingvi had seen men killed before. It was something else in the hall that made him afraid.

When it was finished, Unwin said, "Cart the guts out to the ditch."

The two Danes cut the body down and lugged it away. The cold draught through the opened doors made the torch-light waver over the roof-trees and the many silent people.

Ud pulled Ebba to her feet. "We have a song to

make." As he led her from the hall, no one saw them go.

On the dais Unwin looked at the blood staining the floor and roof-tree. He turned his back on the crowd and, from the wall at the back of the dais, took down the sword, Woden's Promise.

With a hiss of iron scraping iron, he drew the sword from its sheath and swung it through the air. "The Woden-forged sword that must never be sheathed unblooded." He drove it hard back into its sheath. "*That's* how much I care for the old Gods. They are dead. Now you have one God above and one king below. I am the king."

CHAPTER 11

That Passed; This May Too

"I would burn it down," Unwin said, "but the fire would spread."

Men were aloft on the roof of the God-house, unfastening the shingles. Godwin cricked his neck to watch them, and turned to grin at his father. Already holes had been opened in the roof and the thin snow fell through them, into the God-house, to settle on the God-figures themselves.

Some of the men on the roof were in tears, and stopped at intervals to wipe them away. All worked slowly. The God-house was old. Legend said the first Saxons to tread in the land, those Woden's-sons, had built it. Many had entered it every day, stepping into its dark, forest-scented

221

shadows, looking up at the God-figures lit by their altar fires. It had never entered their minds that the God-house would – could – ever be destroyed. They had not known how deeply they loved it until they were ordered to break it apart.

Unwin had ordered its wooden joints to be disjointed, its darkness opened to the light, its stored centuries of sacred air dispersed. The great roof-trees, the shingles, the planking, were all to be carted outside the Borough and burned to ashes. It was no longer enough that the paintings of the Gods be painted over, the God-figures destroyed and Christian paintings and figures put in their place. None of the wood, centuries old and well weathered, would be used again. Every trace of the God-house was to be wiped out, and the children taught that it had housed demons. Their children would be taught that it had never existed.

Many Welsh stood watching. It was not often you saw a building of such size and wealth pulled to pieces. Danes stood among them with glum faces. They worshipped in such God-houses as this: the gods being dishonoured were, though named a little differently, their Gods.

Kendrida was standing near Unwin, where he had dragged her. She was sobbing, her face hidden in her cupped hands. Godwin thought: stupid woman! She raised her head as a stack of shingles came clattering to the ground, and he saw the flesh darkened round her eye, and her split and swollen lips. Stupid, clumsy woman! She'd fallen into the bed-post, she'd said, when he'd asked her what had happened.

Kendrida had loved the God-house. Bringing her children to its altars had made her feel sure that they would live to bring their children to them, and that some memory of her would linger in the God-house smoke to see them come. But now the God-house was broken, her children were taken from her, and Elfgift was offal, thrown into the Borough's ditch. How ready she had been to believe in him, and how easy to fool. She sobbed the harder, for shame, dismayed to find herself so full of tears, but unable to stop.

Godwin, seeing his mother still crying, sighed, and would have gone to her, stupid as she was, but before he could move, his father, big fist clenched, gave her a blow to the head that sent her staggering. "Stop snivelling!"

She took swift, stumbling steps in an effort to save herself, before collapsing to her knees, her hands on the ground. Godwin ran and helped her up. The realization that his mother had not fallen against the bed-post was like a blow to his own head.

"Get away from her!" Unwin said, and beckoned. Godwin went to him, and Unwin put a hand on his shoulder. Godwin turned his face away from his mother. She *was* a stupid woman. And worse than a heathen: an apostate.

Kendrida stood, though trembling. Her head throbbed. People edged further away from her. No one would interfere. She was Unwin's wife. The night before he had told her, and shown her, that she was still his wife. He didn't care, he said, what heathen words she had mouthed. Under Christ, there was no unwedding.

"Now I am king," he had said, "I shall found a monastery in memory of my mother – and that's where you'll spend the rest of your life. You'll die as my wife and you'll be buried in my church."

Her head had been buzzing and aching from his blows, and blood had been running down her face. She had not dared to speak, fearing he might kill her if he started hitting her again. But there had been hours since to wonder how long would pass between her entering the monastery and her burial. A year, perhaps. Time to allow her family to hear that she had become a devout Christian priestess – then she would die suddenly and be buried with all the royal honours her brother could expect. Unwin would marry again: some Christian princess from across the water.

How, she thought, can I get word to my brother? Who can I trust to carry a message? Who can I ask to put themselves in such danger? She looked round at the men so pointedly keeping their distance from her – and then at her own eldest son, standing beside his father with his back to her. A rush of anger rose in her, flushing her face and throbbing harder in her head. Why had Elfgift not been Goddess-chosen, but only a boy?

A crash, and a shaking of the earth beneath her feet, made her start. The great door of the God-house – oak, carved with intertwining dragons, wolves and other fierce creatures – had been wrenched from its hinges and thrown down. Men were standing on the door, their boots muddying the carvings that had been on the inner side. With axes they hacked at it, chopping it into pieces small enough to be tossed into a cart. Kendrida did not dare to leave the place until Unwin gave her permission, but she lowered her head again, until she could see nothing.

"What are you?" Ingvald said. "Maids-at-milking? What did you expect when you came to war?" He was seated on a bench in the hall of his lodgings, at the council meeting he held every day to settle disputes among his men, to dole out rewards, praise and blame. But here was a deputation come to urge him, of all things, to break his faith with Unwin. And the deputation was led by Ingvi.

"You!" Ingvald said, pointing to his brother. "You've spread a feast before the raven, you've fed the wolf – wasn't that what you wanted? What are you griping about?"

The other men hung back. Ingvi stooped over his brother and demanded, "You like what's been done here, then? By that – Christian?" The men, their arms folded, nodded and rumbled agreement through their beards. None of them, Ingvald noted, were too plain in their speech. They left that to Ingvi.

"*You* are the friend of Christians, brother," Ingvald said. "Weren't you angry with me once because I didn't run to stand beside your dear Unwin in the battle-line? Wasn't he a great, proud atheling, seeking vengeance for his brother? And me a close-fisted peasant because I wouldn't fight for him?"

Ingvi dropped down on the end of the bench. "I was wrong."

Ingvald clapped him on the back. "It was worth coming to war to hear that!" Some of the men laughed.

"Unwin broke the Jul peace!" someone said, and roused a chorus of "Ayes".

"And not by honest battle," another said. "By attacking unarmed men from behind!"

Ingvald pointed at the man who had spoken. "You had your axe there! You attacked!"

The man flung out his arms and shouted, "I was sworn to Unwin! What could I do – break my oath?"

"Yet you expect me to break mine," Ingvald said.

"Well," the man said, looking at the ground. "You're a Jarl. It's different when you do it."

There was some laughter, but a third man broke into it, saying, almost accusingly, "You saw those two in the grave-field!"

The laughter stopped. Heads lifted. They looked at each other, and from everywhere came, "Aye – aye." This, Ingvald saw, was what had really brought them to him – the memory of the two in the grave-field, in the darkness and torch-light, looking like the ghost-warriors on the God-house walls.

"The way he fought –"

"– guarding each other's back –"

"– like Odin's Chosen –"

"– the Brothers –"

"– beat them back, not just once –"

The men were shifting, looking away as fast as they caught each other's eyes. There was some unease in them, roused by the memory of the sword-dancers, but whether it was born of guilt or superstition, Ingvald couldn't tell.

"Did you hear that shout he gave?" They had all heard it. The speaker leaned forward and the men all drew closer. "Like Ing before the spears."

"Aye," they said, glancing from one to the other. "Aye – aye."

"Lovern's men couldn't take him. It was some Christian spell brought him down."

Ingvald refused to whisper. "Or Odin broke faith with him – as He will with us all."

That wasn't what they wanted to think, and they were silent until someone said, "Christians!"

"To do that to him!" Ingvi burst out. "To butcher him like a pig! Shameful!"

"Didn't you cut the blood-eagle, brother, on the thane of – where was it?" Ingvald asked.

Ingvi's dark face darkened further with a flush. "That was for the success of the war – and in thanks for the battle!"

"But now you grudge Odin His best sacrifice, the captured king?"

Seeing Ingvi lost for an answer, one of the men said, "It's on Unwin the eagle should have been cut!"

"So," Ingvald said, "you'd not only break your oath to your leader, but kill him as well?" Then he shouted, "What, were you all in love with this Elfgift? You're all in such a flutter over him. He was only a farmer and a bastard too – not much more than a thrall. You don't fret so much over thralls as a rule, little brother. How many thralls and farmers have you all killed since this war began?"

"Are you turning Christian?" one of the men said, but turned away when Ingvald gave him a sidelong look.

Ingvi jumped up from the bench to stand over Ingvald. "He was the old king's son, and Goddess-chosen, and elf-born!"

Even the shamed man raised his head, and they were all nodding and agreeing again. They all knew the song about the beautiful elf-woman who'd been Elfgift's mother, and the story of how the Stone had screamed for him. Unwin might call him a devil, but the Danes knew that elves were spirits, of fields, woods, rivers and mountains, only a little less powerful and magical than the Gods Themselves.

Ingvald sighed. "So the story goes. But one thing I've learned: a story never grows less in the telling and poets are all as big fools for a pretty face and a fine head of hair as you lot."

"So you're Unwin's man!" Ingvi shouted.

Ingvald stood, took Ingvi by the scruff and swayed him on his feet. "I never liked Unwin Eadmundsson. I never wanted to join him. That was your doing – and Lovern's. But I gave my word freely and I won't break it now. You! Ayc, you! What do you want?"

A man had been hovering at the back of the group for some minutes, plainly full of news but afraid to interrupt. Now, as everyone turned to him, he said, "The elf-born's body! It's gone from the ditch!"

Ingvi's head snapped round to stare at his brother, and the other men stared too, as if this was some great happening.

"Look at your faces!" Ingvald said, and laughed. "What have I done, to be surrounded by hare-brains! The body's been stolen for burial. May the Gods favour those who did it – and may the Gods help them if Unwin finds them out!"

A guard opened the door for Unwin to enter the small room. The shutters were closed over the high window, letting in a few pale shafts of grey light. Only one candle burned in the stand, throwing a fragile, gauzy light over the wooden floor and walls. The shadows in the corners were deep.

A clot of blackness moved at the room's centre – a black-robed priest, rising to his feet. Unwin stopped, his arms folded, and looked down at the sleeping bench where Wulfweard lay, one arm crooked under his head, his eyes closed. He wore only a thin woollen tunic, and must have been chilled.

"Atheling, I have prayed with all my power," the priest said, "but the Devil is with him still. He hasn't spoken or eaten."

Unwin turned to look at the room's other bench, where a pile of folded clothes lay beside a plate of bread and a jug of ale.

"I fear, Atheling, that prayer will not be enough."

Unwin was looking at Wulfweard. "Lay a hand on my brother and I will see that hand *off*!"

The priest lowered his head. Having been in Unwin's company since leaving King Lovern, he didn't doubt that the words were meant.

"Leave us," Unwin said.

When the door closed, Unwin seated himself beside the pile of clothes and studied the long, still shape of his young brother. Particularly the face, closed against him. It no longer had to remind him of Elfgift, but did.

Wulfweard knew Unwin was there: he had heard everything. He had no wish to see or speak to Unwin, and so kept his eyes closed, even though, behind his eyes, he saw, again, Athelric's body dumped on the ground, wallowing like a pig's carcass. If he wrenched his imagination from that scene, he saw the axes chopping at Elfgift. He all but felt the weight and edge on his own ribs. The longer his eyes were closed, the brighter and more lifelike the pictures became, until his hearing began to tremble to the cries of pain. Before Unwin had come, he would open his eyes to stare, unseeing, at the goldenness of the candlelight, and the sounds, the pictures, would fade a little. He heard the priest droning without hearing his words. Faintly, before his open eyes, the butchery had still gone on.

Unwin had done that. It was worse than if he had done it himself. At least, then, he would have understood how it could be done.

He felt no anger that Elfgift had failed, only grief that he was gone. The most faithful of men, said the poet, will betray his friend when his flesh turns cold and his corpse chooses, instead, the chill clay as its companion. But the betrayal had been the Lady's, not Elfgift's. Wulfweard prayed that She would help him find the courage to die as well as Athelric and Elfgift had done.

He knew his own death was close. Unwin would kill him: that was clear. They were both athelings, sons of the same father. Either could be chosen king. Alive, he would always be a rival and a threat to Unwin, and Unwin would only tolerate him as long as he was the petted, favourite younger brother, running after Unwin as fawningly as Godwin did.

He put his arm across his eyes, as if he could block from sight memory of a time when he had admired Unwin. That time was done. That he and Unwin were brothers was unalterable, but they could never trust each other again. So Unwin would kill him – or order it done.

The most he could hope for was to be given a sword and allowed to die fighting. Perhaps then, when he was again on that bleak, dark moorland, he would be able to reach the hall where his brother Hunting waited in the doorway. Athelric would be there too. And Elfgift?

Unwin, seeing Wulfweard put his arm across his eyes, sat straighter – but after that one movement, Wulfweard was still again.

Unwin felt all the agony of indecision a hunter feels, stalking a deer through woodland, wary of every twig that may be broken and every branch set rustling. Would too slow and cautious an approach lose the moment and let the prey escape? Would too sudden a movement panic it into running away?

Without speaking, he took up the plate of bread and quietly crossed the room until he stood above Wulfweard. He set the plate down on the broad bench by the boy's head. A slight flicker of the closed lids was the only response.

Unwin considered. He could snap out an order to sit up and listen, or speak the boy's name, or ask if he was hungry. Whatever he said would be ignored: the closed face promised it. So he bent, swept the boy's legs from the bench, seized his arm and jerked him upright. Startled into opening his eyes, Wulfweard looked into Unwin's face.

Wulfweard would have pulled away, but Unwin gripped him by the shoulders and pressed him down on the bench. When he sat quiet, Unwin picked up the plate of bread and, sitting beside him, held it out.

Wulfweard was hungry, and there was no sense in that. He took a piece of bread and ate.

Unwin, watching him, kept his face still but Wulfweard, knowing him so well, could see his triumph.

Wulfweard reached for another slice of bread with his left hand. With his right he reached between their bodies for the dagger on Unwin's belt. They were so close together that once he had his fingers round the hilt, he had to lift his elbow in a straight line to bring the dagger from its sheath. His arm brushed Unwin's, and he saw Unwin's face sharpen.

Wulfweard jumped up and away, snatching the dagger with him. He moved in again, quick, the dagger held to stab. Unwin shoved the plate in his face.

Wulfweard shied away, knocking the plate aside, sending stale bread scattering about the room. Unwin was standing, his hands raised, palms outward. At Unwin's belt hung a sword, dull and plain – Woden's Promise. He had no right to it. Wulfweard shifted his weight from foot to foot, ready to jump from either one, looking for the place and the chance to stick the dagger.

"Wulf, give me my dagger."

Unwin saw a shudder go through the boy. He stared Unwin in the face with open mouth and widened eyes. Unwin's voice, at its gentlest, had brought back many memories of kindness. His arm, that had been ready to use the dagger, lost its strength.

"Wulf, what's the matter?" A question that had been asked many times before.

"You owe me a life! You killed my brother!" Always, as he moved to use the dagger, he shrank back from hurting Unwin. The pull from one impulse to the other set him trembling and his breath came brokenly.

The flesh of Wulfweard's face was drawn tight over the bones and so white that the outline of his lips vanished, while his eyes darkened and fixed. Unwin raised his open hands higher, recognizing the white-faced rage that hardly feels pain. Woden's rage, he would have said, if he had been a heathen. He knew he would have to go carefully.

"Wulf, you're angry with me now. But that will pass."

The boy came at him.

Unwin's body was so long trained, it thought for him, but he moved only barely fast enough to save his life. The dagger's point ripped his tunic and tore flesh, glancing off a rib and drawing plentiful blood. Then Wulfweard's rush had carried him past, and Unwin moved close behind him, locking one arm round his neck. In his free hand he caught Wulfweard's dagger-wrist.

Wulfweard set his feet against the edge of the wall-bench and threw his weight backwards, overbalancing Unwin, who fell, pulling Wulfweard down with him. But Unwin kept his hold – in unthinking reaction, he even tightened it. He rolled on top and used his greater weight to pin the boy down. Taking his arm from around Wulfweard's neck, he used both hands to force back the boy's thumb and wrench the dagger free. He threw it into the far corner.

Unwin drew breath, thinking the fight over, but Wulfweard twisted from under him and was after the dagger. There followed a desperate, bruising struggle on the hard floor, banging knee, hip and wrist bones, raising dust and straw, taking blows from fists, elbows, knees and grunting over them. Unwin gasped for breath, tasting blood in his mouth from a bitten tongue, feeling pain in his lungs. His arms weakened and, astonished, he realized that he might not win this fight. It was then that he drove his knee hard into Wulfweard's belly. Wulfweard's breath whooped past his ear, and the boy went limp, his head thrown back. He gasped for breath that wouldn't come.

Unwin collapsed beside him, breathing hard. Released from his weight, Wulfweard drew up his knees, arms hugging his belly. His breath came in snatched whoops. Unwin put his hand on the boy's head. He knew what it felt like to take such a blow: how the breath strained for seemed to stick in the throat, never reaching the aching lungs. His own arms and legs were trembling from effort, his heart beating over-fast. He shook his head and, breathlessly, almost laughed. He would never have believed that his slip of a brother, weighing no more than a wet shirt, could have so nearly overcome him. All in an effort to murder him. A Woden-born temper – or an elf-born one.

Unwin got to his knees and, taking Wulfweard under the arms, heaved him up. Holding him, Unwin pushed himself backwards along the floor until he was leaning against the wall-bench. Wulfweard tugged at Unwin's hands, locked about his waist, even though his head was tipped back against Unwin's shoulder. His breath still came hard.

Unwin said, "I wasn't going to let you stab me, but –"

Wulfweard stopped trying to loosen Unwin's hold. He folded his own arms over Unwin's and drew up his knees. He leaned back against Unwin, but turned his face away.

"Come back to me, Wulf." Unwin drew Wulfweard's long hair back from his damp face, though Wulfweard tried to move his head away. "Take your oath to me." There was no answer, but then, the boy could hardly draw breath. "It was a devil, Wulf. You couldn't see that – you were bewitched. I had to kill it. Listen, I'm going to make a church here: I shall have it consecrated for Christ's Mass. Take the Host there, and then make your oath to me." He paused, hoping for an answer – unless the weight of his brother, leaning warm against him was an answer. Wulfweard's breath was coming a little easier. "Wulf. I don't want to kill you."

Wulfweard's head rolled on his shoulder, turning towards him. "Do it yourself."

Unwin tried to keep himself from laughing, because Wulfweard had spoken to him. "Do what, Wulf?"

"Don't pay Danes to do it."

Unwin pushed him away and got to his feet. His legs shook under him as he crossed the room, and went out into the hall beyond. The priest was waiting, and looked shocked when he saw the blood on Unwin's tunic, his bruised face.

"What would you do," Unwin asked, "to end this bewitchment?"

The priest folded his hands in his black sleeves. "There is only one way, Atheling. The possessed body must be made no easy lodging for the spirit that has taken it. Withhold food – that, at least, as a beginning."

"Do it," Unwin said, and walked away.

*　　*　　*

Wulfweard, left alone, curled on his side, drawing up his knees and hugging his belly. An old song was going through his head.

> Wayland, fettered, knew misery:
> Stubborn Jarl, he suffered wrongs,
> His hearth-companions Sorrow and Longing
> In his cold, winter's exile —
> But that passed; this may too.
> That passed. This may too.

CHAPTER 12

Rune Song

Elfgift fell up into fiery light, dived deep, and broke his head through the shining surface of a burning lake which lapped around him, brilliant, washing over his skin without burning. Above and around the lake was nothing. The brightness of the fire made the darkness impenetrable.

He waded to dry ground, which was hard and cold under his feet. As he stood, shivering, the fire died, leaving a lake of quiet, dark water. All around him was black: insubstantial shapes of greater darkness against dark.

For an unknowable time, he waited for light. No sounds reached him, no movement. No bird sang.

He stood and called into the darkness, but he disturbed nothing, made no echo, heard no answer.

No day was coming. He walked into the dark.

The stars were spread across a black and freezing sky. Beneath their feet the frost sparkled in traceries on the hard, black ground. Ebba tried to hold her cloak about her as she followed Ud, but her cloak kept flapping open, letting in fierce spears of cold air.

Behind them lay the light, the noise and warmth of the hall and she longed for it.

The Borough gates were locked, but at a word from Ud and a touch of his hand they released their locks with a snap, and sprang open as if afraid. They passed through, and crossed the wooden bridge over the deep ditch that surrounded the Borough, their feet making soft booming sounds.

Ebba didn't like the dark. There was so much of it, stretching beyond the Borough into the fields and orchards, and beyond that, into wilder country. Danger went silent and unseen through the dark. Savage-toothed and clawed bears, that could outrun a horse. Wolves, packs of them, yellow-eyed. Witches, Valkyries, ghosts, all sorts of night-walkers. With Ud she was safe, but she dreaded that he would desert her and all those waiting creatures would gather round her.

Ud led her to the edge of the Borough ditch. It was hard to see where she put her feet, and she felt the ditch pulling at her, wanting to draw her down on to the sharp stakes set at its bottom. Ud walked as surely as if it was broad day.

Then he took her hand, stepped into the ditch and slithered down its steep side. She squealed as she was pulled after him, fearing the sharp stakes and the ghosts which would gather to her cry. But Ud pulled her to him, and held her, and though they struck hard against stakes, they were hurt by none.

Much rubbish had been thrown into the ditch: peelings, broken pots, rags and bones, all now silvered with frost. Despite the cold, there was an over-rich stink of rot. Close by them she glimpsed something long and pale, and smelled the butcher's stall stench of fresh, bloody meat. She didn't want to see, and turned her face away.

"Here I'll light our fire," Ud said. "Here we'll work."

A fire was good: if they were to sit for hours making a song, a fire was very good, but why light it in the stinking rubbish of the Borough ditch? But Ud did as he chose and she made no protest. She merely hugged herself and shivered.

She heard no striking of flints but, in an eye's blink, there was yellow flame and then a high, burning fire made of thick branches that had never been found in the ditch. The sap crackled and spat glowing shreds of bark into the air: the wood split in the fire, the splits glowing gold and red. The pungent smoke stung the eyes and caught in the throat.

In the fire's living light and warmth, Ud and Ebba squatted on a thickness of fallen leaves, on level ground. A sighing and creaking overhead made Ebba look up: high above was a far-spreading roof of firelit branches and ruffling leaves – the canopy of a tree bigger than any she had seen or imagined. By its leaves she knew it for an ash: the tree from whose strong, light wood shields and spear-shafts were made, the tree from which men had been made. Its roots, bigger than wagons, rose from the ages of fallen leaves. Its trunk was so far from the fire that it lay in deep shadow, and was so far round that what she saw of it seemed flat, like a grey-green wall. The stink of rubbish was gone. Now she smelled damp earth, old leaves, water and moss.

From the tree came a din, a constant noise of soughing and rustling, of creaking and groaning. She felt the earth beneath her swell and sway as the giant roots pulled at it. She knew the tree at once: no one could see it and hear it and smell it without knowing it – Odin's Horse, the Tree He hung on, the Tree of the World. So intent was she in gazing at the shifting pattern of flame-light and darkness among the leaves, and listening to the Tree's song, that she hardly saw the long and bloodied shape that lay beside the fire.

Only with the corner of her mind's eye did she see the firelight playing on the sharp stakes and steep banks of the ditch.

Pointing, Ud said, "Fetch my drum."

Leaning against one of the Tree's giant roots was a drum. Ebba walked, knee-deep, through a rustling heap of leaves, releasing scents of loam and mushroom. Near the drum, she saw a glint of dark water. Under the root was a deep, black pool and beside it was a man's head. Nothing but the head, yet it had all the colour of life. The eyes moved, watching her sharply as she stooped for the drum.

She snatched it up and ran, crunching, back through the leaves to the fire. She hid from the head behind Ud.

He took the drum and propped it against his knee. It was flat, a skin stretched over an oval frame. A bone hammer was fastened to it on a leather string, and with it, Ud beat a rhythm to the Tree's song.

"*To Thorny moor you'll come at last...*" High mountains, black against a black sky, leaned and overhung the narrow, thorny valley where he trudged. In the dark, unseen thorns brushed him, and, with a cold sting, drew blood. The only sound was of his own passing. Not an owl called, not a fox screamed.

Then the drum called. A long while he stood and listened, then he followed the sound through the dark, over rock and through thorn.

The fire's heat drew out the stench of the rubbish. Ebba crouched by Ud while he clapped his hands and sang.

"Nine long nights I rode my horse in the wind; pierced through with my spear I rode. None brought me food; none gave me drink. Grasping the runes, I fell back screaming —"

He screamed, and Ebba hugged her knees and bent her head low, hoping the ghosts crowding the darkness outside the firelight would not see her.

"I know one rune: it soothes pain, cures sickness, makes whole. Even the teeth of grief and longing it can blunt! Its name is —" Ud stooped low over the corpse, put his head close to its ear and whispered. Then he raised his head and let a long laugh go into the darkness.

Ebba was startled by the laugh, and jumped, looking round, searching the darkness above them at the lip of the ditch. At such a place and time, laughter sounded like madness.

"A second rune I know: any man who would heal

must know it – only I can teach it! The name of that rune is –" And, again, Ud bent to the corpse's ear and, straightening, laughed.

The drumming was almost lost in a deep and constant noise, like the swaying of the sea or rain blown on gusts of wind and pattering on hard ground. He knew it for the rushing of wind through a forest: the lifting and fluttering of many, many leaves and the creaking of branches, the groaning of trees.

The darkness was split by firelight, and the light showed not a forest but a single, vast ash tree.

A root rose from the dead leaves, and he had to climb it like the side of a hill, setting his feet in the grooved bark. He felt the root thrumming under him as it strained to cling to the earth, and the smell of the wood filled his head.

Reaching the top of the root, he looked down on firelit ripples on black water. A man's head – only a head – watched him from the water's side. He climbed down, treading through clumps of soft, damp moss.

A fire was burning in this space between two of the Tree's vast roots. Against the flames he saw black shapes: a crouching girl, a man with a drum. He went to them, holding up a hand to guard his eyes from the brightness, feeling the warmth slide over his skin. The girl looked up. She had an odd

246

little face with slanting dark eyes. He knew her.

The man was old but strongly made, with wide shoulders and heavy arms. His hands on the drum were big. The skin of his face was lined and crinkled like worn old leather, his long hair and beard grey. One eye glinted in the firelight, the other was a shadowed pit. Elfgift knew him too.

Moving round the fire, he looked down on his own corpse. The body was hacked, marred, but the face untouched, and he studied it curiously, never having seen his own face before. For an eye's blink, he thought it was Wulfweard.

Ebba, from behind Ud's shoulder, saw the ghost stoop above its own corpse. It shuddered like a reflection in rippled water, and vanished into the rise and ebb of firelight and shadow. She gripped at Ud's shoulders with her sharp fingers – but the ghost appeared again, and then she shuddered, thinking, *What am I seeing?*

The fire scorched Ebba's skin on one side, and left her aching with cold on the other. Ud's song went on.

"A third rune I know: with it I can blunt my enemy's blade, turn his staff soft as grass. Its name is –" Ud whispered the name in Elfgift's unhearing ear.

"I know a fourth: if my enemies fetter me with chains and lock me within doors, this charm will break the chains, will turn the locks. Always I walk free. Its name

is –

"A fifth I know: I can stop an arrow in its flight with a glare of my one eye. And the name of the fifth is –"

One-Eye raised his voice over the water-roar of the wind in the Tree. "You were long in coming. Hungry? Here – joint the meat for the pot." He lifted a cleaver from the leaves beside him, and threw it to land at Elfgift's feet, its broad blade glaring golden in the firelight.

The only meat to be jointed was Elfgift's own carcase. He looked at One-Eye, and the old man nodded.

So Elfgift took up the cleaver and crouched beside himself. Into the leaves beside him pattered a small, sharp knife. He worked like a huntsman, jointing and chopping, separating bone from bone.

When he looked up, it was to see a tripod set over the fire, with a brass cauldron glinting above it. The girl was making her way through the leaves, to and from the pool, filling the cauldron with water.

Fetching water in that world was as heavy work as in any other, and with every trip Ebba grew more afraid of the head beside the pool, which seemed intent on catching her out, so closely did it watch her. Her arms ached, and it was hard to lift the bucket so high, to empty it into the hanging

248

cauldron. But the more tired she was, the harder she went at the work. In such a place, in such company, she was afraid to complain.

Elfgift threw the joints of his own meat into the cauldron. Even the head he threw in, as if to make brawn.

In the Borough's ditch, Ud sang. "*A sixth rune I know: if any send me glory-twigs carved with runes, I can turn their power on him. And the rune's name is –*

"*I know a seventh: if fire seizes the hall where my friends shelter, with a word I can douse it. And the word is –*

"*An eighth I know: all men would like to learn it but only I can teach it! If hatred seed in men's minds, I can uproot it – if so I choose! And the rune is –*

"*I know a ninth: if ships are in danger, I can still the wind that makes the spume fly: I can calm the sea – if so I choose! And the rune is –*"

As Ud's laughter carried into the dark, Ebba crouched against his back, hiding her face against his cloak.

The vast branches of the Tree swayed and groaned overhead. One-Eye took a wooden bowl and, with a wooden ladle, filled it from the pot boiling over the fire. He passed it to Elfgift. "Enjoy yourself!"

Ebba peered round Ud and watched every mouthful as the ghost ate itself.

What I am seeing?

She wondered if she was to wake up remembering this. Was she to return to her own world, and to go about the business of eating and talking, while remembering this?

In the Borough ditch, Ud sang. *"A tenth rune I know: I can sing so witches cannot shift their shapes nor even find their way back to their own doors. Its name is –*

"I know an eleventh: when I lead my friends to battle, I can so sing behind my shield that unhurt they fight and unhurt triumph, and unhurt go home. And its name is –

"A twelfth rune I know: when I meet one of my own, a hanged man, I can command him to tell me all he knows. And its name is –

"I know a thirteenth: if I speak it over a babe, his courage will never waver, nor will he ever die in battle. And its name is –"

One-Eye called for Elfgift's help and, between them, they lifted the cauldron off the fire. "Over!" said One-Eye, and they pushed the cauldron over.

Out came the broth in a foaming wave, pouring away, steaming, into the leaves. Bones rattled and spilled. A long thigh-bone lay over the cauldron's lip, as if half-spat from a brazen mouth. The skull rolled and clanged in the cauldron's bottom.

"Now name your bones," One-Eye said. "Pull yourself together!

"A fourteenth I know – it's unknown to fools! Only I can teach it, and its name is –

"I know a fifteenth –"

Elfgift crouched beside the hot cauldron and used his own thigh-bone to bowl his own skull from the cauldron's depths. It was easy to set the skull in place on the leaves, and the many bones of the spine beneath it: the shoulder-blades, the shattered ribs; the arm-bones and the hip's sculpted curves, the long bones of the legs. But the many tiny bones of the wrists and ankles, hands, feet, fingers and toes were hard to find in the leaves.

Ebba went to help him. She knelt beside the ghost, and burrowed her hands in the damp leaves, raising thick scents of earth. Her fingers closed around smooth knuckle bones, still warm from the boiling water. Her flesh tingled at the smooth slickness of the wet bones. She held them out to the ghost, and it took its own bones from her hand. She felt its touch, like the touch of a living hand, and watched it put the bones of its own hand together.

All her life she had wanted to be close to Elfgift, and now she was among his bones, which was funny and she wanted to laugh, but was afraid.

The ghost smiled at her, and made her giddy, as

if the wind soughing overhead through the great branches of Odin's Horse was blowing through her head, setting her every thought and memory whirling.

How can I have this in my head and go on living? How can I dream this and not wake?

People in Jul's Borough – guards – must have heard Ud's strong voice at its long song in the darkness; they must have heard his full, loud laughter. No one came. Perhaps they knew it for a witch-song, and were afraid.

"A sixteenth rune I know: if I fancy, I can have the love of a white-fleshed woman. And the name of that rune is –

"I know a seventeenth: so powerful is it that the woman will be bound to me until I cast her loose. And its name is –"

"Lie down," said One-Eye, and Elfgift lay down among his own bones. One-Eye heaped over him the richly-scented leaves of the great Ash.

Ebba went to help. It was from an ash that Woden had made the first man, and from an elm, the first woman. I am making a man, she thought, out of ash leaves, and ash wood and bones. She paused in the work and put up her hands, dirtied with forest earth, to feel if she had two eyes or only one.

Elfgift lay among his own bones and stretched out his arms and flexed his hands, feeling the bones move under his flesh. He looked up into the wide-spread branches of the Tree, and watched the darkness and the firelight's gilding play among the ruffling leaves. He heard the creaking of the great tree, and its constant soughing, and felt the earth throb beneath him as its roots sucked.

One-Eye bent low over him and he saw the glitter of the one living eye. One-Eye bent lower, put his mouth to Elfgift's and breathed into him. The breath was rank as a wolf's, and the lips cold as clay.

"An eighteenth I know, but never will I tell it, not to the white woman in my arms or even my own sister! The secret held alone is most powerful – only I can teach it, and never will I!

"Nine runes and nine more I learned on the Tree, a hard schooling! These were my words before there were men, and these were my words after my death, when I rose again!"

The fire crackled. The wind blew clouds of eye-stinging, choking smoke about them. Firelight cast a bright circle of light that dazzled. A nearby stake would suddenly be seen, or part of a smashed pot, or the toothed jawbone of a pig poking from the rubbish of the ditch; then the fire would flicker and all would blink into darkness. Beyond that the blackness was a wall, and against the blackness whirled flurries of scarlet sparks. Small flakes of snow fell from the blackness and sizzled in the fire.

Ud took the hands of the corpse and pulled gently. The corpse rose with his pull, and Ebba covered her mouth with her hand and closed her eyes. But, hearing a softer sigh than the wind in the trees, she looked again.

Ud and Elfgift sat facing each other, Ud grasping Elfgift's hands. They sat as if in a small boat, their bent legs interlocked, and they smiled into each other's faces.

Ebba stared from one to the other: the one clothed, the other's naked flesh shining like polished ivory in the firelight. The one grey and bearded, the other fair and beardless. Over Ud's face the firelight played hide and seek, making a pit of his lost eye, doubling the depth of the creases across his brow and above his nose, finding every one of the many seams and crumplings in his leathery cheeks and about his living eye.

Elfgift's face, full in the light, was burnished by it. His eyes shone silver.

Ud reached out a big, veined, wrinkled hand, and drew one thick forefinger down Elfgift's face from brow to chin, like an artist who admires the work he has made.

Ebba was shaking, juddering like a shaken

moppet on a string. She hugged herself tightly, and only shook the harder. She thought: *No one should see this.*

Ud said, "Answer me, if you can: How was the earth made?"

Ebba put her fingers in her ears, not to hear, but heard anyway.

"From the First One," Elfgift said, "who was woman and man, Mother and Father of everything. The mountains are made from First One's bones, the earth from First One's flesh, the sky from the dome of First One's skull—"

"Enough!" said One-Eye. "But answer me this, if you can. Who were the first people, and from where did they come?"

"The dwarfs bred like maggots from the First One's flesh. And then—"

Ud grinned. "Enough! But answer me this, if you can. When my son, Ing, lay on His funeral pyre, what was it I whispered in His ear?"

Ebba was shaking her head, because she didn't want to hear the answer. Elfgift leaned far forward, so he could whisper in Ud's ear.

She saw Ud grinning, his face deeply creased. She saw him nod at the whisper, and nod and nod.

There was a sound among the dry leaves, and something moved in the shadows of the tree. Both Ebba and Ud looked towards the sound: Elfgift turned his head.

A woman came into the firelight, a tall woman and beautiful. Her long hair hung over her shoulders and breasts to below her waist. It seemed dark, but shone suddenly red as she came closer to the fire. Long streaks of grey ran through it. Around her neck was a broad golden collar, from which flashed sparks of light, and there was more gold at her waist.

Elfgift saw her, rose, and went to her. Ebba watched them meet and embrace, and felt pain at her heart, as if it was being crushed between two millstones. *What I am seeing!* That Elfgift never would, never could, be hers. No matter how tenaciously she followed him, how she planned, how she dreamed, his fate and hers had been fated long ago. She could not even be jealous – she did not dare.

Elfgift walked, with the Lady, into the deepening shadows under the tree. Ebba watched, aching, until she saw Ud watching her. His one eye glinted, and he smiled.

She drew a long, aching breath, tipped back her head and looked up. Above her was the freezing, star-filled sky above the Borough's rubbish-filled ditch. She also saw the leaves and branches of the great Ash.

Ud laughed and waved a hand at her. "Go, little one – away with you!" Her head swam, as if she was moving backwards and yet sitting still. "Go tell them how I sang him my runes. Tell them what I've made of him. Go tell them what I'm sending them." Ud laughed. "Tell them to look for him in nine days. Nine days!"

What I have seen! Ebba thought, and lay in the ditch.

CHAPTER 13

Holly Fires

Where the God-house had stood was a stretch of scoured earth, pitted with black post-holes. A couple of the wooden posts still stood, exposed to daylight as they had not been for many lifetimes. Grey winter light shone on the planes made by the axes that had chopped them into shape. To look across that space, at walls of halls that, before, had always been hidden by the God-house, made Ebba's skin prickle. The angles of everything seemed wrong, the shadows fell all awry. Flinching, she looked up, half-expecting to see the trunk and branches of an immense tree.

She saw only the Borough streets, and laughed, and danced along the ground where the God-house had stood. What she had seen! Against that, Unwin's careful destruction of the God-house seemed such a waste of time. Twirling in her dance, she clapped her hands. People passing her shied away. Everyone knew the mad girl.

Their fear made her laugh louder. "This is the eighth day!" she called out. "Tomorrow – oh, what you will see!"

People looked away, pretending not to hear, but they had heard. When she'd gone by, they'd talk, the Saxons and the Danes. Nine days. The mad girl, Woden's girl, babbled constantly of nine days. The number had a magical ring. Nine days Odin hung on the Tree...

And Jul was passing uncelebrated while Unwin prepared for the feast of his new God, Christ. People didn't like that. Ebba heard what they said, though Unwin didn't. An old guest hall was to be sanctified a Christian God-house, and those who had slept there turned out to cram into other halls. It was mostly pagan Danes who suffered, as Unwin cared less about offending them than his Welsh allies. Ebba heard the grumbling. Unwin didn't.

She had watched as all the weapons which had hung on the walls of the old hall were carried out – they could not hang in a House of God, said the Christian priest. Ing bore a sword, Thunor a war-hammer, and Woden a spear, but Christ hated

259

weapons and war – except when the war was led by Unwin.

Overnight Jul had become "heathen" and was to be forgotten. The hall was to be called a "church", a foreign word. Hangings were pulled down because of their "heathen" pictures. Beautiful and ancient carvings were hacked from the pillars and walls or disfigured.

In every hall, not just the "church", the greenery was ordered to be torn down. The same women who had so happily woven the green garlands were set to pulling down every stem and leaf, to sweeping out every red berry. Nor was it enough that it should be thrown on the middens. It was all to be burned. Fires were built in the yards, and the greenery piled on them. Clouds of smoke had risen up, stinging the eyes and throats of everyone. It had hung over the Borough for hours.

Wandering, Ebba came on one of these burned out fires. In the open yard before a guest hall was a circle of grey ash, a ring of black earth round it, where the heat of the fire had melted the snow. In the night, the black mud had frozen again.

Danes and Welsh sat on the bench outside the hall, and women of the Borough hurried past with downcast heads. Ignoring them all, Ebba danced into the ash, kicking it up in a fine grey cloud, stirring up a fresh smell of burning. It was soft about her ankles and settled on her skirt, staining it. Some rose high enough to drift on to her dark hair and face, turning her to an old woman.

What she had seen! Remembering that, the burning seemed so funny that she laughed aloud – and then she remembered Elfgift in the arms of the Lady, and was seized with the extraordinary pain of knowing that she could never, never have even the smallest taste of what she wanted from life. It hurt, it hurt – and yet she continued to laugh in astonishment at how much she had seen and how much she knew. It was knowledge that hurt like the bite of flames and yet made her dizzy and drunk. This, she realized – and still more knowledge opened to her and staggered her – this was why Woden had cut out his own eye to buy a drink of wisdom. This was the pain and the drunkenness that had pierced him like a spear and swung him dizzily on the Tree.

She whirled in the ash, clapping her hands and making a strange sound that was neither weeping nor laughter. Through a haze of ash she saw that one, that dark Dane they called "Troll". He was sitting on the bench among others, gaping at her. Stamping harder, vanishing in a cloud of ash, she sang out music for her own dancing:

"Every winter He leaves us, following the whale's road,
But holly-fires, holly-fires rouse Him from His sleep

And back He comes, back He comes
With sheaves and sheaves of corn in His arms!"

The ash rose round her, and she couldn't sing for coughing or for laughing. So funny that Unwin had ordered the lighting of the holly-fires!

As the ash settled about her, she saw that the Danes had stopped the polishing and oiling of their harness, and were looking from each other to her with a sly glee. They had understood her song.

Ebba smiled at them – and then she spotted, lying at the edge of the ash-circle, a perfect, un-burned, green and scarlet holly sprig. Snatching it up, she danced again, jumping and spinning, waving it above her head.

"Oh the holly and the ivy
When they be both full growed
Of all the trees that be in the wood
The holly tree bears the crown!
Oh the rising of the sun
And the running of the deer –"

Ingvi jumped from the bench and ran through the ash to join her, spoiling his freshly cleaned boots. The girl was an eldritch sight, capering and caterwauling, mad as a hare, covered in grey ash from head to foot. But she was Mad Odin's, and it was Odin's season. Ingvi caught her free hand, and joined her dance and her song.

> "– sweet singing round the fire!
> Oh the holly bears a flower
> As white as any milk
> As Frigga bore Him, our sweet Ing
> And lapped Him up in silk!
> Oh the rising of the sun – !"

More Danes came from the benches and a ring-dance formed, circling and stamping the ash. Their loud, glad singing and their laughter rose in the cold winter's air and carried over the rooftops.

They ended the song breathless, and their circle broke and folded inwards as they hugged, cheering and applauding themselves. Welshmen had come from other halls and were watching, some smiling, some not.

Ebba pulled at Ingvi's arm until he stooped his dark head towards her. He was darker even than she, but his hair, too, was now grizzled with ash. "Tomorrow is the ninth day," she whispered. "He comes back in nine days."

"Mad," said someone, but in Ingvi's dark eyes she saw the light of belief.

"When he comes," he said, "I shall be with him! Count on that, sweetheart."

She smiled, then kissed him and, as he drew

back in surprise, she ran away, calling out. "Today is the eighth day!"

"Mad," said the man again.

"Aye," Ingvi said. "Odin's."

Wulfweard's head seemed full of noise, it ached so furiously. Sometimes he thought the noise was the Christ-priest tramping the wooden floor, haranguing him, exhorting him to make his vows to Christ and Unwin. Sometimes, when he opened his eyes, he was right, and the lurching to and fro of the priest made him sick. Sometimes the room was empty. It might be lit by beams of grey daylight from the high, shuttered window, or by a single candle, or be dark. Whatever. The crashing and banging in his head went on.

To give in had seemed unbearable, to hold out had seemed strong. But his body had weakened faster than his will. His head had begun to ache in a way that scattered thought. Lifting the water jug became hard. He could hardly make a fist. Within him his stomach gnawed as if, starved, it was trying to feed on him.

Oddly, the thought that Unwin would come had helped him endure. Unwin could not have ordered this. Yet he knew that Unwin wanted him dead. His thinking wasn't clear. Unwin would come...

His neck and back and other joints ached with a miserable, grinding intensity. His finger-ends became tender. The slightest pressure bruised them.

Once he had opened his eyes to find the priest's face filling the space above him, peering at him with alarm. The priest had whisked dizzyingly out of sight, and had come back, ages later, with bread and cheese.

The stink of the cheese had set Wulfweard retching on an empty stomach. He thought he would turn inside out, like a shirt pulled off over the head, and might have laughed at the idea if he hadn't felt so wretched. He had pushed the plate of bread and cheese away, so it fell off the bench on to the floor with a crash that hurt his head. He knew he would die if he didn't eat, but he couldn't face the food. He knew he was dying, but couldn't care much about it. If it meant the pain would stop, then so be it.

The hard wall-bench bruised him where he touched it. Lying in the dark, he sank into the pain in his head and body and floated with it, as if carried by a thunderous river. The river was carrying him towards a world he knew. He had been there before.

The pain in his head dulled, and through it, as it cleared, he felt a touch on his forehead. The pain shrank more, and he knew the touch for that of fingers, a hand. A feeling of cold and clarity, of ice-water, cut through the clamour of pain: a blessing.

His lids were heavy, and flickered once or twice before he succeeded in opening them. He looked up into a shadowed face hanging above him, hidden by long, curving wings of hair which fell down on either side. He stared up at it, blinking a few more times, before he saw that it was not the priest, nor Unwin, but Elfgift.

Wulfweard smiled. He had been washed up in the Other World, then. That was why the pain had stopped. And his brother had waited for him. An ease and warmth crept through his joints, soothing the pain of his cold hands and feet, making his whole body restful. It was good to have died.

His eyes closed again, heavily, and he may have dozed for a few moments or slept for hours. What roused him was the sound of rain – no, the rush and sough of wind among many leaves. The touch of a hand was still on his forehead and, when he opened his eyes again, Elfgift still leaned above him, as if no more time than an eye's blink had passed.

He looked about, his head moving under Elfgift's hand. Above him was an overarching canopy, a sky, of weighty branches and ruffling leaves, lit by brightening and fading firelight. The leaves and the firelight played together, neither ever still, making caverns of darkness one moment and intricate weavings of light and dark the next. Here a strength of branches, there a light-gilded leaf. And, as beautiful as was the movement, the light and dark, it was matched by the constant whispering and sighing of leaves and wind.

Wulfweard moved his hand, and it clenched on dried leaves. He lay soft, on thick ages of fallen leaves. The scent of the forest floor rose about him, and beneath him he felt the swell and fall, like breathing, as the Tree's great roots grasped the earth. The last, the very last of the pain left him, and he didn't know if it was banished by Elfgift's healing touch or the presence of the Tree.

He tilted back his head to look up at Elfgift, and Elfgift grinned at his astonishment, then pushed an arm beneath his shoulders and began to lift him up. Wulfweard struggled to sit up himself, but found his body infuriatingly weak and hard to control.

The firelight came from a fire that burned nearby: he could feel the soft touch of its heat. A tripod was set over the flames, and from the tripod a cauldron hung, on chains. An old man sat hunched beside the fire, a cloak wrapped round him, its hood drawn over his head. Where the firelight touched it most brightly, the cloak was blue. When he saw Wulfweard sit up, the old man took a wooden bowl and a large wooden ladle from stones beside the fire, and filled the bowl from the cauldron.

He brought the steaming bowl over to them and, as he came nearer, Wulfweard caught a whiff of strong meat, of rich, greasy stew. His guts twisted and he started to retch painfully.

From behind him, Elfgift's hand pressed hard against his belly. "No," Elfgift said, and spoke another word in his ear, which he neither caught nor understood – but the painful spasms faded and the nausea left him. In its place was hunger, such pure, sharp hunger as he had not felt for days. His mouth dribbled water as he reached for the bowl. The one-eyed man grinned at him, his wrinkled face twisted by the gouge scar.

The full bowl was heavy, but Elfgift held it for him, and the old man gave him a wooden spoon. The food was hot. Its heat seeped through him, bringing strength with its warmth. The very savour of the meat in the mouth, its salt, its dark blood flavour, gave strength. Elfgift was behind him, making a support for his back, and Wulfweard both heard and felt him laugh. The old man, sitting on his heels in the dead leaves, grinned through his grey beard to see him eat so well. The good humour, the warmth of the fire, the shelter of the great Tree, was as strengthening as the food. The food finished, he lay down in the leaves again, and fell asleep to the gentle, breathing rise and fall of the earth beneath him: the pulse of the great Ash.

He woke to the hard bench beneath him, to deep quiet, a sharp cold and grey-lit darkness. His head spun as he sat, but then settled, and he was thankful to find his thinking clear and his body without pain. But he was in the room again, its wooden walls clamped narrowly round him. Long beams of bright, clear moonlight angled down from the edges of the high shutters, fading the darkness. Loneliness, and longing for the beauty of the Tree, brought stinging tears into his eyes, and he caught his breath.

A laugh made him snatch his head round. In a shadowed corner of the wall-bench, Elfgift sat, naked, his flesh catching the dim light like polished ivory, his long hair and his eyes like silver.

Wulfweard started to his feet, and then paused, astonished at the strength he felt. Elfgift rose and, passing by his brother, caught at his hand as he went. The door, at his touch, released its lock with a soft, rolling click, and the door swung inward. Wulfweard felt no wonder – or he felt too much wonder for this to be remarkable. He was led through the door into the hall beyond.

There were guards outside the door, spears in hand, while their shields rested against the walls beside them. One stared before him, the other leaned against the wall with his eyes closed.

Elfgift and Wulfweard stood beside them, as tall, as solid, yet the guards neither glanced at them nor seemed to hear any sound. It set

Wulfweard shivering, to stand so close to capture and yet to seem as insubstantial as a draught beneath a door. He wanted to ask Elfgift: Are we both ghosts, then? Am I dead?

Elfgift, silently laughing at him, reached out and pulled the beard of the open-eyed guard. The guard jerked his head aside, coughed, shifted his weight – but settled to his stand again. Still grinning, Elfgift pulled Wulfweard away.

They ran the length of the hall to the doors, heaved up the bar and put it aside. Pushing the doors open, they ran out into the winter's night.

The shock was like leaping into a winter river. Above them, the sky was freezing black, and every one of the many stars had a hard, icy glitter. The moon was huge, almost full, a bone-white disc with its edge clipped. Beneath their bare feet the ground was hard and thinly covered with sharp, frozen snow. It was not a night to stand still.

Elfgift raised a hunting cry and ran for the gates. Wulfweard, answering, followed. They took different alleys between buildings, calling to one another over the rooftops, meeting where streets opened into yards before parting again. They came together at the gates, which stood open between their uncaring guards. Wulfweard wondered at that, but had followed Elfgift through them and over the wooden bridge before he could do more than wonder. Then they were running down the snowy slopes towards the orchards and the fields and all his thought was needed for keeping his feet. The cold night passed over his skin like the sting of whips.

The yew trees about the grave-field were black masses in the grey moonlight. A golden, leaping light flashed from behind them as Elfgift and Wulfweard leaped up on the wall.

A fire burned at the centre of the grave-field, black shapes crouched beside it. The golden light gilded the grey stone of the inner wall, and washed over the snow-covered mounds and the wooden posts, carved with runes, that told who lay there and who had buried them. Where the firelight didn't reach lay deep, black darkness, or the cold, tricksy dusk of moonlight mingled with snow.

The wind whipped their hair about their faces as they stood on the wall, and the cold scoured Wulfweard through his only clothing, a thin tunic. The black shapes at the fire rose, becoming tall, waiting figures. The brothers jumped down and crossed the graves to meet them.

A bird flew, whirring, past Wulfweard's head and landed on a rune-post near the fire. Even in the light it was black. A raven, its strong beak made to tear carrion. A grave-field, a battle-field bird.

The two waiting by the fire were an old man

and a tall boy. The grey-beard opened his arms and took Elfgift into his embrace, and when he turned and hugged Wulfweard too – in a crushing hug of surprising strength – Wulfweard knew him for Old One-Eye, who had served him meat under the Ash. Now One-Eye wore mail, and a helmet lay gleaming on the ground at his feet.

The boy was hugging Elfgift, and kissing him. Long hair, red in the firelight, fell over his mail, but when this boy turned to Wulfweard, he saw that the hair was streaked with grey, and this was a woman, not a boy. A Battle-woman, dressed in mail, with a sword belted round Her. He knew Her too. She hugged him hard, pressing Her cheek to his. Pulling back, She drew a long knife from Her belt and offered it to him, the hilt to him, the blade across Her hand.

Elfgift was taking an offered knife from One-Eye.

Wulfweard said, "What? Are we to dance the sword-dance again?"

Elfgift grinned. "We are to finish it."

Wulfweard pulled his tunic over his head and threw it aside, so that he was as naked as Elfgift but, he was sure, much colder. He took the long knife from the Battle-woman. The ravens flew up, cawing, and circled above.

Wulfweard moved into the fighting stance from which the sword-dance began, but Elfgift shook his head and held out to him his left hand. Wulfweard put his own left hand into it. Elfgift drew back, pulling their arms taut, and set the point of his own knife to Wulfweard's arm, near the elbow. His glance, which felt like a light slap to the face, told Wulfweard to copy him.

Wulfweard set the point of his own blade to Elfgift's arm. He remembered the true purpose of the sword-dance – to feed the dead with blood, to wake them and call them to Jul. He had tried to stab his brother Unwin, and had not been able to do it. Still less did he think he could cut his brother Elfgift.

The pressing of the knife's point hard against his own cold flesh was a deep, bruising pain but, though it made him grit his teeth, not unbearable. Not as bad as the wretched, miserable pain of starving. There followed the long, white, searing pain of the sharp edge parting his skin from the elbow to wrist. Blood welled up in the track of the dagger, black in the moonlight.

Gritting his teeth harder, he pushed the point of his own dagger against Elfgift's skin, which gave to the steel but resisted. His hand wavered, but the grip of Elfgift's hand on his own tightened. Catching a breath, he changed the angle of the knife and drove it down hard, driving it through the skin, and deeper than he had meant – he dragged it quickly down Elfgift's forearm to the wrist. He thought he could hear the skin tear, like the cutting of silk.

Elfgift released his hand and tossed his dagger from his right to his left. He held out his right hand for Wulfweard's. While blood ran around their left arms and dripped to the earth, they cut each other's right arms.

Elfgift raised his arms and flexed them, to make the blood run faster, down his arms, across his shoulders and on to his chest. He flung his arms wide, blood flying from them in droplets.

"Give us *Barleycorn*, Wulf!"

Wulfweard was rubbing his hand down the cuts on his arms, and flicking the blood from him. He saw Elfgift moving away from him with a half-dancing step, turning, letting the blood fall from his arm on to many graves.

Wulfweard's voice was hoarse and unmusical in the cold, but would the dead care?

> *"There were three kings came out of the West*
> *Their victory to try,*
> *And they have taken a binding oath –"*

Elfgift, from the other side of the grave-field, joined in.

> *"That Barley, our Barley*
> *That our Barley should die!"*

They ran and spun about the grave-field, their arms spread wide, their lively movement making the blood flow faster. It fell and stained the snow dark, but froze and could not sink into the earth.

> *"They ploughed, they sowed, they harrowed him in*
> *Laid sods all on his head,*
> *And they have taken a binding oath*
> *That Barley, our Barley*
> *That our Barley is dead!"*

Elfgift hacked at the grave-mounds with his knife, running from one to another, making holes in the mounds and letting the blood from his arms drip into them. When the cold staunched his blood, he used the knife's point to open the cuts again.

Wulfweard sang:

> *"And dead he lay for a many moon's time*
> *Till the spring rains down did fall,*
> *Then Barley, he raised up his head*
> *And sore amazed us all!*
> *And so he stood till come midsummer*
> *Though he looked both pale and wan.*
> *Then Barley, our Barley*
> *Grew a long beard and so became a man!"*

Elfgift, kneeling on the frozen earth, felt, far below

him, a shifting. Setting his hands against the earth, he let the blood run down his arms to pool about his wrists. "Sing!"

Wulfweard felt the shifting under his feet, and his voice took on a higher, sharper note.

> *"They sent men with sickles so sharp*
> *To cut him off at the knee,*
> *And they rolled him and tied him —"*

His voice faltered and stopped. The grave-field's thin covering of snow was broken jaggedly with black. The grave-field was sprouting.

Elfgift jumped upright, his outstretched arms streaked and dribbled with blood, and took up the song:

> *"They rolled him and tied him round the waist,*
> *Served him right savagely!"*

Wulfweard found his voice again, though his breath caught, and, with the wind scratching at them and tugging at their hair, they sang together, while the ground troubled beneath them.

> *"They sent men with sharp pitchforks*
> *To prick him to the heart*
> *And then they served him worse than that*
> *For they bound him to the cart.*

They carried him round and round the field
Till they brought him to the barn,
And there they made a solemn oath
To end our Barleycorn.
They sent men with crab-tree sticks
To flay him skin from bone
And then they served him worse than that
For they ground him between two stones."

Long, straight ash-staves were growing from the earth. Iron spear-heads glinted at their ends, golden in firelight, silver in moonlight. The earth rose, mushrooming with broad shields, their centres cold gleaming bosses of iron. The hard earth rolled back as if parted by a plough-share – but this earth was being ploughed from beneath.

Helmets broke the earth and caught the moon's light, bare heads came up and bone gleamed. Hands reached and groped, shoulders heaved, knees bent up. Out they scrambled, dressed as they had been for burial, in mail-shirts. Back they reached, into their holes, for the swords that had been laid beside them, for their axes. They lifted up shrunken heads and looked about them. The fire's light shone on noseless faces covered with a hard, leathern skin, on faces half-covered with sodden flesh, on faces that were eyeless and all bone.

They were close about Wulfweard and his voice

dried in his throat. He could hardly draw breath. The knife fell from his hand. He had travelled, in spirit, into the world of the dead, but had never thought to see bones climbing out of their graves in his own, waking world. This was Woden's magic: death magic, fearful.

Elfgift came running, dodging through these standing bones, to Wulfweard's side. He put his arms about Wulfweard, his fist, clenched on the bloodied knife, against Wulfweard's shoulder. Elfgift sang the last of the song, jolting Wulfweard in his arms, trying to shake him out of his fright.

> *"Now here I pour in the nut-brown bowl*
> *The blood of Barleycorn!*
> *Now here we'll drink the season in*
> *With the blood of Barleycorn!"*

Wulfweard, his voice dry and barely above a whisper, joined with the last words:

> *"For the huntsman, he can't hunt the deer*
> *Nor the warrior sound the horn,*
> *The ploughman, he can't drive the plough*
> *Without blood of Barleycorn!"*

The dead pressed close about them, and their every breath was choked with the thick smell of earth and the overpowering stink of the grave.

Hands – fans of bones to which shreds of skin clung – reached towards them in greeting. Bones clasped their shoulders, touched their heads.

Elfgift reached out his hand to them, but Wulfweard put up his hands to fend them off. Quick as bites, bone hands closed about his, and about his arms, closed and clung with a fierceness that threatened to drive the bones into his own bones, intertwining them until they could never be parted. Faces lurched at him, as if pushing forward for a greeting kiss, teeth bared to the dark, eyeless sockets. Wulfweard would have fallen if Elfgift's arm had not been round him.

Yet the dead were crowding to them in love and welcome. Elfgift let them clasp his hand, embraced their wasted bodies, offered his cheek to the touch of their earth-stained teeth, their clay-cold, clay-moist lips. Wulfweard turned his face into Elfgift's shoulder and hid from them, though he felt their touch on his head and back and heard, all round him, a dry whispering and rustling. "The Brothers," the dead said. "The Twins."

Then Old One-Eye and the Battle-woman came pushing through the crowd to them, and the dead host began to beat their spear-heads on shield-bosses, raising a clashing, ringing din in the cold. They turned away and marched on the Borough, their helmets and spear points catching the light of the moon.

CHAPTER 14

Feasting the Dead

Unwin looked down the length of his captured feast hall. In the heat and golden light of the torches, the plundered finery of the guests and the weapons on the walls gleamed, and faces were flushed and damp. On all sides, at every table, were bright crowns of green leaves and scarlet berries: holly wreaths. It was the Danes, the heathens, who wore them.

Even Ingvi Troll, sitting to Unwin's left, wore a green and scarlet crown on his black hair, in defiance of the orders that Jul not be celebrated. On the table before him Ingvi had placed corn-dollies – little straw figures of Woden's goats and Ing's boars.

Unwin showed no displeasure. He could not afford an open quarrel with the Danes. His men, both Christian Saxons and Welsh, had taken their lead from him and had sat down to feast with the Danes, ignoring the Jul crowns and Jul dollies.

To see the Danes flouting his father's orders made Godwin deeply angry, but he had been allowed to take one of the lesser places at the high table instead of sitting with the women on the wall-bench behind it, and he dared not speak his mind for fear of being sent from the table.

It would have been easier to bear if he could have understood why his father said nothing. Was he afraid of the Danes? That thought came hard. Perhaps – he hoped – all his father's men had knives hidden beneath their clothing and, at a signal, were going to turn on the Danes beside them and kill them all, as in an old story. He would like to kill that grinning Troll himself. It would be called treachery and murder, but when people heard the truth, they would change their minds. It was the Danes who were treacherous, first making their vows to his father and then defying him.

A movement drew his eye, and he saw a girl come skipping into the open space before the high table, dancing to the music of her own singing. With distaste, he saw it was the mad girl. Her tiny, skinny body was swamped in a grubby gown of

grey wool, and her tangled dark hair was crowned
with a wreath of dark-green ivy leaves and black
berries – her counterpart to the holly crowns of
the Danish men. She was supposed to be a Saxon
– another traitor! Her looks weren't Saxon. Her
little white face was triangular as a cat's, pointed
at chin and cheekbones, and her eyes were like
sloes from the hedge – long, slanting and black.
She looked more elvish than even the elf's get had
done. Old Welsh blood was in her, maybe.

Everyone at the high table was watching her but
she, being mad, was far more concerned with
pointing her foot and holding her arms just so...
But when her eyes met the Troll's, she smiled and
called out, "He's coming tonight!"

"Who?" Unwin asked.

Ingvi grinned, his teeth very white against his
dark skin. He held up one of his corn-dollies – the
rough figure of a man, its arms outspread.

"Christ," Unwin said, deliberately misunder-
standing. "Christ is coming on Judgement Day,
aye."

Ingvi laughed, and propped the little figure
against a bowl. Unwin turned away. He knew the
figure was meant to be Ing, His arms outspread to
receive the spears in His heart.

The hall was full of noise: the crackling and
spitting of fires and torches, the clattering of
dishes, tread of feet, the din of talk, laughter,

knives on plates – all of it rising into the rafters with the heat, and pressing on the ears so constantly it was hardly more noticed than the air they breathed. Through it pierced a sudden shrill cry: "Hark! Harken!"

It was the command of a minstrel beginning a song and it demanded, in courtesy, silence. The noise dropped away, and people craned for a sight of the minstrel. Unwin himself stared about, baffled. He had commanded no minstrel to sing.

A figure leapt above them – the mad girl, jumping to a bench among the seated men, and from there to a table-top. "Hark!" she cried again, raising her hand, her voice ringing through the silenced hall.

As if she had laid a spell on them, the last sounds died away. Servants stood still, hands were stilled on the boards, breaths were held. From without the walls came the sound, faintly, of metal on metal – blade striking shield, blade striking blade. Axe-music. Sword-song.

Enemies were within the walls! The men of the guard were engaged with them. Who had broken in, and how, was impossible and needless to know. All that mattered was that they be met and beaten.

Unwin started to his feet, looking about him, at the weapons and shields on the walls, at the men at the tables. Weapons were not worn at a

Christmas feast. Though the hall was full of men, they wore no mail, no helmets, and were armed only with eating-knives.

Unwin filled his lungs and yelled, in a voice that he had trained to carry across valleys: "Arm!"

Men sprang up, knocking aside benches, knocking down plates and horns. They jumped on wall-benches and wrestled down shields, lifted down axes. Even the Danes, even Ingvi Troll, obeyed: there was no knowing who the enemy outside was. Unwin himself took down the big, plain sword, Woden's Promise. He wasted no time in fastening the sword's belt about him, but drew it from its scabbard with a snake's hiss.

The men, intent on getting down weapons, scattered Kendrida's maids from the wall-bench. With cries, they ran for the steep stairs to the private room above.

Kendrida herself, darting from her seat, seized Godwin by the arm, meaning to drag him with her to safety. But he pulled away and struck out at her. "Leave me alone, woman!" He clambered on to the wall-bench, reaching for a sword made for a man, far too long and heavy for him.

"Lady!" A frightened maid, almost in tears, pulled at her arm. Kendrida, watching Godwin jump down from the bench with a sword he could hardly lift, wanted both to laugh and scream at him, and was proud of him to the point of tears. It was a man's life to die for his lord if need be, and Godwin – his little boy's face set hard – was looking round for his father, to stand by his side. All the courage of his grandfather and uncles! He was the pledge of the courage bred into her own blood and bone.

"Lady, please!"

The dais was clear, the men having jumped down into the main body of the hall. Kendrida, seeing that she could be of no use there, swept to the stairs, pulling the girl behind her. Tears ran down her face. Grief for her son's loss was already setting its claws in her heart, but it was what he had been born and raised for. On the half-landing she stopped and stood fixed, staring down into the hall below. The maid pulled at her and wept, but could not make her take another step.

Godwin set his shoulder against his father's side, ready to stand with him in the shield-wall. His heart beat thunderously, a din in his ears, a shaking throughout his body, but he felt a great strength of relief. No longer did he have to wonder if he had the courage for this. The hour was here: he only had to act. He was afraid. He couldn't pretend he wasn't, but he had also grown more than himself with anger and excitement, and knew that he could stand.

Unwin, looking down and seeing his son beside him, pushed him away with a thrust of his leg.

"Get to your mother!" He wanted no children under his feet.

Godwin, hurt, retreated to the dais, and climbed on it so he could see over the shoulders of the men. If he watched his chance, he might still save his father's life.

The hall doors burst inwards. Long, cold draughts blew about the flames of fire and torches and set the light fading and flaring, washing about the walls and rafters like a tide. Shadows rose, deepened, shrank. Through the doors came men of the guard, Welsh and Saxon. The first of them were running, faces wild, grinning with fear, without sense. They had – Godwin was shocked to see – thrown away their shields and weapons to run the faster.

They dashed into the ranks of the hall's defenders, forcing them aside, breaking their line as the men hesitated to strike their friends.

The clash of Woden's music grew louder, hard on the ear, and the next through the doors came backwards, fighting, gasping for breath. The shield-wall of the defenders opened again, making passage for these hard-set men.

Then came the attackers, one thrusting a spear down and through an exhausted man, another making a leg-blow with an axe. The cold wind carried their stink into the hall. It whirled in the smoke and turned the fires cold and blue. And, as every living man in the hall drew that stink into his lungs, there broke on their ears a long, savage exulting scream that locked their every joint. A Valkyrie-scream, sounding the call to battle.

And then the sight of the attackers as they came into the light. Weapons stained with blood held in hands that were fans of bone. The divided bones of arms and legs, shreds of flesh clinging between them. Leather skin stretched tight over noseless faces; fleshless teeth bared to eyeless holes. The heart of every living man turned cold and tight within him. Weapons fell from their hands. Their will failed.

Those in the front rank turned and fought those behind them – those who had not yet clearly seen what they faced. They pressed against the sharp blades of weapons, desperate to get to the back of the hall, as far as they could from the things come in from the night. They fell to their knees, crawled over benches and under tables. On a table-top the mad girl danced and shrilled, "Fill the horns, bring bread! The dead are come to the Jul Feast!"

Ingvi stood stock-still, too chilled to move – and so earned the name of a brave man. His shoulder set against Ingvald's thick arm, he felt the tremor that shook his brother. He heard the breath Unwin drew shudder in his throat.

"Stand!" Unwin yelled. "In this hall you boasted of your courage! Now make your boast good!"

The lines of men wavered, as the bravest among them turned. Those who had shields locked them together in a wall. But as the dead pressed forward, casting their choking stink into the faces of the living, the shield-wall trembled.

Out of the darkness, into the golden light, came two who were not dead. They came so lightly and swiftly they seemed to hang in the air, their long hair lifting and floating about them. In their hands they held swords, but were otherwise naked. They were as alike as twins.

Inside the doors, they halted, and the dead warriors fell back and gathered round them like a bodyguard. Against the earth-darkened skin and earth-stained bones of the dead, their living flesh was smooth and shining, though streaked and daubed with dark blood.

A cry which broke from every Dane rose into the rafters. They knew the Brothers who had danced in the grave-field: the ghost-warriors from the walls of the God-house, Odin's Chosen, come to make an end to those picked out by Old Grey-Beard and His Battle-women. They had all seen Elfgift butchered, but now he had not a mark on him, except for the long cuts down his forearms.

Ingvi stared in rapt, disbelieving belief and heard, all about him, gasps and long moans and groans of the same belief and disbelief and bewilderment. He knew that not one among them could raise a weapon against this army. He knew that he could not.

Above, on the stair, Kendrida pressed against the wall and stared and stared. Her mind cried aloud, but made no sense, even to her.

Ebba leaped down from her table-top and ran to Elfgift, throwing herself against him and her arms around him. He held his sword-arm free of her, and pushed her behind him, where she laughed and clapped her hands and danced among the dead.

Ingvi let his sword fall from his hand. He left his brother's side, pushing forward through the few men in front of him. Coming into the space between the lines of the living and the dead, he held up his hands to show he was unarmed and went forward slowly.

Elfgift turned his head and looked at him, and Ingvi stumbled, his head jerking back. Elfgift's gaze had the force of a blow. Ingvi halted, conscious again of his thumping heart. The weight of the gaze pressed steadily against him, and he had to use strength to keep his place and not give way before it. Lowering his eyes as he took the holly-crown from his own head, he pressed forward again. Careful not to meet the elf-born's eyes, he set the holly crown on Elfgift's head – and then yielded to the weakness in his knees, and knelt as if about to take a vow of faith. "My sword, my shield, my faith, Elfgift – all yours."

Every Dane yelled out, echoing the words. They moved aside from the Saxons and the Welsh, aligning themselves with the dead. Even stolid Ingvald left Unwin's side to join his brother. Unwin watched him go and had not the strength to lift his sword against him.

The world had shrunk about Unwin until there was nothing to see but that loathsome thing which stood in the firelight, holding up its holly-crowned head. Everywhere it looked, people ducked and hid their faces, afraid to meet its eye.

When he saw it shining in the firelight and its grace of movement, he could not silence the voice inside him which said, "Beautiful!" And he loathed it more.

He feared it. He had seen it killed. Its blood stained the roof-tree behind him. A thing killed should stay dead – otherwise, how could you know the sun would rise tomorrow or that the earth would stay under your feet? The Resurrection in which Unwin believed was distant in time and place. Not this resurrection. If this thing was whole and alive, then he was nothing for all his rank and courage – nothing but a fool.

His God was testing him!

With this answer to the puzzle, he found breath. God was testing him, as He so often tested the saints, torturing them, driving them half-mad to ensure they were strong enough for the task He set them. He must meet the test.

He stepped forward, clear of the huddle of his men. Elfgift's head turned and the thing's eyes snapped to his face. The impact of the gaze was a blow to the face, and Unwin stepped back heavily before he could brace his heels and make himself stand.

"In the name of the Father, the Son and the Holy Ghost, and with Their help, I shall kill you again; and by Their leave, this time I shall lay you in your grave for good."

Elfgift, naked, without mail or shield, turned to him and smiled.

"But I'll not fight with this sword! Here – take it back!" Unwin threw Woden's Promise and Elfgift caught it from the air. He straightened, a sword in either hand, his hair falling over his shoulders and a holly crown on his head. For an eye's blink, Unwin was caught in staring. "Beautiful!" said his mind. The thing was the very image of a ghost warrior, dancing between swords, inlaid on a shield-boss buried with Unwin's heathen father.

In a sickness of anger, Unwin broke the stare. He wanted to kill this thing so badly, and put it underground where he would never have to see it again. But only God, it seemed, could make it stay there. Under his breath, he began praying.

Elfgift threw his own sword to him, in exchange

for Woden's Promise. Unwin let it fall to the ground. "I want a sword forged by a Christian."

He turned, his hand held out, and found himself standing alone. The Danes had withdrawn from him. His Welsh and Saxons had shrunk back against the hall's furthest wall. Some were crouched on the floor, hiding their heads. None offered him their swords.

A touch on his arm made him look down. There was Godwin, his son. The child's raised face was beseeching, and he held a man's sword – he had to use both hands to offer it to his father. The pommel of the sword, where the blade and hilt formed a cross, was decorated with a gold disc inlaid with another cross of garnets. It had been forged for a Christian, if not by one.

Unwin, feeling an odd, new wonder that this child was of his body, put his hand on the boy's head.

Godwin said, "I shall pray for you!"

Unwin took the sword, pushed the boy aside, and turned away.

Godwin stayed where he had been pushed. Nothing would have made him leave that spot.

Unwin, facing Elfgift, was again staggered by a blow, and couldn't tell if it was the shock of its gaze or its beauty. It waited for him with galling patience, asking for no shield, no helmet. Its only preparation for the fight was to throw aside its holly crown. It didn't even stand at the ready. Woden's Promise, loosely held, pointed at the floor.

Unwin lunged with all the force and aim he had trained for, and for a breath's space believed he had struck home – but found himself staggering and the thing nowhere in sight. Whirling, feeling heavy and blundering, he saw the thing behind him, hair flying, Woden's Promise gleaming in its hand. The light ran in ripples of grey and silver over the pattern beaten into the iron, the inter-woven triangles of the battle-fetters. Unwin felt the pain in his heart, the needle of fear driven there, and he breathed deep, heaved up his sword and charged again before the fear could unnerve him.

Elfgift's shield was his speed. Ducking under Unwin's blow, he came up behind Unwin's back, drawing his sword's edge along Unwin's thigh. Woden's Promise had no weight in his hand: it felt live, as if it was itself straining to bite Unwin. He guided it, but where his will ended and the sword's began – or whether they were the same – he couldn't tell. He saw the blood spring from Unwin's leg, and it was as if his wish had called it out, and then he was at Unwin's other side, while Unwin wrenched himself round, trying to find him over the obstacle of his own shield, and look-ing clumsy. Unwin's blood fell on to the straw on the floor, and there was a shifting of eyeless heads among the dead, a clacking of fleshless jaws.

The sound squeezed Unwin's heart cold. He feared that Elfgift was aiming a blow at him from behind – he could not see the thing. He felt himself lumber as he turned, his arms and legs clumsy, and he raged inside himself. Christ was watching – he could not fail this test! And there was the thing, waiting, as if he was such a contemptible opponent that it had no need to attack. His rage rose higher, but the light rippled along the blade of Woden's Promise, and froze rage into fear.

Sweat pooled in Unwin's hands, ran down his back, into his eyes. He wanted to lie on the floor and howl, but instead aimed a fast, hard blow at the thing's legs. He missed. A cockerel's long crow filled his ears as the force of his missed blow carried him off-balance, sent him stumbling in a circle.

Elfgift had leaped high above his blow and seemed to hang in the air above the sword, crowing in mockery. As he came down, he struck a blow at Unwin's helmet – a heavy blow but mockingly struck with the flat. Struck with the edge, it would have shattered both helmet and skull.

From the onlookers was only a deeper silence. The metallic din of the blow rang round the rafters.

Unwin, his spine jarred, his head dully booming, went heavily to his knees. His shield's edge struck the floor, jarring and bruising the arm it was fixed to. His sword hand, clenched about his sword's hilt, bashed its knuckles on the floor.

Elfgift drew off and waited, but threw Woden's Promise from hand to hand. With every throw the pattern of the battle-fetters rippled and shone.

Godwin watched his father get, too slowly, to his feet. Unwin was breathing hard. Godwin's eyes were stretched painfully wide. He could not look away or even blink. His father was being made game of – and his brother, Wulfweard, stood by and watched. Shame and fury shook Godwin as if a hand shook him by the scruff. He wanted to kill the elf's get. He wanted to kill Wulfweard.

Unwin was hardly on his feet before Elfgift drew blood from his arm above the shield. Unwin swung towards the pain, but Elfgift was gone. Moving as swiftly as the flicker of flame-light, he was already at Unwin's other side, drawing blood from Unwin's ribs. As Unwin tried to turn again, Elfgift threw Woden's Promise high in the air and was at Unwin's other side to catch the sword as it fell. He tossed it from hand to hand and sent its point darting to nick Unwin's leg above the knee.

The light once more showed the battle-fetters along the black blade, and the dead began to beat a rhythm with their spear-butts: a gentle, deep rhythm on the hard floor, setting the straw whispering, their bones rattling, and their disintegrating mail to ringing. Only then did Unwin, the blood beating thickly in his head, his chest choked and strained, understand. The elf's drop was *dancing*. This was the sword-dance, and its purpose was to shed blood. This was the taunting of an animal meant for sacrifice, the cocks set to fight at a funeral, the stallions goaded to fight for Ing, the stags torn apart for Woden.

But he could not fail: he had to win for Christ. While his heart slogged and his sight blurred, while his arms and legs dragged, he forced his body on by sheer will, gathering together all of his strength and rushing at Elfgift. And the light so caught Elfgift's blade that, before his eyes, he saw the full pattern of the battle-fetters, from hilt to point.

There was a tightening about his struggling heart, like the iron band a cooper shrinks about the staves of a barrel.

Unwin was bleeding, and had put too much force into too many blows. He stumbled as he turned and staggered to keep his feet. Elfgift, untouched, untired, appeared again and again on that side where Unwin thought he could not be. The dead turned their eyeless faces to the fight and beat their rhythm on the floor, but the living who watched suffered. Elfgift was shining, quick, lithe, beautiful – but cruel. Even as their eyes followed and admired him, they knew their own likeness was with the sweating, stumbling, failing Unwin.

Kendrida grasped the stair rail as she peered down. Inwardly she urged Elfgift on to the kill, and yet she pitied Unwin. She had not thought she could, but it was her own clumsiness she pitied. Though Unwin had been, if nothing else, a brave man.

Wulfweard kept his head up and his face turned towards the bloody dance, but the tears stood so deep in his eyes that the light had turned them to a golden dazzle. The sound of Unwin's hard breathing and stumbling feet made his heart ache.

Breathless, exhausted, weighted by the battle-fetters, Unwin sank to one knee. Still he set his teeth and struggled to rise against the weight of his shield and his own body. If he lost this fight, he lost everything. He could not endure to live a prisoner or humbled.

He heaved up his head, and again the full length of the battle-fetters gleamed before his eyes. The spell clamped on his mind.

His knees locked and he could not rise. His elbows locked and his sword's point rang on the floor. His heart stuttered: he could not draw breath. His God was not with him, and he was nothing but a fool. He could not force a sound from his throat. His sight dimmed but still, though he could not move his head, he rolled his eyes, wide and white, towards Elfgift.

Throughout the hall, no one moved.

Elfgift circled Unwin lightly, like a dancer. He felt Woden's Promise tugging at his arm, like a leashed dog.

There was no longer any need to kill Unwin. Now he was humbled, few men would follow him again. But there was between them a memory of choking smoke and heaped bodies. Unwin's life was owed him. Woden's Promise tugged insistently at his arm.

Elfgift looked at Wulfweard, who felt the look knock against his face, but had to squeeze the blinding tears from his eyes before he could see. He knew what Elfgift was silently asking him. He looked to Unwin, and at Unwin's stricken face. He felt the unwilling pity a man might feel for a wolf that had torn and killed his lambs, but was now bloodied and crippled itself. He remembered the pain he had felt when imprisoned and starving: that Unwin had ordered it and had not come to him. It taught him the pain Unwin had always known: the pain of loving a brother but knowing him for a threat and an enemy.

Wulfweard felt that the ground, sharp edge of a sword was being driven through his heart by two hands – those of the brother who had betrayed him and the brother with whom he must keep faith.

Wulfweard would have turned away, but Unwin held his eye, and then he could not turn his back. It was as if he could do nothing more for his brother than watch and keep the memory. Then he would do it. He watched.

Elfgift saw that tiny movement – the beginning of the turning away and then the halting of it. Godwin saw it too and suddenly knew what was going to happen, as if he had already seen it. He saw that no one was going to help his father – no one. There was only him to help! And though he was like an ant attacking a bear, he started forward, unarmed, desperate, and threw himself into what seemed like a solid wall, but was only the big ashen shield of the man beside him who flung his arms, shield and all, around the boy and held him. Another man, seeing how fiercely the boy fought, came to help. Godwin saw nothing but the shield's inner curve, and heard his own shouts echoing from its cup.

Elfgift sprang across in front of Unwin as he knelt. Twisting at the waist as he rose, he swung Woden's Promise upwards. The firelight sent its golden light and red shadows through his up-flying hair, over his shifting muscles, and along the sword, turning the black iron gold, rippling along the blade's hammered pattern. The blade hummed as it cut the air, the hum rising until, at the peak of its swing, it rang out in a shriek, like the scream of sharp edge dragged across edge, jarring the heart and stirring the hair of all who heard it.

Unwin, kneeling beneath the blade, heard its scream, and his heart, his breath, stopped. His sight turned to a hopeless darkness, and the shriek rang on and on...

Down the blade swept as Elfgift dropped from the air. The leap seemed a dancer's flourish, but the blade passed through Unwin's neck. A sound of an axe chopping wood, and body and head thumped to the floor, the head a foot from the neck. Blood poured, lifting straw, soaking into the earthen floor.

From the living came not a movement, not a sound. They hid their faces, or stood staring at their fallen king and the spreading blood.

The dead warriors crowded forward, their bones shuffling in the straw, their mail jingling, crowding about Elfgift and the blood. Wulfweard saw that one of them wore a hooded cloak, show-ing blue where the firelight was brightest. He leaned on his spear-shaft over Unwin's body, a grey beard spilling from within his cloak. As he straightened, the hood of his cloak fell back, revealing a face that, if it was dead, was newly dead: the flesh swollen and dark with blood, a bulging eye catching the light like glass, and the tongue stuck from a grimacing mouth. With its long grey beard and thick grey eyebrows, it was a face gruesomely merry, as if the old man pulled this ghastly face in fun. Grey-Beard reached for Elfgift and embraced him tightly, His spear sticking up behind Elfgift's back.

The dead moved again, blocking Elfgift and the Grey-Beard from Wulfweard's sight, but then he saw the blue cloak flourished, and saw it settled about Elfgift's shoulders. And then Elfgift was alone among the dead. There were bald skulls and half-fleshed heads to which darkened, lank hair still clung – but no thick heads of grey hair, no full grey beards.

Wulfweard went among the dead himself, and they laid bone hands on his shoulder in welcome. The blood brimmed at his feet, and he looked down at the carcase of his brother. Tears welled over his lids and clung to his lashes, but now Unwin was dead, the pain had faded and a numbed quietness come to him. A shrill squealing startled him, and he jerked up his head to see the mad girl dancing round the edge of the blood, laughing and dancing because Unwin was dead. He thought that he should be angry, that he should hit her – but he felt nothing.

Kendrida ran down the stairs so headlong, so

carelessly that once only her hand snatching at the rail saved her from falling, but the grip of that hand swung her and dashed her against the steps and rail. She felt no pain. Her mind was filled with Godwin and Elfgift, Elfgift and Godwin. She must reach them, and quickly, though she hardly knew why. She wished to hold them, shake them, guard them. At the bottom of the stair, men blocked her way. She beat on their backs with her fists, screeched at them, shoved them aside. Godwin, Godwin! She could feel the danger tightening about him.

Godwin was fighting the men who held him, battering his head against the shield held over him, kicking and biting until the hold on him slackened and the shield lifted, and he was able to see.

He saw the blood spreading among feet of bones, wrapped in earth-darkened and sodden rags. At the sight, and at the butcher's-stall smell of blood, he stopped short, and a chill calm settled over him. He pushed forward into the dead's carrion stink. In his ears he seemed to hear a buzzing, and there was a prickling over his scalp and down his spine. He came to his father's body lying slumped, and yet the sight made no sense to his eyes. No one could lie so, with their head hidden. Then he saw the head – it wasn't touching the body. There was floor between it and its shoulders. So strange. Beyond the head, still held in his father's outflung hand, he saw the sword. Its medallion of gold, inlaid with a garnet cross, flickered fitfully in the firelight.

He walked in a straight line through the pool of his father's blood, his goal being the sword. Reaching it, he bent down and took it from his father's still warm hand. Unwin gave it up easily.

The sword was too long and too heavy, but now he had cold rage to give him strength. He raised his head and saw Elfgift not so very far from him, with a blue cloak draped about him and his long hair falling over the blue. An old man, with a grey beard and a swollen, ugly face, was setting the holly crown back on Elfgift's head.

Godwin had known hot and flustered rages before, which fogged the eyes and brain. Now, coldly, he chose the place where he would drive the Christian sword – Elfgift's belly. He knew just how he would twist it once he had driven it in. He let his mind order his body, gathering together all the strength, speed and skill he would need. And then he moved.

"God—!" Wulfweard cried out, and moved too late. Kendrida, still fighting her way through the press of scared, numbed men, heard his shout, and screamed out herself, wordlessly, in fury and terror.

Elfgift's head snapped round, and he looked full at Godwin.

A hard blow in the face. A giddy sense of falling. Godwin saw the firelight advancing and retreating among the rafters high, high above, and heard the sound of the sword he held striking the floor. He tried to raise the sword and found his arms fastened to the ground with their own weight. He gasped for breath and heard his own breathing like the tearing of thick cloth. His lungs were turned to wood – they would not fill and his ribs would not lift. Breathless, he felt the beating of his heart speed until it thumped at him. He wanted to cry out for help, but could not make a sound. He didn't know what had happened. He could hardly remember why the sword was in his hand. It was as if the blow that had knocked him down had knocked memory from him.

The hilt of the sword was taken from his hand, and Wulfweard's face appeared above him, then his mother's. He was half-lifted from the floor as his mother gathered him to her, babbling his name and kissing him. He still could not move. He could not find air to make a sound or shape his lips to speak. Staring out from his mother's enfolding arms, he saw dark holes staring at him, and noseless faces, great earth-stained grins. He saw, for an eye's blink, a leaning, tilted, swollen face that glared with a bulging eye and poked out its tongue.

And then Elfgift's face, so like Wulfweard's but

colder, clearer. His gaze rested on Godwin's face with a steady weight. In his mind Godwin began to kick and struggle, to escape the weight of that stare – but however hard he willed it, he could not move or make a sound.

Jarl Ingvald and Ingvi had come up, as if shy, and half-afraid of the dead warriors around them. Ingvald knelt beside Kendrida and gently moved the child's head, took his arms and tried to straighten them, tried to unclench the fists. He looked into Kendrida's eyes and turned to Wulfweard. He would not look up at Elfgift.

"Elf-struck," he said in a whisper, meant only for Kendrida to hear.

Gritting her teeth, Kendrida rose, Godwin in her arms. Both Wulfweard and Ingvi moved to help, but Ingvald was closer. He took much of the boy's limp weight, though Kendrida would not let him go. She turned to Elfgift, her mouth opening and closing, her eyes filled with tears of anger and grief. She wanted to shout that she had given her faith, her love – she had believed. Was this how she was repaid?

She said none of it. Elfgift looked back at her and his lids swept down, covering his eyes, and that eye's blink gave his face an extraordinary gentleness. In that eye's blink, the world was shaken from around her and she was again kneeling at a fireside, looking into Elfgift's face, feeling the fire's warmth of love for him and hearing his voice say, "There is no safety in knowing me..." As the weight of her son's stricken body brought her back to the stink of blood and carrion, she realized that Woden was not the only treacherous God.

Elfgift looked at the paralyzed child, amazed that his mere glance had done so much – and wishing it had struck the brat dead. One child more or less mattered nothing, and this child...

He raised his eyes to Kendrida's face. She flinched from his look, lowering her head, but he felt her grief, as if he had put his hand to cold metal and it had frozen there. The painful chill crept through him. Still, countless mothers grieved for dead and damaged children, and the stars shone still, the corn still grew. He looked beyond Kendrida. Those around her stepped back, turned aside, afraid of his eyes. Only Wulfweard returned his gaze straight, and it was Wulfweard's face he had sought.

Again, Wulfweard knew what he was being asked. He answered, "Help him."

Elfgift smiled, seeming shy and a little sad. "If I spare him now, it's you, Wulf, who will have the killing of him." And the slight widening of Elfgift's eyes asked, *Do you dare that?*

"Help him," Wulfweard said.

Still smiling, Elfgift put Woden's Promise into

Wulfweard's hand, and made to take Godwin from Kendrida. She clung to him – and met Elfgift's eyes with her own, baring her teeth. But though she felt his gaze brush her face like a breeze, it no longer struck like a blow. She let go, and Elfgift took Godwin into his arms.

Handed over to his enemy, Godwin tried to clench his fists, to kick, but his body responded only by the crooking of a finger. Terror screamed in him – this thing would bite him, shift wolf-shape, carry him off, kill him…

Elfgift tilted his head to look down at him, and his hair swung forward to touch Godwin's face with its tendrils – a touch which to Godwin, in his terror, seemed to burn and cut.

But heart-beat by heart-beat raced by, without his coming to harm or suffering any pain, and he was as solidly upheld as if in a warm bed. His heart's thudding slowed. The elf-eyes touched his face, his arms, his chest, with touches like the soft touch of a finger. The mouth shaped a word and a greater warmth closed about him, bringing drowsiness. Dreamily, he felt himself tilting as his head was lifted up, but he was sleeping when Elfgift's lips touched his forehead.

Ingvald, Ingvi, Wulfweard – all had gathered closer without knowing they had moved. Kendrida pressed so close that she embraced both Elfgift and Godwin. Elfgift smiled at her as he pulled away and turned towards the stairs. She followed after him, clinging to his arm. They all followed – many Danes and even Welsh, trailing through blood and past overturned benches, as if hoping to be led to some more peaceful place.

With Godwin in his arms, Elfgift climbed the stairs, Kendrida at his heels. Wulfweard stopped at the stairs' foot, looking up and blocking the way for those behind him.

Elfgift paused at the half-landing and looked down, cradling the sleeping child higher against his shoulder. His eyes moved over toppled benches and tables, food, cups, bowls scattered, drink spilt. Weapons and shields glimmered, abandoned. Men cowered on wall-benches or stared up at him. Living men stood beside the dead. A blood-soaked floor and a headless body. The more he saw, the more he smiled, until he was laughing – and an old grey-beard looked up at him and laughed back.

Leaning forward, holding the child tightly, Elfgift called, "Don't let a squabble spoil the feast!"

The living heard him in mazed silence. The dead beat their spear-butts on the ground.

"Spread the feast for the dead! Isn't it Jul? Serve my guests!"

One moved among the still crowd below – Ebba. She ran and picked up a bench, ran on to another and set it straight, beckoning to others to help her.

Wulfweard walked dazedly from the stairs, set Woden's Promise down on the edge of the dais, and went to help Ebba. Other living men hurried to help him, setting table-boards back on their trestles, picking up horns and fallen joints of meat. One man took a cloak from a bench and threw it round Wulfweard.

Elfgift carried Godwin on up the stairs. The door of the private room slammed as Kendrida followed him inside.

Ebba ran to take dead men by the hand and lead them to the benches. When they were seated, she kissed their faces and put horns into their hands. The living watched her in awe: she was mad.

Finding an unspilled jug, Wulfweard filled horns held out to him in hands of bone. The faces above them had holes for eyes, holes for noses. Their lips were shrivelled to the shape of the teeth beneath, or they had no lips. But they were his people.

"Bring more drink. And bread." Some of the living moved to obey. Wulfweard, pouring more wine, looked down the length of the table and saw, at its end, staring back at him, Unwin.

CħAPTER 15

Web in the Weaving

A strange Jul Feast, the stink of grave-earth mixing with the smell of bread and roasted meat.

It was close to morning when Elfgift came down, leading Kendrida by the hand. He moved wearily, and the flesh of his face was drawn close to the bone. Dead men rose to bring him to the table, and put a horn of mead into his hand.

Now Elfgift brought the living to sit with the dead, sat Ingvald and Ingvi beside warriors who had died fighting their grandfathers, and living Welsh beside long-dead enemies. Kendrida called together her women, and led them round the tables to fill horns and pass bread.

The drinking horn passed from hands of flesh to hands of bone. Living eyes looked into empty sockets. Lips drew back over teeth, smiling, to answer grins that had no lips.

Wulfweard, at the table's end, saw the grey-faced, grey stare of his brother, Unwin. Not even Elfgift could outface the stare.

Birds twittered in the high thatch, announcing the late winter dawn. Then Elfgift led the procession, in the grey cold, through the streets and down through the orchards, to the grave-field. The dead went into their ground again, and the living smoothed the earth over them.

At daybreak the weary living lay down on the floors of the halls and slept almost like the dead, to wake thinking they had dreamed strange and terrifying dreams.

Ebba did not sleep. She roamed from the grave-field to the woods, her feet and hands stiff and tingling with cold. She wandered through the Borough streets, and came to the razed ground of the God-house. There, she crawled to where the great Woden-figure had stood for such an age.

What she had seen!

Sitting there, wrapping her cold feet in the hem of her skirt, she tried to imagine the God-house walls about her again. She knew it would be rebuilt, the God-figures raised again.

In the God-house she could live, and there, what she had seen would not break her apart.

The fire would be lit and would burn always, night and day, never allowed to go out but at Jul, and then relit. Every day the old straw would be swept out and new straw spread. That would be her job. At the Woden-figure's feet, that would be her place.

High above the hall, in the upper room, Kendrida lay warm in bed, hugging Godwin to her, his head beneath her chin. The other children, for that night, slept with maids.

She had watched while Elfgift had worked his healing and now, whispering to Godwin, kissing him and coaxing, she found that he could grip her fingers with his. He could turn his head and answer her, and eat and drink a little. If his legs were still cold and unmoving – well, at least Elfgift had healed some of what he had stricken.

Kendrida could not think of Elfgift without gratitude. Where he could easily have killed, he had spared. He had partly healed and – if she was loving and grateful – he would heal further, she was sure. She could not say he hadn't warned her – "There is no safety in knowing me" – but he forgave. She dared not think ill of him.

"You must not hate Elfgift," she whispered to Godwin, stroking his back. "You don't understand why he is as he is. You must not hate him."

Godwin could only think of Elfgift with fear.

Ingvald and Ingvi sat side by side on a bench at the back of the hall, touching at shoulder and knee. They passed a horn between them, and had little need to put their thoughts into words.

"To Lovern!" Ingvi said, and drank a toast to the Christian king to whose court he would not be returning. "To freedom!"

Ingvald grunted, took the horn and drank glumly. Alliance to the elf-born was not what he would call "freedom".

On the hard sleeping bench of a private room, Elfgift was deeply asleep, far beneath dreams. Over his face and shoulders trailed the long red and grey hair of the woman whose arms were clasped about him. There was nothing to wake or disturb him. The hour of his death, and the manner of his dying, had been fated long before.

Wulfweard woke. A voice had called him sharply, in his dream. "Unwin's-weard! Brother's-weard!" He had known his name and answered.

NOTE

The rune-rhymes with which Ud binds Elfgift in the grave-field, and Ebba's "Ing-rune" are loosely adapted from the "Anglo-Saxon Rune Poem," which gives a rhyme for each of the thirty runes.

In fact, the "Rune Poem" is echoed throughout the book, too frequently to list.

The long song of eighteen runes with which One-Eye resurrects Elfgift is loosely based on "The Words of The High One" from the *Elder Edda*, one of the source books of Norse Mythology.

The questions which are asked of Elfgift at the end of this chapter are also freely adapted from the *Elder Edda*, from "The Lay of Vafthrudnir." In this legend the giant Vafthrudnir unwittingly takes on the god Odin in a contest of wits, the loser to lose his head. Odin's final question, "What did I whisper in the ear of my son Balder as he lay on his funeral pyre?" is unanswerable. Vafthrudnir loses his head.

The song which Wulfweard remembers at the end of Chapter Eleven is loosely adapted from the Anglo-Saxon poem, "Deor". This verse refers to the legend of Wayland the Smith.

The song with which Elfgift and Wulfweard raise the dead is loosely adapted from the English folksong, "John Barleycorn". This song was collected not so long ago, in the nineteenth century, but the paganism of its words has roused much interest. Several recordings of it are available.

The snatch of song with which Ud harps the guards to sleep in Chapter Nine is from another folksong, known as "Jack Orion" or "Glasgerion".